August 24, 1966

Media Books
170 Fifth Avenue
New York City 10010

Gentlemen:

I was delighted when I heard that Thomas Thompson
had been chosen to write the historical novel that frames the
background of Ben Cartwright and his sons on the legendary
Ponderosa. Mr. Thompson, in addition to being a western historian
and novelist, has been closely identified with the Bonanza series
from its very beginning, both as a writer and story consultant.

Beyond that, however, I was eager to see how the real
history of the area would be dealt with, the vastness and beauty and
feel of the country itself, as well as the warm, family relationship
that has kept Bonanza the number one show for so many years.

Having just completed reading the galley proofs of
the Bonanza book, "One Man With Courage", I am excited and
exhilarated. Here is Ben Cartwright as I have tried to envision
and portray him, but placed against a much broader canvas of
history than could possibly be reproduced within the limits of the
television screen. Here is the feel of the country in which the
Cartwrights would have lived. Here is the well researched
background of history that could have spawned a Ponderosa.

I know that the many millions of Bonanza followers
around the world will have a deeper appreciation of the true history
and glamour of the Bonanza days after reading this book, and a
keener interest in the shows to come.

I know I will.

Sincerely,

Lorne Greene

Lorne Greene

LG:mc

BONANZA

One Man with Courage

BY THOMAS THOMPSON

AN ORIGINAL NOVEL PUBLISHED BY

media **M** books
170 FIFTH AVENUE
NEW YORK CITY 10010

FIRST PRINTING, SEPTEMBER, 1966
SECOND PRINTING, FEBRUARY, 1967.

LIBRARY OF CONGRESS CATALOG NO. 66-29144

MEDIA BOOKS IS A DIVISION OF PROFIT PRESS, INC.,
170 FIFTH AVENUE, NEW YORK CITY 10010.

PRINTED IN THE UNITED STATES OF AMERICA.

To my good friends,
the real unsung
heroes of Bonanza—
the men and women
of the TV crew.

1 THE SOUND that did not belong here came again and Ben Cartwright reined up sharply, turning his head into the wind in an effort to hear it plainer. The buckskin gelding's ears flicked forward, for the horse had heard it before his master—the first signal Ben Cartwright had that something was amiss. A bluejay in a nearby thicket chided both horse and rider, and a grey squirrel, halfway through the enjoyment of cutting down a sugar pine cone, started an argument with the jay. The wind sighed softly through the topmost branches of the towering ponderosa pines that surrounded this high meadow, and again the foreign sound that was worrying Ben Cartwright was lost to him. He touched his mount with his heels and Buck moved forward, cautiously, as if aware of his master's concern. The man shifted his weight in the saddle.

He had been riding for four days, and in that time he had talked to a crew that was cutting meadow hay so rich he was shipping several tons of it to England to a friend who owned a stable of race horses there. Leaving those lush meadows along Washoe Lake he had counted a thousand head of his own cattle grazing on the slopes in back of Carson City, the capital of the new state of Nevada. A third day had been spent with a fencing crew of

7

forty men, a day's ride north, and now at the end of this fourth day he was riding through millions of feet of virgin pine, high in the timber country, and at no time in these four days had he been off his own land. The mighty Ponderosa Ranch encompassed a thousand square miles and sprawled from the shores of Washoe to the incredible blue of Lake Tahoe, and Ben Cartwright knew and loved every inch of it.

He was a big man, but it was a lot more than physical size that distinguished Ben Cartwright. There was a confident ease about him that said he would be as much at home in white tie and tails as he was in the boots, well cut saddle clothes and sheepskin-lined coat he was now wearing. That confident ease touched every move he made, and he sat his saddle with the casualness of long experience. Most men respected and admired him, but there were some who feared him and some who hated him for the power and wealth he represented. Women found him attractive, and many of them would gladly have altered his marital status. Ben Cartwright was a widower, and a hint of past tragedy lurked in the shadows around his eyes.

There was a penetrating alertness in those brown eyes. Above the high sweep of forehead, a wealth of snow white hair swept back in an authoritative manner from the great gull wings at his temples to an almost tousled confusion at the back of his leonine head. He was a man of twinkling good humor, as anyone who knew him realized, but he also gave the impression that he could, if need be, become as impersonal as one of the bullets in the holstered gun he carried on his hip. There was a charged, latent energy in the man, such as the energy locked in one of the tremendous coiled springs that cushioned the heavy, steel ore cars in the Virginia City mines. Like the spring, he was there when he was needed, solid and practical and a buffer against shock. Unleashed, he might well burst forth with a potential of damage that had

8

never been calculated into the original sculpture of an outwardly peace-loving family man who had raised three sons. Riding now, he saw Buck's ears flick forward, and that tormenting sound was back again and immediately he knew what it was. It was the ring of axes biting into the trunks of forest giants.

For a long moment Ben paused. He was a man who rarely acted on impulse. Standing in his stirrups he looked around the horizon, making sure he knew where he was, quickly finding landmarks to confirm his position. His features clouded then as he went back over the plans he had made with his two sons just before leaving home. Hoss, his middle son, had a crew of twenty Paiute woodcutters over on the Carson River, taking advantage of the Indian summer weather that could end abruptly at any time. His youngest son, Joseph, was on the annual cow gather with a dozen men, moving the last of the herds from the high country meadows to the lower slopes before the snows started. He had fifty men building a lumber flume that would crawl across granite-faced cliffs and stalk across canyons on spindly trestles. It was costing ten thousand dollars a mile to construct, but when its fifteen-mile length was completed it would be capable of carrying five hundred cords of wood or a half a million feet of lumber a day to the mills down in Washoe Valley. Further back in the hills a logging crew was working long hours to fulfill a contract Ben had for mining timbers, but they were working in what he called a controlled area where he had personally selected and marked every tree to be cut, for he was a confirmed conservationist and a bitter foe of the logging outfits that were stripping every living tree from the Sierra slopes in an effort to supply the demands of the booming silver mines in Virginia City.

Once more he checked his surroundings, and once more he was sure. The sound of those axes was not coming from any one of his own vast operations. It could

9

mean but one thing: there were timber rustlers on the Ponderosa.

Ben rode quickly to the top of a slope where he could get a view of the canyons and valleys below him. The forest stretched endlessly, its dusky green turned to the softness of smoky blue by its very vastness. To his back, beyond the lake that was hidden from here, jagged granite peaks hoarded snow in shadow-laden crevices. Eastward, beyond Eagle and Carson and Washoe valleys, rolled miles of mountains so ruggedly barren and alone they held a stark and fascinating beauty, sharply etched in the flawless desert air. And around and below him, the vast realm of timber—timber that was as valuable as silver, for without it, every mine on the Comstock Lode would be worked out and closed down in a matter of a few weeks, as ore bodies were being worked out and the mines were going deeper, ever deeper. The Comstock was fast becoming the burial ground for entire forests; only the Ponderosa was making a continual effort to control its cuttings. A thin column of smoke caught Ben's eye.

The muscles along his jaws tightened as he watched that smoke column. It was perhaps two miles from here, down on a slope he knew well. He had not authorized any logging in that particular area, nor did he intend to in the future. It was a stand of arrow-straight Ponderosa pines, too young for cutting. There was a good sized creek meandering through that stand, and it was a creek that could rampage badly during spring run-offs. Strip that slope of timber and tons of earth would be washed down to clog the land below. In addition, the grove served as protection to the deer herds during winter snows, and beavers—nature's own flood controllers—had thrown dams across the many switchbacks of the stream. Without thinking about it, Ben drew the rifle from his saddle scabbard, checked its loads and replaced it. A sudden chill touched the almost imperceptible breeze, and he tugged down his hat and turned up the collar of his coat before riding back down the slope.

Now he rode as fast as the terrain would allow. The sound of swinging axes became increasingly louder and soon he heard the undulating grate of the two-man cross-cut saws, with their metallic twanging at the end of each stroke. He topped a rise, and now he could look across at the grove. He saw the quivering in the branches of the tree and heard the shout of "Timber!" and the tree shuddered like a stricken thing, leaned, seemed to hesitate, then plunged downward through thick growth, tearing branches from other trees, smashing its own limbs against the earth. The crash assailed Ben's ears, and he pushed Buck forward, unmindful of the fact that timber thieves were always expecting trouble and were therefore prepared for it. He burst through the timber and the devastation in front of him sickened him.

Fallen trees were piled across each other, splintered and broken, half their valuable lumber wasted, the result of careless felling. Small growth had been slashed out or mashed to the ground. A fire burned limbs that could have been saved for cord wood, and that fire might as well have been burning pure silver, for timber and cord wood made the real life-line of the Comstock. Without it, nothing moved. Without timber, a mine could not be deepened to a lower level to reach richer ores; without cord wood, not a mill or a hoisting works could raise steam in its boilers. The ever-growing towns of the Comstock begged for lumber for their homes and their business buildings, and each home or building meant still another greedy stove demanding fuel.

Ben threw himself from the saddle. "Who's in charge here?" he demanded.

The man who moved forward had a lump of snuff behind his lower lip. He was as tall as Ben, perhaps thicker

11

through the shoulders, the muscles of his arms and back apparent under his flannel shirt. He sized Ben up and spit a brown stream. "That would be me," he said.

"Do you know you're on private land?" Ben asked. He was fighting to keep the anger from his voice.

The big logger looked around at his crew. There were six of them in all. They stood there, leaning on their axes. In the background was a team and wagon, and standing, yoked, were four oxen. A small, gypo outfit, but they were doing their damage. One of the men threw another limb into the fire, "You hear that, boys?" the big logger asked. "He says we're on private land."

"That don't seem rightly possible, Larson," one of the men said. "I think he's wrong, don't you?"

"Yeah, I think he's wrong," the man called Larson said. "I just wanted to see what you thought." He turned directly to Ben. "We think you're wrong," he said.

The calm insolence of the man was almost more than Ben could take. His eyes quickly took in the smashed young trees, the torn earth where logs had been dragged away, the hideous rubbish of limbs and slashings and uprooted brush. In this sort of operation speed was essential, and a good stand of timber could be destroyed forever in a matter of days. None of the men was wearing a gun, and Ben's quick appraisal did not reveal a rifle, but a double-bitted axe in the hands of the average logger was just as deadly as any firearm.

Larson turned his back. "All right, men," he said. "Get back to work."

Larson's back was still to Ben when Ben reached out and gripped his arm. There was no doubt Larson had expected such a move, for he turned swiftly and his entire weight was behind the blow as his fist thudded solidly against the side of Ben's head. Ben staggered back and he could hear the shouts of laughter from the men and he saw them running in to watch the fun. He backed off, wanting time for his vision to clear, wanting to free

12

himself of that heavy coat . . . he wrenched his arms free of the sleeves just as Larson came at him again. There were to be no rules in this fight, and the only fairness Ben could expect would be that the others would stay out of it . . . He sidestepped Larson's rush and deliberately tripped him, then threw himself on top the man.

A boss logger generally became boss because he could whip every other man in camp, and Larson was no exception. He had the strength of a bull and a knowledge of rough and tumble gained through experience and the sheer love of fighting. These things Ben sensed as he pinioned Larson's arms to his sides and rolled over and over through the broken limbs and slashings, fighting for a few seconds that would let him recover from the sting of that first blow. He felt Larson break free, saw him move back.

Ben snapped to his feet, for he knew if he stayed on the ground one second too long he would have the caulked boots of the big logger in his face. His vision was clearing. He had lost his hat, and his hair was in wild disarray around his face, but he was all right now and he was moving, balancing. He was ready for Larson's next bull-like assault. He sidestepped and hit the woods boss three times before Larson knew what happened.

Larson stepped back, startled rather than hurt. He spit out his cud of snuff and actually grinned as he wiped a tiny trickle of blood from the corner of his mouth. "Well, now," he said, "maybe this is gonna be more fun than I figgered on."

"You gonna let him keep that gun on, Larson?" one of the men asked.

"Why not?" Larson said. "He won't have time to use it. You boys stay out of it." He moved in, but this time he moved with caution.

For a moment they circled each other, each man looking for an opening, each wanting the other to make the first move. The loggers were shouting encouragement and advice to Larson. Suddenly one of them pushed Ben and Larson saw the opening he had waited for. He threw an arm around Ben's neck and threw him to the ground. He had told the men to keep out of it but apparently wasn't going to refuse their help. Ben looked up to see the big logger diving down at him. He threw up his feet and caught Larson in the pit of the stomach, spilling him on his head. Immediately Ben was up. He had already arrived at the strategy he must use. Ben was well versed in rough and tumble, but so was Larson. His best chance, Ben decided, was to out-box and out-maneuver the man. He watched Larson get to one knee. There was a certain bewilderment in his expression. He couldn't understand a man who didn't use his boots when his opponent was down.

Time, Ben had thought before, seemed to stop when a man was fighting for his life. Things were happening here in seconds, and yet it seemed he had been facing Larson for an hour. He felt a fist crash against his ribs, felt the jar in his own elbow as his fist found Larson's jaw, felt the smear of blood on his face and did not know if it was his own or the logger's. The shouts of the other men became distant and detached, and there was only that face there in front of him, a face that was mashed now and twisted . . . they clinched and strained against each other and went down and Ben's mouth was full of dirt and he felt Larson's teeth clamp into his shoulder and he twisted from a thumb that gouged at his eye.

He couldn't tell how long they fought. He only knew that his lungs were screaming for air and his legs felt as if they would buckle beneath him and he was searching wildly for a target for his fists and there was no target there . . . only then did Ben become aware of the total silence around him and only then did he realize that Larson was having difficulty getting to his feet. As Ben's

14

vision cleared he saw the damage his lashing fists had done to Larson's face. Blood was running down one cheek from a wicked cut over his eye. His lips were smashed to a pulp, his shirt torn from his body. Ben felt something close to admiration as he saw the big man lurch to his feet, realized he was coming at him again . . . Ben took his time. He swung from hip level and knew he had measured the blow exactly right. Larson went down, and this time he didn't move.

Ben turned to face the others. There was a stunned look of disbelief on the faces of all of them. "Take your tools and get out of here," Ben Cartwright said. He gestured toward Larson. "Take him with you." His six-shooter was lying on the ground where it had long ago fallen from his holster. He went across and picked it up and no one made any move to stop him.

"You don't whip Neil Larson, Mister," one of the men said. "You may stop him, but he won't stay whipped. He'll be lookin' for you, Mister."

"You tell him my name's Ben Cartwright," Ben said. "I'm not hard to find. Now get out of here, because if I have to come back, I won't be alone."

He picked up his hat and went across to stand by Buck. He was still breathing heavily and he wished desperately there was no one here to see him for he would have gone to the nearby stream and buried his swollen face in the icy current. He half turned and saw the men moving toward him, each man with an axe. Only then did Ben make any gesture with a gun. He drew the rifle from the saddle scabbard and levered in a shell.

"I told you to start moving," he said quietly.

The men hesitated, then sullenly turned and tossed their axes aside. One man took the drinking bucket and sloshed water on Larson, and he stirred and sat up. They took one more look at Ben Cartwright standing there with the rifle and started gathering their tools.

15

2 IT WAS WELL on to midnight when Ben Cartwright arrived back at the sprawling, log ranch house that was headquarters of the gigantic Ponderosa Ranch operation. There was a sharp chill in the air, and the fragrance of pine smoke from the ever-burning stone fireplace hung in the air and greeted him long before he came through the pines into the clearing and the complex of buildings and corrals that clustered downslope from the main house.

He was bone-tired, but beyond that the long ride had stiffened his strained muscles and it seemed to him there wasn't a square inch of his body that wasn't battered and bruised. He rode into the ranch house yard, glad now that it was this late, for he wanted a chance to bathe and doctor his cuts and bruises before anyone saw him.

Unsaddling Buck, he thought again, as he had so many times during the past four days, of the great changes that had taken place on the Ponderosa since the discovery of silver on the Comstock Lode. In the first days, before there was a Virginia City, he had run this ranch with the help of his oldest son, Adam, and a few trusted hands. Today, many of the men who worked for him were only names on a payroll sheet, and where once he had worked side by side with his riders and hay crews and fence builders there were now weeks at a time when he did not get out of this house.

Once, the Ponderosa had depended completely on livestock, and although that was still a large part of the operation, the real wealth here now was timber. Millions and millions of feet of lumber were being lowered into the ground to build up the already famous "square sets" designed by a German engineer named Deidesheimer. The town never stopped growing, and the demand was for more and more lumber and wood. It had to come from someplace, or Virginia City would die. The Ponderosa had the greatest stand of timber in the world.

A great shudder of a sigh ran through Ben Cartwright's body. Yes, everything had changed, but that was the way it had to be. Time did not stand still for anyone, nor did Ben expect it should.

Buck gave a grateful snort and trotted through the gate Ben opened and into the pasture beyond. Ben walked slowly toward the house, too tired even to take his bedroll from his saddle. He would take care of it in the morning. He opened the heavy door that was never locked and stepped into the familiar living room. A huge back log was burning in the massive stone fireplace, throwing flickering lights against the hand-hewn beams of the ceiling, playing tricks on the white plaster chinking between the logs. The big sofa directly in front of the fire was too appealing to resist and Ben sank gratefully into it, spreading his hands toward the warmth

The furniture here was in character with the house, scaled to fit the surroundings, and the stairs that led to the bedrooms above were broad and severely plain and utilitarian. It was a man's house, and men lived here, but it hadn't always been so . . . a deep sadness touched Ben and wouldn't let go. He had to get some sleep, he knew. Tomorrow would be a long day and an important one and again he was thinking of the ranch as it once was—the days when a man said what he meant and stood by it. That meeting he had to attend tomorrow in Virginia City would not be that way, he knew. Men would say one thing, but they would mean another, and money and control and power would be god at that table . . .

17

He got up wearily, wishing he could avoid it, knowing there was no way. As brutal and savage as his fight with Neil Larson had been, it was a lot easier than the fight he surely would have to wage with the Bank of California. He went slowly up the stairs and into his bedroom. The temptation was great just to throw himself full length on the bed, but he lit the lamp and examined himself in the mirror.

Neil Larson had done a good job on him, there was no doubt about that. One eye was swollen nearly closed and his lips were badly mashed. He would apply cold compresses, and perhaps Hop Sing, the combination cook, house boy and factotum, might have some ideas. Hop Sing generally had some sort of solution to any emergency that involved one of his beloved "Cartlights." Of one thing Ben was sure: Hop Sing or no, those men at the meeting in Virginia City were going to know he had been in a fight. He shrugged the thought aside. So they'd know. And he'd tell them what it was about. He poured water from the pitcher into the big basin and started gingerly washing his face. In time he undressed and got under the down-filled comforter, sure he would not sleep. It was thin grey daylight when he next opened his eyes.

If anything, he was more stiff and sore now than he had been the night before and his first thought was of a hot bath and a long, good soak. He put on a dressing gown and went downstairs. The fire was crackling merrily through a stack of freshly added pitch kindling, and the smell of newly brewed coffee wafted in from the kitchen beyond the well appointed dining room. He went to the kitchen door and peered in. Hop Sing was busy at the stove.

"Good morning, Hop Sing," Ben called cheerily to the small Oriental in padded shoes and black silk jacket and trousers. "Is there plenty of hot water?"

Hop Sing turned, his braided queue bobbing from

18

under his black skull cap. "You suppose be home early last night," he accused. "I fix suppah. All waste!"

"Sorry, Hop Sing," Ben said. "I got tied up. Now about that hot water . . ."

Hop Sing was staring intently at Ben now, aware of the cuts and bruises for the first time. "Who tie you up?"

"No, no," Ben said. "That's just an expression. I want to take a hot bath, Hop Sing."

Hop Sing moved closer, peering up at Ben's face. "Somebody fight you. I see that. Watsa matter you? One day Hoss fight, one day Little Joe fight, now you fight. Very bad, you understand?"

"Yes, yes. I understand. The hot water?"

"You go sit down by fire. I bling you coffee then fixee bath." He shook his head. "Very bad, fight all the time. Hop Sing don't like."

"Well, I don't exactly like it myself." Ben turned and started to leave the room.

"Mr. Cartlight?"

"Yes?"

"You win?"

"Yes, you could say so."

"Oh, very good!" Hop Sing said, and his smile resembled a sunrise. Ben went into the living room, turning his back quickly so that Hop Sing would not see his amusement.

He waited until Hop Sing brought the coffee, then, being a man who found it hard to remain still for long, moved across to the corner alcove of the big room where he kept his desk and the ranch safe. Behind the desk was a map that was his pride and joy. One of the artists for *Leslie's Popular Monthly* had painted it for him after a visit to the ranch, and Ben cherished it. It made no real claim to accurate cartography, but it did, in its sweeping way, indicate the magnificent sprawl of the land that had become the Ponderosa. He sat down at the desk, sipping his coffee as he shuffled through the pile of mail that had accumulated in the four days he had been away. He stopped suddenly at the sight of a foreign stamp and postmark. It was a letter from his oldest son, Adam.

He read the letter slowly, savoring each phrase, each nuance of meaning, and as he did time rolled back and he and Adam, just out of architectural school, were planning this very house. His middle son, Hoss, already large for his age, was just beginning to discover the mysteries of the deep pine forests and the fern glens and the animals who lived there. He could almost hear the protesting cry of his infant son, Joseph . . . Joseph . . . Little Joe, his wife had called the boy. Ben felt a quick stab of pain and it was a day like other days, and Marie was bending to kiss his cheek and her dark eyes were laughing and she went through that door and into the isolated splendor of a ranch that was a man's dream. For the third time in his life Ben Cartwright knew tragedy. The horse he had so proudly given his Marie . . . how would one know for sure what happened? Who was to blame?

Ben Cartwright shook his head to clear the vision. A man picked up the pieces and raised his sons and built his ranch as a symbol of his faith in the future and a monument to the memory of his past. A million memories ago . . . a million dreams . . . a million tomorrows . . .

"Your bath ready, Mr. Cartlight," Hop Sing said.

"What?" Ben looked up quickly. "Oh, thank you, Hop Sing."

Hop Sing was watching him closely. "You all light, Mr. Cartlight?"

"Yes, of course."

"You takee bath, shave. I fixee face for you."

"Thank you, Hop Sing."

He put down the letter. This house . . . his sons . . . now Adam, the eternal scholar, was in Europe, studying advanced design and architecture and big, lovable Hoss was up there along the Carson with his wood chopping

20

crew and Little Joe was heading up a roundup. Ben felt a sudden stab of loneliness, a driving desire to see his sons. It only heightened his resentment against that meeting in Virginia City, for that meeting was crowding his independence, telling him he must be there whether he wanted to be there or not.

He shaved and bathed and put on fresh clothes—an outfit almost identical to the one he had worn on the range. Roistering, boisterous Virginia City did not judge a man by his clothes. With the aid of some salve and some mysterious ointment Hop Sing insisted on using, he was able to somewhat disguise the fist marks on his face.

He ate hurriedly then, and Hop Sing made no attempt to hide his annoyance. From outside, came the murmur of voices, the creak of saddle leather, the protesting grunts of horses rebelling against the tightening of cinches. The crew going up to meet Little Joe's cow gather was forming. Ben gulped his coffee. Hatless, vest open, he went outside to where the ten men with their mounts and two pack mules were getting ready to leave for the high country.

Half of them were Mexicans from California, with broad-brim, high-crown hats, some of which sported ball tassels around the brims. They were the finest horsemen anyone could find in this part of the country, and they were at a premium as vaqueros, but they were also at a premium in the mines. Because they were Mexicans, many mine owners assumed they must know everything there was to know about silver, because romantically, silver was linked to Mexico and beyond that to Peru and to Cortez and far, far back into the dim reaches of history. It was because of this that many of the Mexican phrases had been adapted by the Virginia City miners, and many of the Mexican superstitions, also. It was not uncommon for a Mexican crew to move into a non-producing mine with a simple contract that however long it took the Mexicans to get out of "borrasca," or non-paying rock, that same length of time would be allowed them to work the "bonanza" they were convinced they would find.

Ben Cartwright had tried time and again to convince his vaqueros that there would be more bonanza in a permanent job on the Ponderosa than there would be in the intermittent splurges on the Comstock. But in this day of complete speculation—when everyone from washerwoman to nabob was engaged in buying and selling Comstock stock—it was hard to convince any man that a steady job was to his advantage. It was even harder to convince a romantic Mexican or Californio.

Ben moved over to José Bettencort, who had been longest on the ranch and who had therefore assumed an unofficial position of command. Ben gestured toward the pack horses. "You taking a chuck wagon up with you too?"

"Si," José said. A big grin spread across his handsome, leathered face. "Little Joe told us before he left always remember we might meet Hoss."

Ben chuckled dutifully at the old and worn joke about Hoss's legendary appetite.

"Tell Joseph I had to go to a meeting in Virginia City. I'll try to get up his way in a day or so."

"I tell him, Señor Ben," José said.

He swung into his saddle with the ease of a man who was born to a horse. The others mounted as if at a signal, and it was almost a cavalry movement in its precision. Ben stood watching them ride out of the yard and into the pines. The chuck wagon moved out from behind the barn and swung behind them.

Again he felt that tug of loneliness, a sense of being left behind. He thought of the meeting—of William Sharon of the Bank of California and of James G. Fair, Superintendent of the big Ophir Mine and of John W. Mackay, the likable little Irishman who was Superintendent and part owner of the Kentuck.

Fair, Mackay and Cartwright, Ben thought with growing anger. *The only three men left in the State of Nevada who haven't sold their souls to the Bank of California.* And immediately he was thinking of the fifth man who would be at that meeting: Matt Vogel. Matt Vogel and Ben Cartwright had tangled before. They would tangle again.

He went back to the house and, from old habit, buckled on his gun belt. He had told these men he would not make any commitment without his sons being present, but still they had insisted on this meeting. He saddled and rode, taking the causeway across Washoe Lake and the road known as the Ophir Grade. A solid line of teams and wagons hauling lumber and supplies to the mines clogged the road and slowed his progress. Every one of those outfits belonged to Matt Vogel.

It was exactly noon when he topped the grade at the Divide and turned his horse into the main street of the teeming city called Virginia. The meeting loomed like a dark threat to his security, and he missed his sons like sin.

3 SPIRITUALISTS AND FORTUNE TELLERS of every description abounded in Virginia City. They were consulted on every subject from how to cure a bunion to where to sink a shaft that might cost a hundred thousand dollars, and they were believed by washerwoman and Bonanza King alike. One of these—a phrenologist, he was—had once told Ben that he sensed a definite "mental telegraphy" at work between the four Cartwrights. They all pretended to be greatly impressed and later, over beers, they had a good laugh about it. Right now, however, the phrenologist might have made his point. Hoss Cartwright was thinking about his father and he had been all day. It wasn't really a worry. Just a nagging concern that he had kept to himself.

Here in the canyon along the upper reaches of the Carson River the sun had come slowly this morning. But now, at noon, the heat burned thickly through the pines and soaked into the hulking frame of Ben's middle son, sprawled out on the cured grass of this open flat. His concern for his father's affairs was not so strong at this moment as to keep him from relaxing.

Tipping the scales at nearly three hundred pounds, this was a man whose heart was as big as his frame. His face was like a map, charting every emotion in mobile undulations that ranged from squinting, almost homely contortions of protest over any injustice toward man, beast or insect to explosive blossomings of an all-encompassing grin or wide-mouthed laugh that could not be ignored by anyone within the radius of its influence. Sensitive and terrified of his own strength, he was inclined to back off from trouble, but anyone who had ever taken one of these gestures for weakness had learned to regret it. Upon occasion—and this was one—he could look as innocent as a new-born babe.

The air was pungent with freshly cut pine wood and the remnant smoke of a noon campfire. New and cured needles blended their scent in an understanding as old as the mountains themselves. Jim Willy, the Paiute, lying on his back, chewing on the long needle of sugar pine, hands laced behind his head, squinted up at the incredibly blue sky and said, "Hey, Hoss. You know that old log we were looking at? I got five dollars says I can saw through it faster than you."

Hoss Cartwright didn't even move. His eyes were

squeezed shut against the brightness of the sun. "Where'd you get five dollars?" he said.

"Sold some scalps," said Jim Willy.

Again Hoss failed to move, but he did wince. "You know something?" he said. "If you'd lived in the days when the whites were fighting the Indians, you'd have starved to death."

"What do you mean 'in those days'?" asked Jim Willy. "You and me and Little Joe still fight, don't we?"

"Look," said Hoss. "If you want to go on being straw boss of this wood cuttin' outfit quit talkin' so much and let your men get their noonday nap."

"If I was the really big boss of this outfit," said Jim Willy, "I'd forget the noonday nap and get some work done."

"You go right ahead," said Hoss. "Soon as you get about sixty cords cut, let me know."

Jim Willy dug his shoulder blades contentedly into the thick carpet of aged pine needles. "Must have been a lot better in the old days," he said. "In all the reading I've done I can't find one place where it says a Paiute worked for a living."

Hoss half turned, squinted one eye at his Indian friend. "What makes you think it's changed?" he said.

The young Indian picked up a handy clod, tossed it accurately and hit Hoss in the stomach. Hoss pretended to be mortally wounded, although in fact he had barely felt the impact.

"You know something, Injun?" Hoss said. "You could be put back on the reservation."

Jim Willy grinned up at the sky. He was a handsome lad of twenty-three, his features fine-chiseled in the manner of his Shoshone ancestors, his lean and muscular frame accented by the familiar wearing of well-cut clothes. He liked to tease with Hoss about being an Indian, but beyond that he never considered the fact that

25

he really was one. Had anyone asked him suddenly, he would have like as not said he was a Cartwright. He certainly considered himself one.

Vaguely, Jim Willy knew he had been picked up by Ben Cartwright out beyond Pyramid Lake during one of the great *pogonip* freezes—the white death that was the scourge of the Indians of that region. Whether his mother and father had died or lived, he did not know. Ben had brought him to the Ponderosa, and he had been raised as one of the family. He had gone to school with Little Joe, vied with him in his lessons, risked his neck on his first bucking bronco to show Joe up and in every other way had grown up as a brother with the Cartwright boys. If secretly, as he sometimes did, he thought of the fact that he was an Indian and therefore different from them, he did not show it, and, he hoped fervently, they did not realize it. The last thing on earth he wanted was to make them feel sensitive about his race.

Hoss half turned and looked at his young friend. A great feeling of well-being swept through the big man's frame, momentarily driving out the worry that had been nagging him. There was a great sensitivity in Hoss, especially where his family was concerned, and that sensitivity extended itself also to the land that was the Ponderosa, for to Hoss the Ponderosa and his family were inseparable. His eyes were wide open now as he stared through the interlacing of needles above his head and listened to the whisper of the small wind that came down from Lake Tahoe in a sigh. That sigh could grow to a shout here in the canyons and blast out as a roar across Washoe Valley to turn, finally, into a howling Washoe Zephyr as it swirled up against the Virginia Mountains and piled down the slope of Mt. Davidson, where it could rip the roofs from the jerry-built houses and send geysers of dust whipping through the streets of the town. Hoss thought of that and he thought too of how ambition could grow, just as a breeze from Tahoe could grow, until it was a smashing, destroying force, sweeping everything before it.

The pleasant relaxation of the noon rest was gone. He was again worried about his father. They were putting pressure on him there in town, Hoss knew, and it was the pressure of ambition—the ambition of two men. He forced himself back to the work at hand.

"Hey, Injun?"

"You speak me?" Jim Willy said.

"Heap big chop wood," Hoss said.

"Just remember, friend," said Jim Willy, "I'm the straw boss here. Pick yourself up an axe and start slugging away at those pine butts. When you figure you've got a cord, let me know and I'll gladly come measure it for you."

Hoss got to his feet, stretched luxuriously and accidentally kicked Jim Willy in the ribs. "Pardon me all to the devil," said Hoss.

Jim Willy was getting to his feet, looking off toward where the twenty Paiute wood cutters were just now moving back to their work. He looked at Hoss, rubbed his chin, spit across the center of his lips and said, "You know something, friend? I doubt your scalp would bring much anyway. I think I could get a lot more for Little Joe's."

*   *   *

Little Joe Cartwright lined the bone bead front sight into the notch of the semi-buckhorn rear sight and slowly lowered the rifle down onto the target. The majestic buck lifted its head and half turned, as if somehow sensing the lethal bore of death was on it. The smooth stock of the gun was cool against Joe Cartwright's cheek, the metal of the trigger yielding against the pressure of his curling finger. There, for this one second, Little Joe Cartwright had the power of life and death in his hands. Slowly, he lowered the rifle. *I wouldn't want somebody to have that*

27

sort of advantage on me, he said to himself. The big buck seemed to understand. Slowly, almost arrogantly, he turned and walked into the undergrowth. Joe Cartwright stood up slowly. "Next time," he said.

He went across to his horse and thrust the rifle back into the saddle scabbard and swung into the saddle. Cochise, the black and white pinto, lifted his head expectantly. Joe reached down and patted the pinto's neck. "You'll get your chance to chase cows," he said. "Before this drive is over you'll be sick of it." He reined the horse around and started riding along the ridge.

This was the high meadow country where the snows rarely left. Great patches of grass stretched between split granite peaks, and down through improbable gulleys small trickles of snow water gurgled unexpectedly, watering meadows of startling greenery between the deceivingly smooth boulders, which from a distance appeared small but which, as one approached, became twice the height of a man on horseback.

This was the northwesternmost reach of the Ponderosa. The shoulder of Mt. Rose thrust itself into the sky beyond the north end of Lake Tahoe. With his cow gather completed, Joe Cartwright had appointed himself a committee of one to make this last swing up into this isolated area to check against the remote possibility that a stray or two might have drifted up this high. He hadn't found a single Ponderosa steer, and secretly, he hadn't expected to. This was a little extra treat he allowed himself every year when it was time to move into the high country to gather the cattle in preparation for the drive into the lower slopes and the rich meadow hay of the Washoe Valley.

This was the time of year Joe Cartwright loved most— the frost on the blankets in the morning, the acrid sting of a pine-knot fire, the tang of the first bubble of coffee in a smoke-stained pot that somehow held a flavor even

Hop Sing could not duplicate. Joe's handsome young face twisted in a grin of pure contentment.

Still in his early twenties, the youngest son of Ben Cartwright had a lot of living ahead of him, and the realization manifested itself in every movement he made. He was a devilishly handsome kid and he knew it and was completely delighted by it. What might have seemed conceit in someone else appeared in Joe Cartwright as supreme but healthy self-confidence. He could ride, he could fight, he could love; and he saw no sense on earth of denying any of these facts. If once in a while, as he sometimes did, he got far enough out of line that people resented him, he could turn on a boyish charm backed by a laugh so completely contagious no one had ever been able to resist it. Jim Willy, the Paiute, Joe's greatest admirer, swore Joe had learned that laugh from a bluejay that had been crossed with a grey squirrel, for it was a cackling, high-pitched, ear-piercing sound that was downright devilish with sheer animal delight. Once Joe cut loose with that spontaneous cackle of his, people turned on the street and total strangers smiled in response. Hearing it, you immediately knew: Joe Cartwright's secret was that he loved life.

He was grinning now, without even knowing why he was grinning, as he reached down and patted the neck of his favorite pony, Cochise. Suddenly the grin faded as he looked out across the vast expanse of timbered slopes and far below, through a veil of trees. At the distant foot of the canyon he caught a blue wink of Lake Tahoe. There was a sudden somberness in him—a thing unusual to his nature. He moved Cochise slightly so that he could get a full view, and in this moment he admitted to himself why he had left his crew and come here alone as he had before. He had wanted to see this particular spot again.

It wasn't the lake itself that held him, although this was the most spectacular azure jewel that God had ever put on the face of this planet. At an elevation of over six thousand feet, the expanse of Tahoe was hugged by timbered shores exceeding imagination of man. West lay the granite ribbed summit of the Sierra, and rising above the water Mt. Tallac bore an eternal cross of snow. On the south shore, magnificent meadows formed summer grounds for the Ponderosa cows and their calf crop. To the east, the timber swept down the slopes to the very doorstep of the Ponderosa ranch house itself. This was nature at her magnificent best, and Joe Cartwright felt it. But for this particular moment his attention was focused on one grove of trees, one rock-laden promontory that thrust into the lake. It was a place he knew well. As a small boy, he had gone there the first time with his father. He still went there alone when he was troubled and wanted to think things through. He went there in a way a man goes to church: for solace and a chance to understand himself, if only for a moment. It was the place where his mother was buried.

For a long moment he looked at this distant sanctuary he had come to love, then his thoughts turned again to his father and to his oldest brother, Adam, and to his brother Hoss. To an outsider, Little Joe was perhaps the least sentimental of the Cartwrights. Joe, in moments of self-searching honesty, worried about the fact that he was the most sentimental of them all.

With characteristic impulsiveness, he reined Cochise, touched him lightly with his heels and headed down the canyon. The annual fall gather of cattle had been a success, he was confident of that. He had a good crew; they had done their work well, and the last of the gather was moving toward Spooner Meadow. Additional hands would be riding up from the Ponderosa headquarters within the next day or so, then the big drive would start: down into the low country, moving the cattle slowly, letting them graze as they drifted. There was always the possibility of a quick snow at this time of the year, but the distance was not so great as to make it disastrous. Joe Cartwright rode easily back toward the main cow camp, the mood of quick depression gone, a man completely at ease with himself and the world around him.

He was never able to remember precisely what it was that made him duck low in the saddle and at the same time draw his gun. There was no time to think about it. The warning was there—the sudden sound of horses where none should be. The unmistakable click of the cocking of a gun. He was half way to the ground when the angry crack of a rifle slammed against his eardrums.

He thought first it was a deer hunter, for the Tahoe country was being discovered by more and more people, and some of them were not used to the ways of guns. He rolled behind a rock, lest the phantom rifleman decide to try again. There was silence, and Joe cautiously raised his head. "Watch where you're shooting, you crazy fool!" Joe yelled.

"I know where I'm shootin'," a nearby voice drawled. Joe turned slowly.

The man was mounted, holding the rifle casually across his pommel. He was tall and thin, and Joe could not recall having seen him before. He wore a stubble of beard, but his clothes were neat, even expensive—the clothes of a saddleman. From the cut of his high-crown hat, Joe calculated him as a man from the Southwest; from the easy way he set his saddle, Joe was positive he was a man used to cattle. Joe stood up slowly.

"I ought to take that gun away from you and bend it around your head," Joe said. He had the hot temper of his Creole mother and he was never able to control it completely. "You better start doing some talking," he said.

A small and not unhandsome grin lifted one corner of the stranger's lips. "I just had my say," he said, and the drawl was almost insolent. "You're on posted land. Get off."

Joe knew that his mouth had dropped open in spite of

anything he could do about it. The idea of someone sticking up a "No Trespassing" sign in this trackless wilderness was almost laughable. He took a second to recover, but disbelief was still in his voice.

"That's the craziest thing I ever heard of," Joe said. "But even if it was so, it wouldn't mean anything to me. Once in a while a few of our cattle drift up into these high pastures. I was checking in case they had, that's all. I'm Joe Cartwright of the Ponderosa."

"They call me Stevens," the man with the rifle said. "They tell me some folks cut down trees that don't belong to 'em. I'm here to see they don't."

For a long moment Joe looked at the man and then, in spite of himself, he started to laugh, and that high-pitched, infectious and short cackle rattled back and forth in the thin mountain air. The man in front of him was suddenly so out of place. "Look," Joe said. "Do you think I got a cross-cut saw or an axe in my saddle bags?"

The faint grin lingered around the rider's lips. "I wouldn't rightly know," he said. "There ain't many trees where I come from." He looked Joe over. "You say you run cattle?"

"That's right."

"Too bad I didn't see you first. Cattle's more to my liking."

"Holding that gun on me doesn't make me inclined to offer you a job."

"I can only handle one job at a time," Stevens said. "I try to do the best I can with it while I got it." He gestured with the rifle. "My boss says keep people out of here, so get out."

There was no mirth in Joe now. "I got a notion to yank you out of that saddle," he said.

Stevens tilted the rifle. "You better get a notion not to." He whistled shrilly, and two riders came out of a thicket of turning aspen.

For a moment Joe stared at them, for he knew them

both. One was a thin, cadaverous man who rode hunched over in his saddle as if his chest hurt. Joe recognized him as "Lunger" Smith. He was a notorious Virginia City "chief," as the gunmen who operated up on the Divide between Virginia City and Gold Hill were called. He wore a long-tailed coat and a curled-brim bowler hat that appeared too small for him, and his black boots were neatly shined. He looked at Joe with his faded, amber eyes and his lips twitched slightly, his only gesture of recognition. The presence of the man was like the presence of death, and Joe knew immediately that whatever was going on here, it was something more than ordinary business. But as startling as the appearance of Lunger Smith was, the appearance of the other man was even more so. Not more than two weeks ago Joe had spent a rowdy evening in Virginia City with the young man who now sat there holding a gun on him.

"What's the matter, Pete?" Joe asked quietly. "Run out of something exciting to do?"

The young man called Pete shifted his weight uneasily and the drawn gun in his hand suddenly became obviously awkward—so much so he shoved it back into the holster. Lunger turned his amber eyes that way but said nothing. Stevens, with only a twitch of his lips, made a note of the gesture.

"You two know each other?" Stevens asked.

"We know each other," Joe said.

"Look, Joe," Pete said. "There's nothing personal in it. I had to have a job. I told you that the other night."

"I offered you one, didn't I?" Joe said.

Stevens was looking from one young man to the other. "Maybe you don't pay enough," he said. "My young friend here has got lots of ambitions." He half turned toward Pete. "Ain't that so, Pete?"

Joe didn't take his eyes from Pete Wilson's face. Pete was just Joe's age—their birthdays were one week apart. They had compared notes on that. In spite of the wide difference of their backgrounds, they were a lot alike and had become fast friends that one summer Pete had worked on the Ponderosa. Pete was a top-notch rider, but there was a great impatience in him that made it hard for him to stick to one job for any great length of time. He wanted to go places in life and that was admirable, but he wanted to go there at once, even if he had to take every short-cut. And even this was understandable to Joe, for along about this age a young man got the feeling he was standing in a tub full of molasses, trying to walk but getting nowhere . . .

"Like I say, Joe, there's nothing personal." Pete was miserable and Joe knew it.

"In that case, maybe you won't mind saying who you're working for."

Pete glanced across at Stevens, apparently got the confirmation he wanted. "Matt Vogel," Pete said. "He's starting up a big timber operation around here. He's moved in a lot of equipment. We're guarding it."

Joe tried to conceal his surprise and wasn't sure he had been successful. Stevens said, "When the man hired me he said don't let no trespassers come around. He didn't tell me about any exceptions."

The cowboy's meaning was clear, and Joe Cartwright knew better than to argue with a gun. He moved across to Cochise and swung into the saddle. He didn't look at Stevens. He looked directly at Pete Wilson.

"Let me know when you have a day off," said Little Joe Cartwright. "Maybe we can get together and have some fun." He hesitated a long moment and then said, "I'll tell Ellen I saw you."

He saw Pete stiffen, and for one swift second he wondered if, in his anger, he had gone too far. Ellen was Pete Wilson's wife. Before marrying Pete she had been engaged to Little Joe Cartwright for two years. Joe wished he could take back the sting he had given his one-time friend, but he knew it was too late. He wheeled his horse and rode back down the slope.

And now all the joy of the annual cow gather was gone, and the moment of memory as he had viewed his mother's grave was behind him. He had learned a lot here in the past few moments, and he had learned nothing.

Why was Matt Vogel going into the timber business? Matt Vogel was one of the most successful transportation company owners in the country. Was he expanding? Had he, too, been caught up in the all-consuming wave of ambition that seemed so closely allied with the mines and the sudden wealth and the speculation so rampant it swept everyone into a whirlpool of desire? He didn't know. But he did know that, whatever the answer, it would affect, even threaten, the Ponderosa.

He came to an open meadow and gigged Cochise into a full run. He had to get back to the cow camp in Spooner Meadow, for this was his job, his first obligation. But beyond that—hopefully as soon as tomorrow—he would go over to the wood camp and talk to Hoss. It was almost as if something were pulling at him.

If Matt Vogel was making a big move of some kind, Ben would know about it, this Little Joe knew. Everything that happened these days was connected with mining in some way or another, and the *Territorial Enterprise* in Virginia City had the best mining editor in the world, and that mining editor was a close friend of the Cartwrights . . .

Shadows slipped swiftly down the eastern slope of the Sierra and the temperature dropped rapidly. *Four weeks since I've read a newspaper, Little Joe thought. A lot can happen in four weeks.* He felt a sudden urge to have the cattle drive finished so that he could have a night in Virginia City.

4 IT WAS NEARLY nine o'clock at night, but it could have been high noon or four o'clock in the morning and it wouldn't have made any difference. The streets would still have been swarming with people, for Virginia City never slept, and at any time one-third of the town was underground and two-thirds above ground, and it was hard to say which group made the most noise. William Wright, mining editor of the influential *Territorial Enterprise,* felt the wooden sidewalk tremble beneath his feet and knew it was an underground blast—an old and familiar feeling that constantly startled newcomers from "down below," as San Francisco was called. A miner came down the sidewalk, weaving slightly. He lifted a hand and from old habit said, "Howdy, Dandy!"

William Wright answered the greeting, liking the feel of it. He knew everyone on the Comstock, and his pen name of Dan de Quille had become so familiar he sometimes forgot he had any other.

Standing there in front of the *Territorial Enterprise* office, leaning his long, lank frame against a post, Dan de Quille drank in the sounds of his adopted town and read a message in every separate one of them. That intermittent blast of steam with its peculiar ear-splitting suddenness was the hoist at the Gould and Curry Mine. The long, metallic rumble was loaded ore cars; the crashing shudder, the rich silver-bearing rock being dumped in the hoppers. There was the quick clang of the signal bell at the Hale and Norcross, the distinctive, sharp but more dis-

36

tant whistle was from the Yellow Jacket over the Divide in Gold Hill, and that rhythmic thumping that could lull a native to sleep and drive an outsider to drink was the reassuring sound of stamps in the mills below the town. Always the tramp of boots on boardwalks as men moved to and fro in a seemingly aimless procession; always the profane shouts from the saloons; always the high-pitched laughter from the girls on North D Street who were paid to laugh. Above the town, standing as a backdrop and a sounding board, was Mt. Davidson. The sounds drifted up through the thin, high air, hit the mountain and reverberated back.

From up beyond the Divide, similar sounds drifted across from busy Gold Hill, and a man could stand here and imagine a steady stream of humanity moving like ants through the earth beneath his feet, while another army swarmed above ground at the mills along the Carson River and through the forests, cutting wood for the voracious furnaces and timber for the ever-deepening mines. An exciting place. A place to stir a man's imagination and fire his soul . . . and yet tonight there was a certain sadness in the thin-faced newspaperman. The sounds were there—all of them—and they were sounds that meant the mines were working again and the depression was on its way to being over. Dan de Quille sighed deeply. Things would never be the same again, he knew. *You can't stop progress,* he said to himself, trying to shake off the mood. But the feeling of nostalgia and sadness did not leave him.

He started sauntering up C Street toward Taylor where the office of the Bank of California stood, and he thought of William Sharon, that precise, dapper little man who was rapidly becoming the most powerful force on the Comstock. Sharon had arrived here when the mines were in "borrasca," as the miners said of depression times. The bank he represented had been more than anxious to make loans, and at fair interest rates, too . . . but loans

37

became due and had to be paid, Dan thought gloomily . . .

Yes, things had changed, and they would change a lot more. A few months ago Dan had known fifty men who were actual mine owners; now only their names remained. Hale—Norcross—Belcher—Best—Gould—Curry . . . these had been flesh and blood men. Some sold out foolishly, some borrowed too heavily from the benevolent Bank of California. There were very few individual owners left, and the ranks were getting thinner every day.

His thoughts turned immediately to his good friends the Cartwrights, and to the Ponderosa Ranch he often visited. He had known Ben a long time now, and sometimes, when these moods were on him, Dan would sneak away for a few days on the Ponderosa and he always came back restored. But lately even that had changed, he thought gloomily. Ben Cartwright was deeply involved in mining stock in the Hale and Norcross Mine. That giant flume he was building was to deliver timber and cord wood to the mines, and there was talk that, once it was completed, it would be possible to flume down hundreds of tons of ice from the frozen lakes—ice desperately needed to cool the mines as they went deeper and deeper into ever-richening veins, through ever-increasing heat and foul air and waters that reached temperatures as high as one hundred and seventy degrees . . . The mines . . . everything revolved around the mines. Even the Ponderosa, once the self-contained domain of a man and his sons, was now becoming dependent on the mines and the mines dependent on the Ponderosa. He had noticed the unrest in Ben this afternoon when he had talked to him —unrest that reached deeper than just momentary impatience caused by the temporary delay of his meeting with William Sharon and the others. *No*, Dan thought. *Ben Cartwright feels it too.* Ben Cartwright was not a man who would stand against progress. But could progress of this magnitude and a man's dreams live side by side?

A little nightcap might be in order, Dan decided, and he went on up the gently sloping street and angled across at Taylor and entered the Crystal, the so-called millionaires' saloon. A dozen men spoke to him and a dozen offered to buy him a drink as he moved up to the bar, but he grinned his thanks and shook his head. Most of the men in the saloon were dressed alike—in rough miner's garb. Some were millionaires and some were muckers, and tomorrow the status could well be reversed. There was no way to tell them apart. To one of the more insistent Dan said, "Sorry, Pete, it's just not my night to howl."

"What's the matter, Dandy?" one of the miners said. "Them wild tales you write catching up with you?"

Dan's grin broadened. It was meant as a compliment, and right now a compliment was something he could use. Around here, the bigger the lie a man could tell the more popular he became, and Dan de Quille, through his anecdotes—or "quaints," as he called them—in the *Territorial Enterprise*, had become the most popular newspaperman in the West. He thought of Sam Clemens, his erstwhile cohort on the paper, and of the wild hoaxes he and Sam had pulled . . . Sam was calling himself Mark Twain now and doing well. He showed a lot of Dan de Quille's influence in his writing. *I owe Sam a letter*, Dan thought. *I'll get to it first thing tomorrow* . . .

Dan bided his time until his favorite bartender, Quincy Malloy, came waddling down to stand in front of him with the hang-down look of a blood hound who has failed to find a scent. Quincy, Dan knew, was also the favorite of Ben Cartwright, and Dan, the newspaper man again, wanted to know what time Ben Cartwright had left town. The length of Ben's stay could well be an indication of just how hard Sharon and Vogel intended to push him.

"Evening, Quincy," Dan said.

Quincy had a way of sidling up to a man at the bar. It was a way that said he knew all there was to know, but a way that also said he might or might not reveal it. Quincy set out a brandy without being asked. He made a point of knowing what each of his customers drank and a further point of knowing each man's capacity.

"Anything going on?" Dan asked as he poured his brandy.

Quincy glanced up and down the bar then moved closer to Dan. "Big things upstairs," he said.

It wasn't unusual for something big to be going on in the elaborate Washoe Club upstairs. Quincy probably meant a poker session with higher than average stakes, but you never knew. Dan made a series of interlocking wet circles on the bar with his glass.

"Anything special?" he asked.

Quincy half-turned so the others at the bar could not see his lips move.

"Ben Cartwright's still up there," Quincy said.

For just a moment Dan de Quille's hand froze, the glass halfway to his lips, then he downed the drink.

"The rest of them too?" he asked.

"Had supper together, the five of 'em," Quincy said. He was pouring another brandy, a sure sign he considered himself a part of the family, for every customer poured his own. Quincy had a way of covering his words with the glug-glug of the bottle.

Dan felt that old stir of excitement familiar to any newspaper man. Maybe the story wasn't there yet, but it was shaping up. He tried to visualize the men around that table up there in the well-appointed club room. William Sharon, probably looking like a smug little Santa Claus, the unlimited wealth and power of the Bank of California behind him, treasurer of the big Hale and Norcross Mine. James G. Fair, an expert miner and a man who dressed like one, was Superintendent of the Ophir.

John W. Mackay would be there, too. He was a mine timberer by trade, but he was a shrewd as well as genial little Irishman of whom it was said he "had a nose for ore." Dan de Quille thought of the other man he knew was at that meeting—the enigma of the lot. Big Matt Vogel was a self-made man with the driving power of a steam engine and a frightening desire to succeed. And then there was Ben Cartwright, the most independent of them all . . .

The mood that had been on Dan de Quille was immediately back. This was the new way of things. Corporate lawyers—consolidation—amalgamation—absentee owners—struggles for power . . . and to some men, that first million dollars meant only a club to be used to beat out more millions . . .

He tried to think of the Cartwrights and the Ponderosa caught in this grinding mill of greed that was raping the Comstock. He saw slopes denuded of timber and streams that once held trout and ran crystal clear turned to sluices of mud, and he saw the Truckee and Carson rivers reduced to trickles because there was nothing left to hold back the run-off. The ceaseless demand for timber and wood had led to that, for men were moving through those forests like mowers through wheat fields . . . Only one man really seemed to care about tomorrow: Ben Cartwright. One man alone.

And immediately the words of Andrew Jackson flashed into the mind of Dan de Quille: *One man with courage makes a majority.*

Don't let go, Ben, he said to himself. *Don't let go. A man does have a right to a dream.*

5 THERE WERE no cards on that corner table in the elaborate Washoe Club upstairs above the Crystal Saloon, but the five men sitting there were playing poker nonetheless, and they were playing for high stakes. If there was any animosity among them, one would have been hard put to find it; but there was in each of them a deadly intent concealed behind the relaxed and polished manner, the casual gesture and the friendly smile.

The supper had been excellent; the brandy was superb, the cigars the best money could buy. Typical of the time and the place, the affair had been comfortably informal and the men were dressed accordingly. Under different circumstances, Ben Cartwright, a man of good taste and appetite, would have enjoyed himself thoroughly. But Ben Cartwright was astute enough to know he had not been invited here solely for his company, although up to this point William Sharon, the host, had made it seem that way.

Sharon was not an impressive man to look at. He was small, and his jutting, lower lip gave the impression he was always pouting. Above his penetrating blue eyes his hair receded from a high forehead. Of all the men at the table, he was the only one over-dressed—almost to the point of foppishness—and this was a well-known affectation of his. He had been educated to the law, and this stood him in good stead in his present capacity of manager of the Virginia City branch of the powerful Bank of

42

California. At one time he had been in the real estate business in San Francisco and had made a modest fortune. He had lost it all gambling in Comstock mining securities on the San Francisco Exchange. Ben Cartwright had often speculated that Sharon's driving ambition to become King of the Comstock was based on a desire for revenge against the men who had broken him. Whatever it was, he had displayed a ruthless willingness to seize and force a profit, regardless of cost to others.

The conversation was still general, but subtly and surely it had drifted closer and closer to two subjects— the Hale and Norcross Mine and the Ponderosa. Sharon said, "Of course, as long as you don't borrow the money from me, it's none of my business, Mr. Cartwright. But I can't see where this flume you are building justifies the tremendous expenditure."

"Then call it a gamble on my part," Ben said. "Although I don't consider it so. My son Adam and I had discussed this for a long time before he left for Europe. He drew up the preliminary plans and Philip Deidesheimer has gone over them inch for inch . . ."

"I read all that in the paper," Matt Vogel said. "That flume still won't do nothing I can't do with my teams."

"Again a matter of opinion, Vogel," Ben said. There was always an unmasked challenge when these two men spoke to each other.

"You got plenty of timber down on the lower slopes to take care of those timber contracts you got with Hale and Norcross," Vogel said. "What are you doing up in that high country anyway?"

"I believe my views of controlled cuttings and sane logging methods have been made abundantly clear," Ben said. The sudden stilting of his speech was the only outward sign of a growing and seething anger.

Matt Vogel chuckled, deep in his throat. He was a dark, handsome man, perhaps even larger than Ben himself.

43

"Somebody was telling me you made a talk someplace about how every time you cut down a tree you ought to plant a seed."

Ben's face flushed. "We'll do something along that line or denude the entire Sierra," he said. "Is that what you want, Vogel?"

Matt Vogel leaned forward slightly. "I accept things the way they are, Cartwright. You go ahead with that 'posterity' speech of yours all you want. If you want to build something folks will remember you by, you can buy a tombstone for a lot less money than you're putting into that flume."

Ben Cartwright's control was a magnificent thing to watch, but his contained anger was making itself felt all around the table. "I wasn't aware that I was trying to erect a monument," he said tightly. "I'm running a ranch that's owned by myself and my three sons." He made a long, pointed pause and shifted his gaze ever so slightly so that it now included William Sharon. "It happens to be a ranch that is not for sale."

"It will be when somebody offers you enough money," Matt Vogel said easily.

If Matt Vogel had wanted to give a capsule summary of his character, he couldn't have done it any more succinctly. Money was Matt Vogel's god—his entire philosophy of life. He got his start working a hydraulic claim across the mountains in the California gold camps. In time he ran six hydraulic giants. He saw nothing ugly in the devastation wrought by the huge nozzles that washed out hills and forests and clogged swift running streams with mud thirty feet deep . . . nothing at all wrong in this, the most destructive of all forms of mining. He saw instead a certain beauty in the power of his monitors, for they were rending the earth apart to make Matt Vogel rich.

There was nothing devious about this big man. Tough,

44

rugged, completely self-made, he had started here on the Comstock as a teamster—a job he took to give himself a chance to look around. Within a few months he had taken over the company that hired him, and in the few years since that time he had taken over one transportation company after another until now he was recognized as holding a monopoly on the highly lucrative business upon which the very life of Virginia City depended. He owned hundreds of horses, mules and oxen, and no man could travel as much as a mile without seeing one of Matt Vogel's sixteen-mule jerkline outfits. He was proud of his position; he could still handle any outfit he owned better than his top drivers could handle it.

Ben raised his eyes and met Vogel's gaze squarely. "There's not that much money in the world, Matt," Ben Cartwright said.

The uneasiness around the table was too apparent to ignore now. William Sharon cleared his throat. "This is all very interesting, gentlemen," he said, "but we're all busy men and I'm sure you realize I did have some business on my mind when I asked you to come here . . . Perhaps if we get to it . . . ?"

John Mackay was enough of a diplomat to recognize an opening when he saw it. He moved into it smoothly. "Since Jim Fair and I are not part of the idle rich," Mackay said, "it just might be a good idea if we got our talking done and got to bed at that."

There was a mildness in Mackay, but beyond that there was the confidence that comes from physical fitness, for Mackay was a health faddist and a man who worked out every day at Bill Davis's Gymnasium on South C Street. Ben liked Mackay, a practical little Irishman with a keen sense of mining, and he had been involved with him on one or two minor deals.

"That's the whole trouble with the mining business today," James Fair growled. "All talk and no action. That's

45

the reason the mines are losing money—a bunch of kid-glove miners trying to run things out of a San Francisco office."

"Was that aimed at me, Jim?" Sharon asked.

"If you want it to be," James Fair said.

There was nothing to like about James G. Fair, and he worked seriously at seeing the impression wasn't changed. He considered himself a miner, first, last and always, and he dressed the part—flannel shirt, shapeless felt hat, denim pants and stout, much-battered boots.

Matt Vogel said, "One of the few times we agree, Fair. I ain't much for talk either." He turned to Sharon. "Go ahead and tell 'em what's on our mind, Bill."

Ben Cartwright noticed two things. The pronoun "our" and the familiar use of Sharon's first name. He knew Sharon well enough to sense he had resented both.

"All right, gentlemen," Sharon said. "I'll put it plainly. You all know Mr. Ralston, the head of the bank, spent the last week here in Virginia City."

"A fact that would be pretty hard to ignore," Ben said. "There was little else in the newspapers."

"Mr. Ralston is a rich and important man, Mr. Cartwright," Sharon said.

"A mighty powerful one, anyway," Ben said.

"Isn't that one and the same thing?" Sharon asked, quietly.

"As far as I'm concerned," Vogel said. Ben knew that Vogel had long admired Sharon—simply because Sharon was a ruthless businessman who was doing exceedingly well. Now, suddenly, it seemed that Vogel was considering himself part and parcel along with Sharon . . .

"Why don't you get to the point, Sharon?" It was Fair again, always blunt, always direct.

Sharon was a superb business man and he was an actor. If he wanted something, he could seem almost pathetic. He wanted something now. He looked around the table and suddenly he was tired, a little bit of helplessness in him, a man who wanted only to do good, asking for help and understanding. "You men," he said. "All of you here." This time he included Vogel. "You know the Comstock as well as anyone alive. There's no need for secrets among us." He paused. "The reason Mr. Ralston came up here was because some of the Board of Directors of the Bank and many of the stockholders were beginning to lose faith in the Comstock."

"The main lode ain't even been touched yet," James Fair growled.

"I know that, Mr. Fair," Sharon said. "So do the rest of us. But you all know the Bank has poured money into mine after mine that has run into borrasca and we've seen a number of mills fail . . ."

"Mr. Mackay's Kentuck is still producing," Ben said quietly. "The Hale and Norcross is enjoying a small bonanza. Mr. Mackay hasn't borrowed any money from the Bank and neither have I in behalf of the Directors of Hale and Norcross." Ben's eyes held Sharon's gaze. "Is there any connection between our not borrowing money and the success of our mines, Mr. Sharon?"

For the first time Sharon lost his composure and let his anger show through. He was speaking to Ben now, ignoring the others. "Mr. Cartwright," he said, "when I first came here from San Francisco I came armed with a dozen letters of introduction, addressed to you. Those letters were from some of the most influential people in the State of California. I came to you before I spoke to anyone else, and I came to you, assuming I had an ally. You've fought me, every inch of the way, Mr. Cartwright. You've advised people not to borrow from the Bank. You've made statements to the press. Why, Mr. Cartwright?"

"Because I don't like your method of operation," Ben said softly. He saw the exchange of glances between Fair and Mackay and knew they agreed with him.

"Maybe we don't like yours," Matt Vogel said.

47

There again was that personal pronoun, and there again was that unmistakable annoyance in Sharon's expression. "I've helped a lot of mills and a lot of mines since I came here," Sharon said. "I've loaned out over three million dollars . . ."

Ben leaned forward slightly. "How many foreclosures have you made, Mr. Sharon?"

Sharon did not back down a bit. "It's my job to protect the Bank's money," he said. "That will continue to be my job. As for those foreclosures, the Bank owns seven mills at the moment." He sat back, a man who knew when to make a dramatic pause. "In order to protect the Bank's investment I mean to consolidate those mills into one, gentlemen. They will be Bank owned and Bank run."

He waited then, knowing there was no longer any need for backing and filling or beating around the bush. There wasn't a man at that table who didn't know what that meant. A group of mills, controlled directly by the Bank, would be a crushing monopoly, for any mine that refused to send its ore to a Bank mill would immediately have economic pressure brought to bear. There would be no further loans or extensions on notes to anyone who dared defy the Bank.

"And I'm putting my teams and wagons into the pot along with Bill," Matt Vogel said. His voice was strangely soft for him. He was smug—sure—a man who had grown in stature with a single, swift stroke.

"Where do Mr. Fair and Mr. Cartwright and I fit in?" John Mackay finally asked. With that simple question he had aligned himself, Fair and Ben into a team.

Sharon came directly to the point. "I've never claimed to be a philanthropist," he said. "I am willing to pay for what I get. I need all three of you." He held up his hand to indicate he wasn't finished. "Mr. Fair and Mr. Mackay, I consider you two perhaps the best mining experts on the Comstock."

"Thank you," Mackay said. "But if the truth were known, Dan de Quille could overshadow us both."

"If I wanted to align myself with a newspaperman I'd buy the paper," Sharon said.

"You seem to have left me out," Ben Cartwright said. He knew, now, why he was wanted.

"With Mr. Vogel going along with us, our new corporation will start with control of the mills and the transportation," Sharon said. "With the help and knowledge of men such as Mr. Fair and Mr. Mackay, we'll soon be able to get control of the mines."

"But you can't work those mines without lumber for the square sets to shore them up and you can't fire those mill boilers without wood. So to have complete control, you must have timber," Ben said quietly.

"Exactly right, Mr. Cartwright," Sharon said.

Ben, Fair and Mackay exchanged glances. Sharon leaned back in his chair, every inch the businessman now.

"It's a gigantic enterprise, gentlemen," Sharon said. "The profits could amount to millions." He laced his hands across his vest. "I see no need to divide those millions among a bunch of faceless stockholders and depositors in the form of interest or dividends."

"You mean to keep the money among the board members of this new corporation," Ben said.

"That's right," Sharon said. "And that's what I'm offering you here tonight, gentlemen. Places on the board of a new company to be known as Union Mill and Mining Company." His voice became businesslike and matter-of-fact. "In return for the chance I'm giving you to become rulers of the Comstock and perhaps as wealthy as any men have ever been, I will, of course, have to have your complete cooperation and a few concessions."

"Such as the Ponderosa," Ben said softly.

"Yes, Mr. Cartwright," Sharon said. "Such as the

Ponderosa. We also must have control of the Hale and Norcross Mine." He let the silence lie around the table like a thick blanket of fog, then he took a watch from his pocket, glanced at it, stood up. "I would hardly expect you to give me an answer on such a momentous opportunity without at least sleeping on it. There will be several other directors, of course—mostly extremely wealthy men from San Francisco, including Mr. Ralston himself." He pulled himself to his full and not very impressive height. "This, gentlemen, is why Mr. Ralston came to Virginia City. After seeing my operation here, he gave me carte blanche to go ahead with the Union Mill and Mining Company. If you wish to come by my office, I shall be glad to go over all the corporation papers with you, individually or severally."

"I'm not going along with you, Sharon," Ben Cartwright said quietly.

Sharon turned slowly. "Mr. Cartwright," he said, "you are either with me or against me. The Union Mill and Mining Company is not a sentimental dream. It is an accomplished fact." He smiled. "Good night, gentlemen."

Matt Vogel was on his feet immediately, like an obedient dog at the heels of his master, but this was a dog who would also leap at a man's throat and tear at his jugular vein, Ben Cartwright knew. He sat there, stunned by the enormity of what he had just heard.

"He's not bluffing, Ben," John Mackay said finally.

"No, John," Ben said, "he's not bluffing."

* * *

Dan de Quille, seated at a corner table, saw William Sharon and Matt Vogel come down the magnificent winding stairway into the noise and hubbub of the Crystal Saloon. He was immediately on his feet, moving across to them.

"Good evening, Mr. Sharon," Dan said.

50

Sharon turned on him coldly. "I have no statement to make at this time," he said.

"Is it true that Mr. Vogel here has leased several thousand acres of timber land up around Lake Tahoe?"

"That's a matter of public record," Sharon said sharply.

"And only the beginning of it," Vogel said.

Sharon's lips tightened. "When I have something for the press, I'll let you know," Sharon said. "Good night, Mr. de Quille." He moved swiftly through the crowd, Vogel right at his coattails. Once they were outside, Sharon turned to Vogel angrily. "You talk too much, Vogel," he said.

"Now that's funny," Matt Vogel said, "because listening to you upstairs there I got the same feeling about you."

"Do you think you're going to get anyplace making threats against Cartwright?"

"Yeah, I'm gonna get someplace," Vogel said. "I'm gonna get every stick of timber on the Ponderosa."

"You're not going to do it by hiring the kind of people you've been hiring and you're not going to do it by going around shooting off your mouth to newspapermen . . ."

Matt Vogel's voice was suddenly deadly and quiet. "You listen to me, Sharon. You run the bank, you make the loans, you say the big words. I don't understand just how this corporation is gonna work; I just know it will. I know if we . . ." he punched a thumb against his chest— "and that includes me—I know if we control the mills and the transportation and the water in the Carson River and all the timber in this part of the country that corporation is gonna get mighty rich, and I'm gonna get rich right along with it." His nostrils flared. "You promised me I'd run the transportation and timber end of it." He reached out and gripped Sharon's lapel. "I been waitin' a long time for this kind of chance, Bill. If you think you're gonnna squeeze me out just because I owe you a half a million dollars, you got another guess

51

comin'." His breath was rasping. "I mean to have the Ponderosa, Bill. I'll be mighty obliged for any help you can give me in getting it, but if it comes right down to it, I'll take it any way I can, but I'll take it."

He let go of Sharon's lapel, turned abruptly and moved off, heading down the hill toward D Street. The high-pitched and piercing laughter of a drunken woman stabbed through the night air.

William Sharon pulled his coat collar up a little higher. He needed Matt Vogel. He knew that. But sometimes big business made strange bedfellows and this was one he didn't like. He felt a sudden chill in the air. He was afraid of Matt Vogel. The big teamster had all the elements of a potentially dangerous man.

William Sharon walked on up the hill toward his boarding house. The Comstock had bilked him out of one hundred and fifty thousand dollars once . . . he meant to have his revenge . . . he meant to strip that same Comstock of millions. Only two things in the way of success now: the Hale and Norcross Mine and the Ponderosa Ranch. *Only one thing,* he thought: *Ben Cartwright.*

The feeling of violence that touched him with that fleeting thought frightened him. He walked on rapidly.

6 THE WINDING STAIRWAY that led down from the Washoe Club to the Crystal Saloon was an architectural masterpiece. The double curve was so graceful, the supports so nonexistent, it seemed like a stage setting winding its way into mysterious upper reaches of elegance. The handrail was worn to a magic patina by the work-roughened hands of millionaires. Adam Cartwright, who knew about such things, always claimed this was one of the finest sets of stairs in existence, and because Ben had a particular affinity for his oldest son's thoughts, he had, almost subconsciously, always lingered a moment when coming down from the club rooms. But tonight the emotion boiling in him far outweighed the pleasant thoughts of Adam and other past memories. To have to stand by and watch the rape of the Comstock and be able to do little about it was bad enough, but the mere thought of someone encroaching on the Ponderosa . . . Ben went through the door into the busy saloon. He was amazed when he found himself standing at the bar with a glass of whiskey in his hand and Quincy watching him closely.

"You *did* say whiskey, didn't you, Mr. Cartwright?" Quincy asked.

If he had asked for the drink, Ben didn't remember it but he was embarrassed to admit it. "Yes, Quincy. Thank you." Quincy moved off, but not before he had given Ben another long look. Quincy knew his customers and there was very little that missed his gaze. In addition, he was an incurable gossip, and his mind had started buzzing when he saw William Sharon and Matt Vogel coming down ahead of the others. Fair and Mackay were still up there. Quincy wished he could have been a mouse in the woodwork . . . Someone called and Quincy moved on down the bar.

For a long moment Ben stared into the amber liquid in front of him and there was a hypnotic effect to it—almost like looking into a crystal ball and seeing floating pieces of the past. Foremost and always was the Ponderosa—not just a ranch, not just a stand of timber or a thousand square miles of lush beauty. This was the place where Ben Cartwright had known he must put down his roots and build a monument to the three women he had loved in his life and to the living needs of the three sons they had given him. The Ponderosa was as much a part of him as the blood in his veins, and the mere thought of the destruction of logging crews moving up its timbered slopes, stripping its trees and fouling its streams and leaving its hills naked and exposed victims of erosion set that blood in his veins to boiling . . .

"So you're taking up all-night drinking," a voice at his elbow said.

Ben turned quickly, startled, for he had momentarily forgotten where he was. He was greeted by the familiar, thin face of Dan de Quille with its humorous dark eyes and its feeble black beard.

"Dan," Ben said. He had a great fondness for de Quille and looked forward always to Dan's frequent visits to the Ponderosa. Neither man had ever stopped to analyze it, but there was a perfect understanding between them on things esthetic. Ben never had to explain how he and his sons felt about the Ponderosa. Dan de Quille knew. Ben gestured toward the untouched jigger of whiskey, half apologetic. "As a matter of fact, I don't know why I ordered it."

"Quite a chill in the air," Dan said.

"Yes," Ben said. "I imagine it's pretty cold outside."

"I wasn't referring to outside," the newspaperman said.

A half-smile touched Ben's lips. "You don't miss much, do you?"

Dan returned the grin. "That's the way I make my living." He motioned for a brandy as Quincy moved back down the bar. Quincy poured and didn't leave. He busied himself at wiping glasses but his ears were fairly vibrating. Dan looked at Ben, winked, and deliberately raised his voice a decibel.

"You don't say!" he whistled. "A hundred million dollars!"

Ben glanced at Quincy, then at Dan and caught that

54

familiar, roguish glint in his eye. "Of course it wasn't cash," Ben said soberly. "But the IOU's on that table were as good as gold, you know that."

Quincy dropped a glass and broke it. As he bent over to pick it up, his ear was close to Dan's face. Dan dropped his voice. "A thing like that gets out, it could ruin some of the biggest men in Nevada."

"I knew you'd see it that way," Ben said. "There are some things that just can't be allowed to get into the newspapers."

"In the public interest," Dan said solemnly. He sighed. "Thank the good Lord for men like you, Ben." He paused. "How about the baby?"

Quincy was no longer even making a pretense of not listening. He was leaning forward, mouth open, hanging onto every word. Ben Cartwright removed his hat and held it against his chest and assumed a funereal mien.

"The child will never know," he said.

Quincy's eyes were bugging. "Somebody up at the other end of the bar is calling you, Quincy," Dan said.

"What?" Quincy said. "Oh." He moved off, but he glanced back a couple of times.

Ben started to chuckle. "You shouldn't do that to Quincy, you know that. It's really mean."

"Not at all," Dan said. "He thrives on it." He winked. "Besides, I've gotten some of my best stories this way. I just wait a couple of days and then let Quincy tell it back to me. By that time he's forgotten where he heard the beginning of it and he's filled in all the empty spaces."

They both laughed, but the laughter in Ben was short-lived. Dan watched his friend's face closely.

"You shouldn't let Matt Vogel get under your hide, Ben," Dan said quietly.

"Does it show that plainly?"

"Afraid it does. He and Sharon weren't very happy

when they came down those stairs and neither were you." He gestured toward the drink. "I was watching you. You didn't even remember ordering that drink."

"I never liked having my mind read," Ben said, not unkindly.

"We've known each other quite a while, Ben."

"Long enough that I know you're waiting for me to say something about what happened up there."

"Guilty as charged. You going to say it?"

"Nope."

"Didn't figure you would."

The two men looked at each other and grinned.

"I already know quite a bit," Dan said.

"You usually do. Let's turn it around. Is there something *you* want to tell me?"

"Why, Ben," Dan said in mock dismay, "you wouldn't want me to cause the *Territorial Enterprise* to lose the sale of a copy of tomorrow's paper, would you?"

"So Sharon's that sure of himself," Ben said.

"I won't try to bait you, Ben," Dan said. "The only information I have is what I've picked up from Matt Vogel." He grinned. "Matt has never been exactly bashful."

"Nor particularly likable, so far as I'm concerned," Ben said.

"But successful," Dan said. "And I'm afraid that's all that counts with him." He downed his drink quickly. "I saw Sheriff Coffee a little while ago. He said if I saw you to tell you he's waiting for you up at Beth Kelly's boarding house."

Ben bristled immediately, in the manner of a man who feels an old and trusted friend is meddling in his affairs. "Seems to me Roy's taking a lot for granted," he said. "He doesn't even know for sure whether I'm staying overnight in Virginia City or not."

Again that pixie grin was dancing around the corners

56

of Dan de Quille's eyes. "Maybe he was just taking a chance that you might possibly drop by Beth Kelly's on your way out of town," Dan said.

Ben felt something strangely like a flush touch his cheeks. He said something that sounded faintly like "Harumph!" and he did not give Dan de Quille a formal good night. He stepped outside, pulling up the collar of his sheepskin-lined coat. Dan stood at the bar, looking after Ben's departing figure, chuckling softly.

By golly, he found himself thinking, Ben and Beth *would* make a mighty handsome couple at that!

*   *   *

The air was thin and cold and it burned in Ben's lungs as he made the steep climb toward B Street. The constant jar of the stamps shook the night. The earth beneath his feet trembled from a blast, deep in the bowels of the teeming earth. A whistle shrilled with eardrum-splitting abruptness. The sound of boots on wooden walks was like a muffled drumbeat, and floating above it all, as if detached, was the sound of human beings . . .

For one brief interval, there with Dan de Quille, teasing Quincy, Ben had felt a moment of ease, but now the dark thoughts were back and pressing in on him. He thought of Beth Kelly and wished Sheriff Roy Coffee had picked a different night for a visit. Sometimes it was good to just sit alone with Beth in her parlor and visit . . . as often as not Beth said nothing, but she still had a way of understanding. *If Roy Coffee is waiting for me to have a hand of cribbage,* he thought . . .

Virginia City, sprawling, impersonal, noisy, was crowding in on him, leaving him no life of his own. Virginia City was alive and it would continue to grow so long as silver remained in the mines. The furnaces and the stoves and the heaters in the cribs along D Street would impersonally burn their thousands and thousands

57

of cords of wood. The yawning mines would devour their millions of feet of timber and give back their millions and more in silver.

Ben Cartwright had helped create this town. In the early days he had grubstaked half a dozen miners; some had failed, a few had struck it rich. Then came silver, and again Ben had had a part in it. He had helped finance Hale and Norcross, and when those two men had sold out, Ben had held onto his share of the mine. As Virginia City grew the Ponderosa grew—far beyond Ben's wildest dreams. And now, he thought somberly, the economy he had helped create was turning on him, threatening to devour him.

He moved toward the warm and yellow lights of Beth Kelly's boardinghouse and climbed the familiar stairs to the long porch that ran across the front of the towering house that had once been a millionaire's mansion. He remembered when Beth Kelly reigned as mistress of that mansion; he remembered when big, boisterous Kevin Kelly had held parties here that were the talk of Washoe . . . and he remembered the night when Beth Kelly had come to him on the Ponderosa and told him that big Kevin Kelly was dead.

Once again the stock market in Comstock shares had collapsed; once again there were bodies in San Francisco Bay. And this time a lovable, big Irishman was dead in a mansion in Virginia City with a pistol clutched in his right hand.

Ben moved up the stairs. He turned on the porch and looked around, for the view was magnificent from here. Up the slope from B Street were the most substantial of the homes, and B itself, once the main street of the town, was fast giving way to C Street, a block below. Standing here he could look directly down on the chimneys of the houses on D Street, so situated was the terraced town. The moon rose suddenly out of the east, and the miles of barren hills were stark outlines against the sky. Ben breathed deeply of the incomparable air. Virginia City . . . a wild, gay, thriving metropolis, the most famous city in the West. Virginia City . . . grasping, gouging, demanding more and more, destroying the earth as it belched forth silver . . . Ben forced the mood aside as he twisted the doorbell. He did not want Beth Kelly to see him this way. It was Sheriff Roy Coffee who opened the door.

"What are you doing here, you old goat?" Ben said, stepping inside.

"Show proper respect for the law and I might answer you," Roy Coffee said.

They were old-time friends, these two, and they argued a lot just to make sure the genuine affection between them wouldn't become too apparent. They shook hands warmly.

"How you been, Roy?"

"Good, Ben. You?"

"Can't complain. You been busy?"

"The usual," the Sheriff said. "A little cuttin' and shootin' up on the divide . . . big saloon fight down in Dayton . . ."

Ben looked up quickly. "Dayton isn't in your county."

Roy Coffee scratched his jawbone, a characteristic gesture he had, and squinted one eye nearly closed. "Well, I tell you, Ben," he said. "I got a sort of working arrangement with the sheriff of Lyon County. Way he looks at it, Dayton is closer to me than it is to him and since it gives him more trouble than any other town in his county, he's sort of deeded it to me."

Ben shook his head. "Roy, you amaze me."

Roy chuckled. He was an amiable man, his greying hair starting to thin. He had a habit of smoothing his moustache with his thumbnail and he seemed to weigh ponderously every decision, from a not infrequent hanging to the studying of the bill of fare down at the Sazerac. A person meeting him for the first time was apt to get the feeling he was somewhat indecisive and most certainly easygoing. More than one criminal had made the mistake of making that snap judgment of the popular Storey County Sheriff.

"Been meaning to get over to see you," Sheriff Coffee said. "Seems like every day they pile more paper work on a man."

"It's the same at the ranch," Ben said. He was looking around the room, and now he moved so that he could see into the dining room, then he obviously craned his neck to look down the hallway.

"No sense twisting your neck," Roy Coffee said. "She's out in the kitchen."

Ben shot Roy the annoyed glance of a kid caught with his hand in the cookie jar. "I'll just go say hello . . ."

"She knows you're here," Roy said.

Ben caught the subtle change in Roy's voice. He looked at his old friend quickly. "Anything wrong?"

"Not with Beth," Roy said. "She's prettier than ever." Roy was suddenly serious. "How did the meeting go?"

"You any idea of what it was about?"

"Yeah. Pretty good idea," Roy said.

"Sharon will never get the Ponderosa, Roy," Ben said quietly.

"Matt Vogel's the one you got to keep an eye on." He caught Ben's questioning glance. "He's hiring up two-thirds of the riff-raff in this town . . . as loggers."

"Loggers?"

"Sharon's putting up the money, I'd guess, but it's Matt Vogel who's leasing and buying up every square foot of timber land he can get his hands on." Roy paused. "He's just about got your Ponderosa surrounded, Ben."

Ben pursed his lips and again the anger was running through him. "So that's his game. Surround me with logging crews and then 'accidentally' start moving onto the Ponderosa . . ."

Roy Coffee put a hand on his old friend's arm. "I want you to remember something for me, Ben."

"What?"

"Nevada is a state. There's all sorts of duly constituted law—including me. Don't you and Hoss and Joe try to take things into your own hands." He broke off suddenly as the door at the end of the hall opened and Beth Kelly came toward them, both hands outstretched to Ben.

"Ben Cartwright," she said, "am I only imagining that I was supposed to have supper with you tonight?"

He took her hands and smiled down at her. "The business meeting I told you about turned into a supper meeting. I should have sent word . . ."

"It don't matter," Roy Coffee said. "I took your place. Fine meal, too."

Ben was still holding Beth's hands. He turned on Roy with a scowl and said to Beth, "Has this old goat been bothering you again?"

"No more than usual," Beth said, and her affection for Roy was there in the musical lilt of her voice. "I've missed you, Ben," she said simply.

"I've missed you, Beth," he said.

She turned then, her manner changing completely. "Do you two want me to serve your cake and coffee while you're standing up?"

"You and Ben go ahead, Beth," Roy Coffee said. "I got to stop by the jail."

"Oh must you, Roy?" Beth said.

"Don't coax him," Ben said.

Roy made a false pass at Ben's middle with his fist and Ben made a show of dodging the blow. "Just remember," Roy said, "I keep myself in shape."

He moved toward the entry hall and Ben went with him. For a moment he stood there, his hand on the door knob. "I meant what I said, Ben," he said quietly. "I don't want to see you get yourself in trouble."

61

"I don't want to see it either, Roy," Ben said. "But I won't back down to them, you know that."

Sheriff Roy Coffee gave a deep sigh. "Yeah, that's the trouble, Ben," he said. "I know that."

He opened the door and went on out into the night. Ben turned and went slowly back into the parlor. Beth was just entering from the hall, carrying the coffee service. "Stand there a moment," Ben said.

"What?"

"I want to look at you."

She stood there, holding the elegant silver coffee service, the light from the crystal chandeliers touching her face with highlights and shadows.

She was a small woman in perfect maturity of figure and poise. The dress she wore was of green velvet with black piping—plain, yet elegant in its plainness. The color was perfect for her, accenting the deep auburn of her hair. Ben Cartwright was never sure of the color of her eyes. They changed, according to what she wore. Tonight they were green. A small flush touched her cheeks and she suddenly seemed much younger than her thirty-eight years.

"Oh, Ben! You're silly!" she said. But she was not displeased. She came forward and set the service on the table and he moved across to assist her. For a moment their shoulders touched. They half turned toward each other, then, as if at a danger signal, they moved apart and she started to pour the coffee. "How was your meeting?" she asked.

Ben settled himself in his favorite chair and took the cup she handed him. "Not pleasant," he said. "Has everything been all right with you?"

"Full house," she said.

He set his cup down carefully. "Beth," he said, "if you were to sell the house and . . ."

"Ben, don't start that again," she said. "I'm perfectly

capable of making my own way and that's exactly what I intend to do."

Ben held up a hand. "All right, all right! I should know better than to argue with you after all these years."

There was a long silence between them.

"How are the boys?" she said finally.

"Fine. Just fine."

Again that long silence. "Do you want to talk about it, Ben?" she said softly.

He looked at her and in this moment he wondered why he fought so valiantly against falling in love with her. She was everything any man would want.

"Sharon and Vogel," he said then. "They have a plan shaping up that would give them complete control of the Comstock. They want the Hale and Norcross and they want the Ponderosa."

She had lived with wealth a good part of her life. She understood business and the complete ruthlessness of it when it was ruled by greed and ambition. "I have ten feet in Hale and Norcross," she said. "It's all the stock Kevin had left." She reached out and touched his hand. "It's yours if you need it, Ben."

"Thanks, Beth," he said. "I'd hate for our people to lose control of the mine."

"It's the Ponderosa you're really worried about, isn't it?"

"Yes, Beth. It's the Ponderosa."

She looked at him for a long time, searching his face as if she were trying to etch it into her memory.

"You don't need me there, Ben," she said. Her voice was barely audible. "You have your sons."

7 BEN CARTWRIGHT stayed in town that night. He went to his favorite, small hotel and luck was with him, for the room he preferred, in which he had slept many times, was vacant. It was the quietest room in the place, but it could not shut out the vibrant and familiar sounds of Virginia City. He looked at his watch and it was two o'clock.

He was tired, physically and emotionally, but the refreshing sleep he craved came only fitfully, and in the moments between sleep and wakefulness he kept seeing the faces of Sharon and Vogel and Fair and Mackay.

Suddenly he was looking at the tallest pine tree of the Ponderosa. It was a magnificent giant, a living thing, swaying in the gentle breeze that swept down from Lake Tahoe, the great scales of its bark warm and brown-yellow and redolent of the pitch that flowed in its veins. It quivered, as if with a chill, and now there were men at the base of this symbol of life and each man wore the face of Matt Vogel and the tree was bleeding pitch and now it fell with a terrifying crash and it landed across the ridgepole of the Ponderosa ranch house . . .

Ben Cartwright sat up in bed with a suddenness that set his heart to pounding. The sound and tremor of an underground blast still lingered in the room, and thin daylight streamed under the lace curtain at the window.

He got up and started to dress. His eyes burned and his muscles were cramped but, above all else, he wanted to get back to the ranch.

64

He ate a hurried breakfast in a small restaurant where he had not eaten before, not wanting to see anyone he knew. The food was bad, but he barely tasted it anyway. Then he hurried down to the stable where he had left Buck.

The stableman had once worked on the Ponderosa and Ben usually indulged the old fellow to the extent of listening to the retelling of some reminiscence he had heard a hundred times before. This morning Ben cut him short and was immediately sorry for his abruptness. He could feel the old man watching him, hurt and a little bewildered as Ben rode on without looking back.

There was a bite in the air that sharpened every scent, from the various chemical fumes of the mills to the pungent tang of the native sage.

At first there had been small timber on these nude hills. It was gone now, and the heavy Chinese population had taken to digging up the roots of the trees that had already been cut and burned for firewood. These trees had once fed the Indians of the region, for pine nuts were a staple of their diet. Now the Chinese wood peddlers could be seen moving up and down the streets, packing the bundles of gnarled roots on their backs. They found ready customers and they found a diminishing supply of roots.

He rode up the hill and turned his horse onto the Ophir Grade and headed down toward the valley, where steam clouds from a hundred geysers stood sharply white in the frosty air. Ahead he heard the team bells of the first of Matt Vogel's huge, twelve- and sixteen-mule jerkline outfits and he knew he would pass a solid line of these wagons hauling produce and firewood and lumber up the grade to Virginia City.

He was alone, and yet, he was not alone. Even here he could not escape Matt Vogel.

* * *

Hop Sing, the super-efficient, amiable, yet explosive little Cantonese who ruled the Cartwright house with an iron hand had forgotten just how long he had been on the Ponderosa. Had he stopped to think about it, he would have remembered he had come from one of the California placer camps across the mountains when the first excitement of the Nevada strikes trickled its way across the Sierra. As was the way with his countrymen, he knew that the average miner, in his eagerness to get rich, would leave enough tailings behind to supply a diligent and industrious man. Hop Sing was an industrious and diligent man.

He did, at times, think back to his first meeting with Ben Cartwright, for that meeting had much to do with the loyalty and affection he now felt for the entire family.

He was not a man to hold a grudge, and he had long ago forgiven the two men who had beat him half to death that day. It was in Johntown—a squalid clutter of shacks up the canyon from Dayton, a place set aside for the "heathen Chinee." Hop Sing and his countrymen did not complain. This was the way it was here in this new land, and so, this was the way it would be. Now and then a bunch of drunken miners would swoop down upon Johntown and wreak havoc, just for the devil of it. A favorite pastime of the miners had been the tying together of several Chinese by their queues. The merrymakers would then fire bullets around the feet of the howling Orientals. Hop Sing remembered a time when one of those bullets had gone astray.

For just a moment some of the old hurt was back with Hop Sing as he once more felt the boots of the two drunken miners. He had rolled on the ground in a vain effort to escape the punishment and it was then he saw the big man get out of the buggy and come running toward the miners.

Hop Sing would never forget the magnificent strength of rage he had seen in Ben Cartwright. That was the first time he ever saw it. Through the years he would see it again upon occasion. He could even remember what Ben Cartwright was wearing—a fine suit of clothes with a white shirt and a dark string tie, his boots polished. He saw him descend on the two miners like some great machine of destruction, saw him grab them by the nape of the neck, one with each hand, and he heard their heads crack together until they fell senseless on the ground . . .

A lady was kneeling beside him. "He's hurt, Ben," the lady said, and there was soft music in her voice.

He felt himself being lifted into the buggy . . .

The bruises healed and the broken bones mended, but the memory of the man who had come to his rescue and the sound of the lady's voice stayed with Hop Sing. He asked, here and there, and he learned of the Ponderosa and the great house that was in the process of building. There was a grown son, a middle boy and a new baby . . . the lady of such a house could use help, Hop Sing decided, and unannounced and without being able to speak more than a few words of English he went there and moved into the kitchen. No one had asked him to come. It was something he had to do. And it had been that way ever since. There was no formal arrangement, no mention of salary. The salary worked itself out; the formal arrangement still did not exist. Hop Sing trusted the Cartwrights; they trusted him.

He thought now of the tragic accident that had taken Mrs. Cartwright away from them and he remembered the long days of sorrow when Ben did not even speak to his sons. The Cartwrights had needed him more than ever then, Hop Sing knew. He took care of the infant known as Little Joe; and with the kindly and sensitive middle boy, Hoss, already huge for his age, he learned of the flowers and the wild life and the mysteries of nature on the Ponderosa; and from Adam, the oldest, he learned to speak English in his own, inimitable way.

As time went by, the little Cantonese became more and

more a part of the family. He loved them devoutly, but he clung with bulldog tenacity to his privilege of telling his "family" what he thought of them, and to his status of complete independence. The manifestations of that independence were sometimes a little startling to the Cartwrights.

Every so often Hop Sing would decided to take a trip to San Francisco to see one or more of his many relatives. The Cartwrights were never—or seldom ever—privy to these decisions. Ninety percent of the time their only indication that Hop Sing had gone "down below" came at the breakfast table, when they would find themselves being served by a total stranger. This stranger, it always turned out, was a cousin of Hop Sing's. Whence he came or where he went, they never knew. They only knew that a total stranger seemed to know more about their kitchen than they themselves did; and, with rare exception, "cousin's" service would be as good as Hop Sing's.

It was ten o'clock in the morning now. Hop Sing had finished his kitchen work and was outside clearing the frost-bitten vines from the small plot of ground he kept behind the main house where he raised a few vegetables in the comparatively short growing season of the Sierra's east slope. Hop Sing muttered to himself as he worked, for he was worried. His sensitivity to his "family" was as accurate as a good barometer is to changes in weather. There was a feeling of trouble on the Ponderosa . . . Hop Sing had sensed it for some time.

He picked around his nearly depleted garden, enjoying the odor of the soil, momentarily entranced by the deepening yellow of huge, crooked neck squash, the first he had been able to raise. The sound of an approaching horse caught his incredibly sharp ears and he looked up and saw Ben Cartwright riding out toward the barn. Even from here Hop Sing could tell that Ben had troubles on his mind. With no hesitation at all Hop Sing decided

68

on a course of action. His pigtail bobbing, he hurried on cushioned soles back into the main house.

*　　*　　*

Generally, the mere act of coming home could lift a great load off Ben Cartwright's shoulders. He was essentially a modest man, but he was also an honest one. He was fully aware that the Ponderosa and its sprawling main house were beginning to be the talk of a continent, for many persons of importance, passing through Virginia City, had been invited up to the Ponderosa. Ben was always the gracious host, but he was not above bragging a bit in front of his sons after the world-famous guests had left. He had built this ranch with his own hands; he was continuing to build it with the help of his sons. He was darned well proud of it and darned well proud of his sons and he didn't give a hoot if the whole world knew it.

This was the mood that nearly always struck him as he rode into the area of the main house, but this morning the feeling was not there. The upgrade traffic on the narrow, twisting Ophir road had been an irritation, because it constantly reminded him of Matt Vogel. When he reached the causeway across Washoe Lake one of those rare, freak breezes had assailed his nostrils with the acid fumes from the ore mills at the town of Ophir and with the smoke from the burning slashings of the big lumber mills at Washoe City. He had wanted, for just one moment, to forget mining and lumbering and Vogel and Sharon, but there was no escape from any of it.

He turned Buck loose in the corral and strode toward the main house, still deep in thought. The high-pitched, accusing voice, stopped him short.

"You no come home suppah, you no let Hop Sing know, you makee food cold, I quit. Good-bye. I go San Francisco."

Lost in his thoughts, Ben was caught completely off guard by the outburst. There in front of him was the familiar figure of Hop Sing, his little round cap perched on his head, an old carpet bag in his hand.

"Hop Sing! What in the devil are you talking about?" he demanded.

"You hear, you know!" Hop Sing chanted. "I quit!"

"Now wait a minute!" Ben said, his temper beginning to rise. "You know we're having guests for supper next Saturday!"

"Let Mister Hoss fixee suppah. Good-bye."

He turned abruptly and started off, the carpet bag banging his short legs. Ben made a sudden dash and got in front of Hop Sing.

"You listen to me, Hop Sing!" Ben bellowed. "Week after next you can quit and good riddance, but we're having guests! Now you get back there into that kitchen and if you come out again . . ."

"You no yell at me Mister Cartlight!"

Ben put up both hands in a characteristic gesture of apology. "All right, Hop Sing. All right . . . I lost my temper."

"I losee plenty food. You no come home last night. You no tell Hop Sing."

"How in the devil was I going to tell you?" Ben said, his exasperation growing again. "Do you think there's a private telegraph line from Virginia City to the Ponderosa?"

"All light," Hop Sing said. "I go back kitchen, next Saturday I fixee suppah. Then maybeso quit, you savvy?"

"I savvy," Ben said. He hated that expression and he had a strong feeling Hop Sing used it just to annoy him. He would never know for sure. Hop Sing turned abruptly and headed back toward the house, entering at the side door. Ben stood there staring after him.

So help me, thought Ben. *If I don't have troubles enough* . . . then abruptly he started to grin. One thing sure, you never knew which way Hop Sing would jump next.

Inside the kitchen, Hop Sing pulled aside a curtain and peered out carefully. He saw the grin on Ben Cartwright's face, and that smile that resembled sunrise bathed his own features. *Old Chinese saying,* he thought. *Little worries soothe big headaches.*

Hop Sing kicked the old carpet bag into a closet. It was perfectly empty. It had been right along. He hummed a little nasal sing-song as he began work. A big lunch would be good for Mister Ben.

The beef stew smelled delicious and Hop Sing was proud of it. The potatoes had come from his own garden. He dipped up a spoonful, blew on it carefully and tasted it. Just right . . . just the way Mr. Hoss liked it. He stood there, the spoon raised to his lips, then slowly he put it down and went into the living room. Ben Cartwright was standing in the open doorway, his feet spread, his hands on his hips. Hop Sing didn't have to ask. Something else had gone wrong.

Quietly he moved up alongside Ben to where he could see the barnyard and the hitching rail in front of the house. Hoss and Little Joe, coat collars turned up against the chill, bedrolls behind their saddles, were riding toward the barn. He saw Ben Cartwright move out to meet his sons.

More trouble, Hop Sing thought. *Mr. Hoss and Mr. Joe not come home unless something wrong.*

He went back into the kitchen and looked into the stew pot. There was plenty. He did not know why he had made enough for everyone. He just had.

Unobtrusively, he took down dishes and started setting three places at the dining room table.

8 HOSS AND LITTLE JOE saw their father leave the house and start toward them, and they both recognized that certain set of his shoulders that said he was bracing himself for bad news. Hoss looked at his younger brother with concern.

"Now don't go off half-cocked and get him all excited," Hoss said. "After all, nothing really happened . . ."

"Nothing happened?" Joe's voice was high pitched. "Some yahoo takes a shot at me—your own brother—and you sit there and say nothing happened?"

Both men swung out of their saddles and started leading their horses toward the barn.

"You said yourself he wasn't really shootin' *at* you," Hoss said.

"Shooting near me is enough," Joe said.

"Could be just like Pete Wilson said. They were hired to guard some equipment and this Stevens fellow got a little over-enthusiastic——"

"Next time he can get over-enthusiastic with somebody beside me——" He broke off. "Oh, hi, Pa!"

Ben stood there looking at his two sons. Joe was trying his best to appear casually unconcerned.

Hoss overdid it. He lifted one big hand and grinned too broadly and his voice was too hearty. "Yeah, hi, Pa!" he said.

Ben said, "What are you two doing here?"

"Got to worrying about leaving you alone so long," Hoss said.

"Yeah," Joe said. "We were afraid you might get lonesome and trade off the Ponderosa for Beth Kelly's boarding house." Joe let loose with his contagious laugh.

Ben expelled his breath. "All right, you've had your fun. Now what's wrong?"

"Nothing, really, Pa," Hoss said seriously. "Just a few things come up that we thought the three of us ought to talk over." He gestured off with a jerk of his head. A dry, little old man of indeterminate age had come out of the barn and was walking over to them. He walked with a decided limp, and even a layman could have told that the elbow of his left arm had been smashed beyond repair. He had the build of a Bantam rooster with the neck of a turkey and the face of a woodpecker.

"Time you two was gettin' back," he said without preliminaries. "In my day I could have had that wood cut and them cows delivered to market two weeks ago." He glared at the two boys. "You want them horses put away or you mean to stand there holdin' 'em all night?"

Hoss studied the man carefully, his mobile face creased with worry. He looked at his brother.

"What do you think, Little Joe?" Hoss asked. "You trust Kirk to put 'em away or should we do it ourselves?"

Joe studied Kirk, then said to Hoss in a stage whisper, "How does he look to you, Hoss? You figure he's sober?"

Kirk was one of the first men to ever go to work on the Ponderosa. He was a devout Mormon who had settled in the little town of Genoa in the early days when it was known as Mormon Station and all this country was a part of Utah territory. True to his sect, he was completely opposed to spirits, and so far as any one knew, he had never touched a drop of anything stronger than water in his life. He had been severely banged up in a Ponderosa roundup in the early days. Since that time he held an honorary position on the ranch. His official

73

duty was to do exactly what he desired to do, and he did his duty well. Hoss sized up Kirk carefully.

"He can still walk without staggering too much," Hoss said. "Let him take 'em, if that's what he wants to do."

Kirk emitted a sound that combined all of his physical attributes—chicken, turkey, woodpecker. He led the three horses off toward the barn.

"Well?" Ben said, when the three of them were alone.

A wagon was rumbling into the yard. It carried some odds and ends of posts and half a dozen men. They had been hired on a temporary basis to put up a rail fence around a twenty-acre pasture where Ben was experimenting with a strain of grass new to this part of the country.

"We can talk about it in the house," Hoss said. He gave a deep sniff and his grin spread all over his face. "See there, Joe? What'd I tell you? Hop Sing *is* making stew!"

"I should have known better," Joe said disgustedly. He reached into his pocket, took out a silver dollar and slapped it into his older brother's hand. To Ben he said, "He told me five miles back he could smell Hop Sing's stew and I bet him a dollar he couldn't."

"Never miss," Hoss said.

They started toward the house and Ben briefly put his arm around the shoulders of his two sons.

"I'll have to admit it's been a little quiet around here without you," he said.

Hop Sing opened the huge planked door and let them in. For one moment the warmth of the living room engulfed them all and shut out any thought of trouble. Here was familiarity—the yawning fireplace with its crackling pine logs, the faint pleasantness of wood smoke and a linger of cold air that had rushed in through the open door and was now moving toward the fire for warmth. From the kitchen came the delicious aromas of splendidly cooked food.

74

Hop Sing grinned at his three favorite people. "Mister Hoss," he said. "Little Joe. Glad to see you home."

"Thanks, Hop Sing," Hoss said, shrugging out of his coat. "That is stew I smell, ain't it?"

Hop Sing looked from one to the other, knowing them so well. A little lie wouldn't hurt, he decided.

"Not ready yet," Hop Sing said. "You take off coats then sit by fire, talk." He turned and went back into the kitchen before anyone could argue with him.

Hoss and Joe threw their coats across a chair and both sank down on the big sofa in front of the fire. "Dog gone it, Pa, sure is a nip in the air for this time of the year, you know that?"

"We had snow by this time last year," Ben said.

"No foolin'?" Hoss said. From his expression one would gather that this was a mighty important piece of information.

"All right, boys," Ben said quietly. "As glad as I am to see you, you didn't ride all the way home to talk about the weather."

There was no sense stalling any further, Hoss knew. He looked across at his younger brother. "You want to tell him, Joe?"

"You tell him," Joe said. "I'm the big alarmist, remember? I'm just the one who got shot at."

"Shot at?" Ben's voice was explosive, demanding.

"Now, Pa," Hoss said, "don't go gettin' all up in the air . . ."

Little Joe had held it in as long as he could. He blew up all at once. "Up in the air?" he yelled. "A guy's taking pot shots at me, ordering me off of my own land, backing himself up with guns and for the past two days you been telling me not to get up in the air and now you're telling Pa——"

"Dad bern it, Joe, you told me it was only one warning shot and from where you tell me it happened you wasn't on your own land——"

"What do you want me to do, take a surveyor with me?"

"Now hold it! Hold on, both of you!" Ben said.

"Some day I'm gonna punch that big moose right smack in the mouth," Joe said.

"You just come ahead any time, Little Brother," Hoss said.

The two moved toward each other and Ben got between them. "Shut up or I'll take a stick of stove wood to both of you!" Ben yelled.

Hop Sing poked his head through the door, looked at the three Cartwrights, shrugged and went back into the kitchen. It was just as he figured. They needed to talk. Like Hop Sing, the Cartwrights believed in being individuals.

"Now does somebody who has some semblance of control of himself want to tell me what you two are doing here and what the shooting and shouting is all about?" There was definite temper in Ben's voice.

"All I told Joe was, like you always told us, he ought to look at all sides of a thing," Hoss said.

"You ever try looking at all sides of a bullet?" Joe said.

"Hoss, you keep still and let Joseph say what he has to say," Ben said.

"Never did try to stop him," Hoss said. "Go ahead, Little Brother."

Joe shot Hoss a look that was not entirely flattering and said, "Pa, you know that opening about a mile up above Sheep Meadow?"

"Yes," Ben said too quickly. "I know it very well."

"Well, I went up there . . ."

There was a lot unsaid here, a certain knowledge by Ben that Joe had gone there for that view down to his mother's grave. For just a swift moment there was a dark-eyed woman sitting at this very table . . . "That's not on the Ponderosa," Ben said.

"That's what I tried to tell him," Hoss said.

"Let him tell it, Hoss," Ben said. There was a new quietness in his voice.

"All of a sudden it doesn't amount to much, I guess," Joe said. "I rode up there and some riders came in and said I was on posted property and they ordered me off."

"The shot?" Ben said.

"I guess when you think of it, it's like Hoss said." He shrugged eloquently. "Just a warning shot——" The anger was always close to the surface with Joe and it came back now. "What in the devil would you have done, Pa? I've been up there a dozen times."

"I would have done exactly what you did," Ben said.

"That's all I was trying to tell him, Pa," Hoss said.

"Did anybody ask you?" Ben asked quietly.

Hoss settled back, momentarily sullen. Ben looked back at his youngest son. "Did I hear Hoss mention Pete Wilson?" Ben asked.

"Yeah, he was there," Joe said, and in a way this admission bothered him more than the fact that the man called Stevens had taken a shot at him. "I don't think you can really blame Pete," Joe said lamely.

"You've never quite forgotten her, have you son?" Ben asked.

Little Joe was immediately on the defensive. "Look, I had a dozen girls," he said, that typical braggadocio creeping into his voice. "I hope I have a dozen more. I like 'em all."

"If I had your conceit," Hoss said. "I'd go on over to Araby or one of them places and get me a harem."

"There's plenty of you for a lot of women," Joe said.

"Would you care to get back to the point or not?" Ben asked.

Joe got up suddenly and started to pace. "Pa, I don't know what to tell you. All of a sudden, in a place where I've been a dozen times before, somebody shoots a warning shot over my head and then rides out and tells me to

77

stay off the property, that Matt Vogel has leased it." There was almost a reluctant admission in his voice as he glanced at Hoss. "I went back and made sure everything was all right with the cows and then I went over to see what Hoss thought." He spread his hands. "Any of it make any sense to you, Pa?"

"Yes, Joseph, I'm afraid it does," Ben Cartwright said.

Hoss looked at his father quickly, his face itself a question mark.

"I went to that meeting with Sharon and the others," Ben said. "It was rather revealing. After that, I talked to Roy Coffee."

"What did they want of you, Pa?" Hoss asked.

"My life blood, as far as I can see," Ben said.

Hop Sing came in from the kitchen. Too much talk could spoil a meal. There was time afterward. "You no eat now," Hop Sing said, "I put stew outside."

Hoss started to chuckle. "That's Hop Sing's interpretation of range slang," he said. "What he means is, 'come and get it or I'll throw it out!'" They laughed, but they all obediently moved toward the dining room table. Hop Sing could, at times, mean exactly what he said.

*　　*　　*

Late in the afternoon the wind picked up and the fingers of winter plucked at the last leaves on the yellow aspen at the edge of the meadows. The horses stood with their rumps to the cold, and Hop Sing's chickens walked with a sidewise gait, their feathers turned back, and their cawing complaints spoke of a change in the weather. Beyond the barns and down the slope, Hoss Cartwright's prize brood sow rubbed her back against a post and found no comfort. The first snow of autumn was in the air.

Winter was barred, inside the ranch house, and yet it could make its presence felt, even through the log walls. There was a gust, and a wisp of smoke hesitated in the chimney of the perfectly designed fireplace. There was a rattle, and a sudden film of steam was on a window pane. Ben Cartwright got up and put another log on the fire. It was only late afternoon, but the darkness was moving down the mountains, absorbing the pitch-black of the pines as it came, descending, velvet, soft and complete on the gentle slopes around the Ponderosa ranch house.

"I think that's everything we talked about," Ben Cartwright said.

The two boys sat, staring into the coals of the fire, each one seeing a different vision, each one finding a different answer. They were like two men going to the same city but arguing about which road would be the best to take to lead them most quickly and safely to that final destination.

"Matt Vogel's made the first move," Joe Cartwright said. "I say we let him know right quick we're not backing down to him."

"Joe, dog gone it, ain't you heard anything Pa's said in the last two hours?" Hoss complained.

"Not much that's made sense," Joe said hotly.

"You watch your tone of voice!" Ben said.

"All right, Pa, I'm sorry," Joe said.

"I wasn't asking for an apology," Ben said, "but I would like to keep this within the realm of discussion, if that's possible."

"Go ahead, Pa."

Ben watched his sons closely, then went across and sat down at the desk in the little alcove in the corner. He turned and glanced briefly at the map that represented the Ponderosa. "Pull up a couple of chairs, will you, boys?" he said then. "There are a few things I want to go over with you."

He took a key from his vest pocket, unlocked a drawer of the desk and took out a ledger. As Hoss and Joe, bringing chairs from the dining room, moved in close to him, he looked up at his sons.

"Did it ever occur to you that someone shrewd enough

79

and determined enough could bankrupt the Ponderosa?" Ben asked.

Hoss and Little Joe Cartwright looked as if someone had hit them in the face with a sledge hammer. Ben looked from one to the other.

"We've never had secrets from each other," Ben said. "There are a few things in here you should know about."

As his sons watched him, Ben opened the ledger.

* * *

"Hard to keep supper much longer, Mister Cartlight," Hop Sing said. It was the fourth time he had said it. Darkness had long since settled on the Ponderosa and it had brought a noisy wind with it. A branch Ben had meant to cut down a long time ago grated against the shakes of the roof.

"You go ahead and dish it up, Hop Sing," Ben said. He closed the ledger.

Hoss looked at his father with something close to apology. "I guess Joe and me just got in the habit of letting you and Adam look after the money end of it," he said. "All those bookkeeping figures sort of make me dizzy."

"Where do you figure they'll move first?" Joe asked softly.

Ben shrugged. "How do we know? Roy Coffee wouldn't say Vogel is surrounding us with timber leases unless it was so. They could move in anyplace. We can't just go hire men off the street and we don't have a big enough crew to patrol every inch of the Ponderosa border."

"Looks to me like we couldn't afford it even if we could hire 'em," Hoss said.

"I've put a lot of money into the flume," Ben said. "It's going to cost a lot more to finish it."

"Yeah, but Pa, you'll make that money back in three months when you start moving lumber and cord wood down it. What you'll save on teamsters alone—"

"I'm afraid Matt Vogel has thought of that, too," Ben

said. "That's just one more reason he's determined to put us out of business."

"Let him try," Hoss said. "Just let him try."

"He will," Ben said.

He got up and it was a signal for the others to move across to the table where Hop Sing was putting out platters of food. A sudden gust of wind ripped at the eaves. As he sat down Ben said, "First things first. The weather's making up, Joseph. You've got to get back up there first thing in the morning and get José to start those cattle moving down."

"Yes, sir," Joe said.

"Hoss, go by and tell Jim Willy to take charge of the woodcutting operation."

"All right, Pa," Hoss said.

"Then go on over and keep an eye on that crew building the flume. They're probably the least dependable of the lot. I had to hire them catch as catch can, and if you think help is scarce now, wait until Vogel starts hiring his logging crews."

Joe looked at his father, a worry in his expression.

"Something on your mind, Joseph?" Ben asked.

"You said to tell José to start the cattle moving? You want me to stay with them?"

"No, Joseph," Ben said quietly. "I want you to pick a couple of men—of your own choosing. I want you to start riding the borders of the Ponderosa."

"Pa," Hoss said. "You know how Little Joe sort of——"

Ben Cartwright looked directly at his youngest son. "I trust Joseph implicitly," he said. "I know he'll never start anything without consulting with you and me first."

There was a long silence between the three of them. Hop Sing came in and saw them sitting there.

"You eat! Now!" Hop Sing said.

He slid back into his kitchen, but in a matter of seconds he was back. He looked from one to the other. "You expect company?" he asked.

81

"No, I didn't," Ben said. "Why?"

And then they heard it, the unmistakable sound of a horse. All three men stood up. "There's no need of the fabled geese of ancient Rome or even a watch dog around this place so long as we have Hop Sing," Ben muttered. He looked at his sons. "You expecting anyone?"

Both boys shrugged. The horse was being ridden up to the hitch rail now and there was the definite sound of a man dismounting.

"Don't shoot! Me friend!" a voice called out in the night.

"Dan de Quille!" Joe said. He moved quickly to the door, flung it open. "Dan!" he said into the night. "Come in out of the cold, you ink-stained wretch!"

Hoss had moved over to the door and as Dan came in, Hoss threw a bear hug around him. "Howdy, Dandy," Hoss said. "You're just about a week early for that party we invited you to but welcome anyway!"

"Always welcome, Dan, you know that," Ben said.

Joe closed the door and Dan came into the room, pulling off his gloves.

"Dog gone if you newspapermen don't always know when it's time for a drink or something to eat," Hoss said. "Come on, pull up a chair."

"I'll be delighted," Dan said. "But before I do, I want to make my position clear."

The three Cartwrights exchanged glances, sensing something in the voice of the tall, thin newspaperman.

"Anything wrong, Dan?" Ben asked.

"I'm here on business."

"What's wrong?" Ben asked.

"Late this afternoon a run started on Hale and Norcross stock," Dan said. "Someone is trying to take control away from you." He looked around at the three of them. "I'm asking this as a newspaperman, not as a friend. Do you intend to fight it?"

Ben Cartwright looked at his two boys. He had explained to them in detail, shown them the figures. This was the move he dreaded most. This was the move that could start the Ponderosa on the way to bankruptcy.

Ben said, "Well, boys?"

Hoss and Joe looked at each other. There was no outward sign, but Joe had given Hoss consent to answer for them both.

"We're gonna fight it, Dan," Hoss said. "With every cent the Ponderosa has. You go right ahead and quote us."

Ben Cartwright turned his head. He felt something stinging the corners of his eyes.

9 SPECULATION in mining stocks came as natural to the average resident of Virginia City as eating or breathing. The various brokerage offices were open day and night, twelve months a year, and when an off-shift mucker or a timberer or a brand new millionaire wasn't hanging around a saloon, he was probably watching the board in front of one of the exchanges. The sale of one share of stock could often cause a panic in San Francisco. Fortunes, real and imaginary, were made and lost within a matter of hours, and there wasn't man nor woman, it seemed, who didn't own "feet" in one mine or another. Because of its economic effect on the rest of the world, Virginia City had grown to be the most famous city for its size and age that America had ever known. Every man was a Bonanza King—or at least a potential one—and every man lived and spent—or wanted to spend—accordingly.

There was an exhilaration in the very air, and the intoxication of it never failed to touch Ben Cartwright. Even this morning, faced with a battle for shares and proxies that could well cost him a fortune, he still felt the stir of excitement as he rode into the outskirts of the town.

The produce, lumber and wood wagons were nose to tail all the way up the Ophir Grade, and here at the Divide they clashed head-on with the loaded ore wagons starting down to the mills along the Carson and along Washoe Lake. The result was sheer bedlam that backed up the entire length of C Street as the shouting and cursing mule skinners negotiated hairpin turns with their twelve- and fourteen-mule outfits. Riding the off-wheeler and using a single jerk line, one of these drivers could, by tossing a pebble at one of his lead mules, practically double the huge ore wagon and trailer back on itself. Harness bells jangled, chains rattled, wagons creaked, dust swirled and men cursed at the tops of their lungs. Buggies piled up in two- and three-block jams, waiting to get across a street, and Chinese wood peddlers, hidden under their bundles of roots, darted and ducked under the very feet of the threshing teams. The sidewalks were packed with pushing, shoving, jovial mobs, and the tinny sound of honky-tonk pianos vied with the chime of the team bells.

Ben Cartwright turned to Dan de Quille, who had ridden in from the ranch with him. "This traffic gets worse every day," Ben said.

"Or better," Dan grinned, "depending on how you look at it."

It took them well over half an hour to get through the incredible jam and up to the stable where they put up their horses. The well-known brokerage office of George Thomas Marye handled all of Ben's affairs, and he headed that way immediately. Dan fell in step alongside him.

"Don't you have to get back to the newspaper?" Ben asked.

"You're news, Ben," Dan said. "I'm working."

There was a direct telegraph wire to San Francisco from the Marye office. Outside the tall building that housed the firm was a machine known as "The Electric Stock Indicator and Reporter." This device, constructed principally of iron, stood on a tower on top of the building. It could be seen from all central parts of Virginia City.

There was such a crowd in front of the brokerage office that Ben stopped, deciding to watch the stock dial from a distance. He saw at once that there was, indeed, plenty of activity in Hale and Norcross.

The list of the important stocks was painted around the circumference of a glass dial, and a large indicator hand pointed to the name of the stock as the proper figures appeared opposite the name. With the direct wire connecting the Marye indicator with the San Francisco office, this stock dial moved simultaneously with the stock dial in San Francisco. As Ben watched, he saw Hale and Norcross move from two hundred and fifty to two hundred and sixty-five dollars a share.

There was no way to keep a run of this sort secret. Everyone knew who owned major blocks of stock. Ben saw two men he didn't know—but who obviously knew him—whispering to each other, pointing him out. The stock could well triple before night, Ben knew. If people started selling and Sharon got hold of the uncommitted shares before Ben and his management group got hold of them he would lose control in the matter of a few days . . .

Ben pushed his way through the crowd with Dan at his side and almost immediately their way was blocked by a little prospector known to Ben as Scotty McCoy. Scotty was having a little trouble focusing his eyes as he bore down on Ben and the thin, bearded newspaperman.

"Dandy!" Scotty yelled. "I been up all night looking for you." He looked around, blinked owlishly at Ben and said, "You can hear this, too, but don't tell nobody, Mr. Cartwright." Then, in a voice loud enough so that practically half the people in Virginia City could hear it he said, "I've hit it at last, Dandy! It's bonanza for me!"

"Good for you, Scotty," Dan said. "Good for you. I hope it's like the Mexicans say." Dan scratched his chin and squinted at the sky. "Let's see—you been in borrasca quite a while. You ought to have about six years in bonanza, at that rate."

Ben and Dan started to move on, but Scotty moved with them.

"It's all right for you to hear this, Mr. Cartwright," Scotty said. "I trust you."

"Thank you, Scotty," Ben said.

By now the traffic had piled up on the street again, and there was no way to cross on over to the Marye office. Ben watched the stock dial, only half hearing Scotty.

"You're right, Dandy," Scotty was whooping. "Six years I was in borrasca. But I don't need no six years in bonanza! Just give me six weeks!"

The hand on the stock dial moved again and stopped on Hale and Norcross. Three hundred dollars a share.

Scotty bumped into Ben as he fumbled in his pockets, first one and then the other, and in a moment he triumphantly extracted a handful of beautifully embossed guilt edged stock certificates.

"Here it is, Dandy," he confided, his voice conspiratorial now. "Ink still wet on 'em." He thrust several of the instruments toward Dan. "Want you to have 'em, Dandy. Forty feet in the Sweet Heather of Scotland." He punched Dan in the wishbone with a wobbly finger. "That's what

I call her, Dandy. Sweet Heather of Scotland. Here. Here's forty feet. Make you a rich man."

Dan accepted the stock certificates without argument. It was expected of him. He had a drawer full of such certificates back at the office and in time he would have a second drawer full. All a man had to do to become rich here was go up on the mountain, scratch around a bit, file a claim, give it a grandiloquent name and borrow money enough to have some stock certificates printed.

Ben stared at the stock dial as if hypnotized. He had to start buying, he knew that, and every time he bought up a share that price would jump again. It was as he had explained it to Hoss and Little Joe. Sharon was throwing the wealth of the Bank of California against the Ponderosa in this, his first move. He was hopeful Ben would spend so much money trying to keep control of Hale and Norcross that he would seriously damage the operation of the ranch itself, and then, hopefully, need to borrow money. Sharon would be right there to lend it.

Scotty looked up at Ben and put a finger to his lips, then moved closer to Dan de Quille. "Don't want too many people to know," said Scotty. "Run the price of feet up too high. But if you want to say something in the paper . . ."

"All right, Scotty. I'll come out and take a look at it. I never print anything about a new mine unless I've seen it, you know that."

"Everybody knows it, Dandy," Scotty said. "That's why we trust you." Again that glance around. "Don't care what you say, Dandy. Just tell the truth. When you see the Sweet Heather of Scotland, you just tell the truth."

"I'll do it, Scotty," Dan said. "You can count on that. Looks like we can get across, Ben."

Ben and Dan started to move on, but Scotty wasn't through with them yet. He turned suddenly and there was a great afterthought in his mind—the sort of small thing that comes to a big financier and mine owner who has just given away perhaps a million dollars. He became intensely sober as befitting a tycoon and he snapped his fingers.

"I almost forgot, Dan," said Scotty. "Could you give me the loan of two bits? I've promised to meet some business associates in a saloon near here."

"Of course I can, Scotty," said Dan, and forthwith produced the required coin. Scotty pocketed it soberly.

"You'll be worth a million come morning," said Scotty.

"I believe every word in your truthful head," said Dan.

Scotty moved off into the swarming mass of humanity, as happy as a lark. Ben looked after him, shook his head. "There's something rather sad about it, Dan," he said.

"There's no sense trying to change it, Ben," Dan said. Someone jostled him, nearly knocking him off his feet. He paid no attention. This was perfectly normal for the sidewalk area in front of a stockbroker's office. He glanced at Ben and said, "Have you heard the latest?"

"Concerning what?" Ben said.

"There's a group trying to set up a company to bore a hole through Mt. Davidson."

"In Heaven's name what for? Some sort of a water scheme?"

"Nothing as dull as that," Dan said. "You know how early the sun goes down here. They figure with this hole and revolving and adjustable mirrors set on time mechanisms they can catch the afternoon sun on the other side of the mountain and reflect into Virginia City so that we'll have several more hours of daylight."

Ben shook his head in disbelief. "The devil of it is, they'll probably sell a lot of stock, even in a scheme as crazy as that."

"They already have," Dan said.

They pushed through the crowd and went into the bedlam of the stock brokerage firm office. Traders were shouting, waving certificates, speaking a gibberish all their own. Women as well as men pushed and shoved and

88

there was even a sprinkling of Chinese. Muckers and millionaires vied with each other in their frenzy to buy or sell shares. The place was as noisy as the inside of a bass drum. Ben pushed and shoved his way through and entered one of the offices at the back of the room.

The man at the desk was young, and Ben did not recall having seen him before. He stood up quickly. "Mr. Cartwright," he said. "We were just getting ready to send a messenger out to your ranch. There is considerable activity in Hale and Norcross—"

"I know," Ben said. "Is Mr. Marye in?"

"He's in San Francisco," the clerk said. "I have been in touch with him by our telegraph and he has asked me to assist you in any way I can." He offered his hand. "I'm Walter Harker."

Ben shook hands and sat down in the chair the younger man indicated for him.

"How does it look?" Ben asked quietly.

"As of this moment, Mr. Sharon can count more votes than the present management."

"You're taking my shares into consideration?"

"Yes sir, I am."

"How many non-committed shares outstanding?"

"Enough to give you a majority, if you could control them all."

"Then that pretty much decides it, doesn't it?" Ben said.

"You want a permanent buy order, regardless of price?"

"That's right," Ben said. "Regardless of price."

"That's what Mr. Marye thought you would want," Harker said. "I shall telegraph him at once." He cleared his throat, a little embarrassed to talk of money with a man of Ben Cartwright's stature. "Mr. Marye said I was to put no limit on your account."

"Thank you," Ben said.

He spent the rest of the day on other ranch business,

but always, whenever he was within sight of it, his eyes were drawn to that stock indicator. The price on Hale and Norcross was holding steady now, and that could well be an indication that all quickly available shares had already been purchased. If that were so, the search was now getting under way for small blocks and even individual shares . . . Ben found himself turning toward Beth Kelly's boarding house.

He didn't dare leave town, he knew. He thought of the money he was pouring into that experimental V flume— a project in which he had every confidence. He was sure he could cut the cost of transporting lumber and cord wood by at least a third and, because it would enable him to start controlled logging in some of the finest stands of timber in the Sierra, he would be able to increase the yield from this important source of Ponderosa income.

Damn Bill Sharon, he thought. *Why did he have to hit me right now?* Immediately he answered his own question as being a little foolish. In business raids of this magnitude you didn't wait for your opponent to be in his strongest position. It had been a long time since Ben Cartwright had worried about money. It seemed strange to him, but it was no less real.

He wondered about James Fair and John Mackay, knowing they were watching this fight for control of the Hale and Norcross almost as closely as he himself was. He thought of the people he knew who held stock in the mine —old friends who would go along with the present management—and he thought of Sharon putting in a new management. He knew what would happen then, for he had seen the Bank do this before. Every share of stock would be assessed to the limit. Word would go out that Hale and Norcross had "struck a horse," whether the vein had actually petered out or not. There would be panic selling and the stock would drop to a price where the assessment far outdistanced the value.

It wasn't just sentiment, though, that made Ben Cartwright determined to fight to keep control. It was a matter of dollars and cents with him, too, for if Sharon and his people took control, Ben's existing contracts for wood and mine timbers wouldn't be worth the paper they were written on. That business would go to Matt Vogel.

Ben stopped on the porch of Beth Kelly's boarding house. He turned and looked back.

The dial of the stock indicator on top of the Marye building glowed like a staring eye in the night, lighted by the only electric light in Virginia City. That light was the ingenious creation of an amateur inventor. It consisted of an insulated steel rod projecting about five feet above the rod of the tower. On the top of this, thirty-six small steel wires, or rods, branched outward and upward. They were arranged similar to the ribs of an umbrella turned inside out. At the upper end of each of the steel ribs a small cord of silk was fastened, each holding suspended in the air an India-rubber balloon, four inches in diameter, at a height of some five hundred feet. This was how the electricity was collected from the atmosphere and brought down the central rod. A ground wire was almost in contact with the atmospheric rod and between the two were placed the carbon points which produced the light.

As Ben watched the glow of that Cyclops eye, the pointer moved across the dial. Hale and Norcross now stood at four hundred and fifty dollars a share.

Someone had made a purchase. Whether it had been himself or the Sharon group, he had no way of knowing at the moment. He turned and rang the doorbell. It was Beth herself who came to the door.

"I've expected you," she said softly. "Come in, Ben."

10 THIS HAD BEEN a day to remember for Matt Vogel. He had met early with William Sharon and some other important people from San Francisco and he had been a part of the beginning of the full-scale raid on the Hale and Norcross Mine. Having supper now in his favorite place, the Sazerac, he had rosy visions of Ben Cartwright, reeling from financial blows, down on his knees begging Matt Vogel to buy the Ponderosa timber at his own price. Matt had another glass of champagne.

Everyone here in the Sazerac knew him and everyone called him by name. He had a special corner table that was his alone, and there wasn't anyone in the place who didn't fawn over him. In return, Matt Vogel was notoriously generous with his gratuities.

He took great pride in knowing exactly what to order. A specialty of the house here was fresh oysters with scrambled eggs—a delicacy that had come across the mountains from the California placer camps and was known as a Hangtown Fry. To wash it down, champagne, of course, and there it was at his elbow in an ice bucket and he hadn't even had to ask for it. This was elegance, and Matt Vogel liked it.

He belched loudly and said to the man across the table from him. "So you figure you can round me up a hundred men, that right?"

The man across the table watched him intently. His name was Cameron and he had the shady reputation of being too closely allied with the underworld elements of the

Comstock. It was said he had some education in the law, and perhaps he did. At any rate, it was a known fact that Bruce Cameron had more than a nodding acquaintance with several judges who had a reputation of being extremely lenient with the gunmen and hoodlums of the area. Matt Vogel didn't care about such things. If Bruce Cameron could do him so much good, that and that alone was what counted.

Cameron said, "I'll find you all the help you want and any kind you want if the pay is right."

Matt Vogel leaned forward suddenly and pointed his knife at Cameron's chest. "You ever hear anybody accuse Matt Vogel of being cheap?"

"You asked me a question, I answered it," Cameron said.

"Get me the help, you'll get paid," Vogel said.

"I might have to bail a few of them out of jail."

Vogel looked up slowly and his voice dropped. "I ain't buying pedigrees," he said, "I'm buying men that will work for me."

He went back to eating, then looked up suddenly as he saw the change of expression on Cameron's face. A familiar voice said, "Howdy, Cameron." Sheriff Roy Coffee was standing by the table.

"You here on purpose or by accident?" Cameron asked.

"What's the matter, Bruce?" Roy said. "Guilty conscience?"

"This man's my guest," Matt Vogel said. "Why don't you do your law business during office hours?"

"I do an awful lot of my business after dark," Roy said. He turned and sauntered off. Vogel glared after him.

"I don't know how he keeps getting elected," Vogel muttered.

"Don't sell him short," Cameron said. He hesitated. "As I was saying, Neil Larson will make you a good woods boss——"

A waiter came over and whispered in Vogel's ear and

Vogel took his napkin and wiped his mouth. "You send them right in here," Vogel said.

The waiter hesitated a moment. "The lady, sir," he said. "She's rather young."

"I said show 'em in here," Vogel said.

"Yes sir," the waiter said.

Vogel turned to Cameron. "Neil Larson. Can't place him. Sounds all right."

"Like I told you," Cameron said, "Larson isn't very fond of Ben Cartwright."

"I won't hold that against him," Vogel said. "Neither am I."

"He went down to San Francisco on a trip," Cameron said. "I'll have him come see you as soon as he gets back."

"Yeah," Vogel said. "You do that."

Cameron left, and as he moved through the tables he stepped aside to let a young couple through. He bowed slightly, and Pete Wilson with his wife, Ellen, both looking ill at ease, came on across to Matt Vogel's table. Vogel stood up rather heavily and he made no attempt to hide his open appraisal of Ellen.

"So this is the little lady," Matt Vogel said. "Sit down, sit down. You don't have to be afraid of me." The waiter was pulling out a chair and Ellen sat down primly.

She was a startlingly blonde girl, no more than twenty years old. The dress she wore was inexpensive, but Ellen was one of those girls who could make any garment look elegant. Her eyes were a deep blue, and her lips, somewhat full, were moist and red with natural color.

"I'm sorry if we're late, Mr. Vogel," Pete Wilson said. "It's quite a ways in from our place . . ."

"Well, maybe we can change all that," Vogel said. "Get you a place here in town." He leaned forward and put a hand on Ellen's hand. "You'd like that, wouldn't you?"

"I like it very much where we are," Ellen said. "Pete and I have always talked about a little ranch."

"I've never said I wouldn't take advantage of something better if it came along," Pete said quickly.

"No, of course you haven't," Ellen said. She had made a mistake and she showed it.

"You two had supper?" Vogel asked.

"Yes. You see when I stopped by our place to pick up Ellen——"

"Don't matter," Vogel said. "You want something else, order it. I keep a credit here." He started eating noisily and Ellen watched with a certain revolted fascination. Vogel looked up suddenly. "Well," he said directly to Pete, "get on with it."

"Everything's fine," Pete said. "Those forty men you hired showed up day before yesterday. They went to work right away on the log skids."

"That hay get there?"

"Yes sir, two loads of it."

Vogel grunted his satisfaction. He looked up and now he was watching Ellen. "I'm hiring a lot more men," he said then. "What with my teams and my lumber interests I'll be running the biggest outfits on the Comstock." He switched his gaze to Pete, then back to Ellen, and his meaning was completely clear. "I like young people who want to get places," he said. "There'll always be a place in my organization for the right man."

"A chance is all I ask, Mr. Vogel," Pete said.

"Man makes his own chances," Vogel said. He thought that over a moment and decided he had just said something quite profound. It was worth repeating. "Man makes his own chances."

"Yes," she said.

Vogel moved swiftly, jabbing his dinner knife toward Pete with such unexpectedness that Pete instinctively moved back.

"What I buy is loyalty," Matt Vogel said, punctuating with the dripping knife. "When you report to me you tell

95

me everything that's been going on, you understand that? Not half of it, not ninety percent of it. You tell me everything."

"Hasn't been much more of importance," Pete said. He was becoming uncomfortable.

"I don't hire you to figure out what's important and what ain't," Vogel said. "I'll make the decision." He gulped the rest of his champagne. "You want to start over?"

Pete gave a dull but accurate account of every move he, Stevens and Lunger Smith had made in the ten days since they had first gone up to the high country. From time to time Vogel would grunt or interrupt suddenly and ask Pete to repeat some minor detail, ballooning it out of actual importance. Pete glanced at Ellen. She sat with her hands folded in her lap, her eyes downcast.

"We ran into Joe Cartwright," Pete said. He saw Ellen look up. Pete rushed his words, wanting to be over this part of it. He tried to keep it light. "Of course Stevens didn't know who it was and he fired a warning shot over his head . . ."

Matt Vogel had put down his knife and fork, Ellen was staring at her husband.

"Tell me about it," Matt Vogel said. His voice was strangely soft.

Pete Wilson had never been so miserable in his life. "Well, like I told you, we checked those survey lines first thing we did. He was on your land, all right."

Matt Vogel started to chuckle. "Little Joe Cartwright. Did you drive him off?"

Again Pete glanced at Ellen. "He just sort of left on his own, sir."

"I knew that Stevens was a good man," Matt said. "I knew it the minute I laid eyes on him. You want some champagne, Mrs. Wilson?" he said.

"No, thank you," Ellen said. "As a matter of fact, I think if you two are through with your business Pete and

96

I had better get back to the ranch. There's so much to do since he's been away."

"All the more reason we ought to sell the place," Pete said.

All the softness had left Ellen's features. "I like it there," she said. She stood up.

Pete got to his feet awkwardly. "Anything else, Mr. Vogel?"

"The supplies for the camp? You take care of that?"

"First thing when I got in town."

"Good boy," Vogel said. He turned quickly as the waiter moved up alongside him. "That will be all, Emil," he said grandly.

"I have a message for you, Mr. Vogel," the waiter said. He hesitated a moment, then without lowering his voice added, "Mr. Sharon wants to see you at his office. Right away."

Pete and Ellen Wilson had heard it, and Matt Vogel knew it. A quick shot of anger ran through him and he felt exactly as if someone had whistled at him or snapped his fingers and said 'Hey, boy! Come here!' He looked at the Wilsons quickly, aware they were watching him. To the waiter he said, "You tell Bill Sharon I'll see him when I'm damn good and ready."

The waiter nodded and backed off, and immediately Matt Vogel was worried. Suppose the waiter took him at his word? Forget it, he told himself. He was sure that wouldn't happen. He deliberately poured one more glass of champagne, intending to toy with it, but instead he found himself gulping it. He stood up suddenly. "Keep up the good work, Pete," he said. "Mrs. Wilson, you're way too pretty to keep yourself hid out." He hauled a watch from his pocket and glanced at it. "I got a lot bigger things to do than go running over to Bill Sharon's office." He turned and waved his hand to the bartender. "Give the Wilsons here anything they want and put it on my account," he said.

Pete Wilson stood there uneasily. He glanced at his wife and she was staring off after the departing form of Matt Vogel.

"You want to go home, honey?" Pete asked.

"Yes," Ellen said.

They moved through the restaurant and saloon and out onto the sidewalk. The wind had picked up and there was a faint skiff of snow in the air. He put his arm around her to protect her from the chill but she moved away from him and walked quickly to where they had left the buckboard. He was almost clumsy in his efforts to tuck the robe around her.

He climbed into the seat and took the lines and before he could lift them she said, "I want you to quit, Pete."

"Quit?" he said. "I just got started. Honey, this is what we been waiting for!"

"It's not what I've been waiting for, Pete. You're no more than an errand boy for that man."

"I suppose you'd rather have me working for three dollars a day on the Ponderosa!"

"Yes," she said.

He put down the lines, taking a quick turn with them around the brake rod. "We finally got it out in the open, didn't we? I told you I explained to Joe there was nothing personal in it!"

"I don't want you wearing a gun, associating with people like Lunger Smith, licking the boots of a man like Matt Vogel!"

"Why? Afraid Little Joe might get hurt?"

She turned and faced him squarely. "I'm afraid you might get hurt," she said. "I didn't marry Little Joe. I married you."

"And I let you down. Go ahead and say it."

She put a hand on his arm. "I won't say it, because it's not true."

He picked up the lines again. His jaws were set. "I

never had nothing in my life, Ellen. Neither did my folks before me. I won't live that way. I won't let you live that way." He cracked the lines sharply against the backs of the bays and the light wagon moved smartly out into the stream of wagons in the street.

"The ranch is all I ever wanted, Pete," she said.

"You think so now," he said. "Some morning you'd wake up and you'd think of the Ponderosa and all that could have been and you'd start hating me . . ."

"Pete! How can you say a thing like that?"

"I won't let it happen," he said. "I love you too much for that."

They drove in silence a long way.

"You're not going to quit working for Matt Vogel, are you?" she said finally.

"That's right, Ellen," he said. "I'm not going to quit."

*　　*　　*

William Sharon sat in his small office at the corner of C and Taylor streets, shuffling through a pile of papers. He looked up suddenly as the door opened and Matt Vogel came in without knocking. A quick irritation crossed Sharon's features. He picked up the latest copy of the *Territorial Enterprise* and shoved it across the desk toward Vogel.

"Have you read this?" Sharon asked.

Vogel glanced down at the paper and saw the article under Dan de Quille's by-line. He looked across at Sharon. "You mean this interview with Ben Cartwright?"

"Yes, that's what I mean."

Vogel didn't get the significance. "You knew he'd fight you for control of Hale and Norcross."

"That wasn't exactly what I had in mind," Sharon said. "I was referring to those statistics on the V flume he's building."

Vogel snorted. "He's been talkin' about that flume for

the past three years! I already told you—let him keep throwing his money away. The sooner he goes broke the sooner we'll take over the Ponderosa, won't we?"

"You don't have any more faith in that flume than you do in a railroad eventually running into Virginia City, do you?"

"I'm a teamster," Matt Vogel said. "You got enough mules and oxen and wagons and equipment, that's all you need. Somebody's always coming up with some new-fangled idea but I ain't seen the horse go out of style yet, have you?"

"Yes, I have," Sharon said. "In many cases it's been replaced by the steam engine."

Vogel blustered ever so slightly. "I didn't say I was against progress. What I'm saying is, he puts all that money in that flume and then he cuts off all the timber at the head of it . . ."

"He claims he won't cut off the timber," Sharon said. "He claims he can log the area for years."

"Then he's nothing but the dreamer you said he was," Vogel said.

"If he can cut the price of cord wood from seventeen dollars a cord to fourteen dollars a cord and the price of timbering from twenty-nine dollars a thousand to twenty-one dollars, he won't be a dreamer," Sharon said. "He'll be a millionaire."

"He won't even be in the wood and lumber business," Vogel said. "I'll have control of the whole thing by then."

"I hope you do, Matt," Sharon said. "Because in spite of the fact that you're going to be one of the directors of our new corporation, you personally still owe the Bank a half a million dollars."

Vogel flushed deeply. "You ain't gonna let me forget that, are you?"

"No, Matt, I'm not," Sharon said. "I'm a banker."

There was a note of warning in Vogel's voice. "Don't get no fancy ideas about closing me out, Sharon," he said. "Even if you foreclosed on my timber holdings I'd still have my teams and wagons. You'd have to have me to move your wood and lumber and ore."

"Yes, I suppose I would," Sharon said. He wasn't even looking at Vogel now. "Unless Cartwright proves to be right and the Union Mill and Mining Company takes over his flume and builds some additional ones of their own."

"You can't float ore down a flume," Vogel said. He was getting belligerent now and he could feel the effects of the champagne.

"You can haul it on a railroad," Sharon said. He squared some papers and the entire conversation became no more than just that—conversation.

Vogel smarted under that threat of the railroad. He had heard this before, a dozen times. Several franchises had been granted to build a railroad from Carson City to Virginia City, but nothing had ever come of it. Nothing ever would, Vogel was sure. He said, "Anything else on your mind?"

"Yes," Sharon said. "Sheriff Roy Coffee was by to see me."

Vogel puzzled over that a moment. He couldn't figure how Roy Coffee could possibly fit into any of his or Sharon's schemes. "He's apt to drop in anyplace, ain't he?"

"I suppose he is," Sharon said. He looked up quickly and fixed Vogel with a stare. "But I don't like him dropping in my office suggesting I've been hiring employees of questionable character."

Here was another area where Vogel and Sharon would never see eye to eye. Many of Vogel's teamsters, swampers and stable hands had police records a mile long. So long as they did their work, Vogel didn't care, and he never questioned what they did on their time off. He often bailed them out of jail in time to go to work Monday mornings and he was openly proud of the reputation his men had for toughness. Vogel's teamsters always arrived with bells on, as the saying went, indicating they

101

had not had to be assisted or pulled out of a mud hole someplace along the road. Had this happened, they would have had to turn their prized team bells over to the one who assisted them.

Sharon, on the other hand, had an impeccable reputation, which he prized highly. He was ruthless in business and he was soundly hated by many, but the foppishness of his attire was more than surface deep. One of his favorite sayings was, "Roll with swine and you'll soon smell of swill."

Vogel said, "I don't see what business it is of Coffee's."

Sharon gave no indication he had even heard Vogel.

"That crew you sent up to the north shore of the Lake," Sharon said. "Sheriff Coffee intimated—and strongly, I might add—that they aren't exactly typical loggers."

Vogel relaxed noticeably. "Oh, that," he said. "Yeah, I hired some boys who could scare people off if need be. I'm moving some expensive equipment up there and I need somebody to guard it. Anything wrong with that?"

"No, I suppose not," Sharon said quietly. "Provided you make sure everyone knows it was Matt Vogel who hired them and not the Bank of California."

"I stand on my own two feet," Vogel said. "I've never tried to hide behind the Bank's skirts."

"Don't try, Matt," Sharon said quietly.

The interview was over as surely as if Sharon had slammed the door on him and Matt Vogel knew it. He got up and left the office without even saying goodnight.

Outside the snow had increased noticeably and the sting of winter bit into Vogel's flushed cheeks. He had been put in his place tonight and he didn't like the feel of it.

He was no fool. He knew he was traveling in fast company. The fastest he had ever known in his life. He knew as well as any man that there was no room here for sentiment nor even for loyalty. The only thing that gave a man security in an operation like this was if you were in-

102

dispensable. *And that's what I'll be,* Matt Vogel thought. *Just as soon as I take over the Ponderosa.*

He walked on into the stinging bite of the wind-driven snow.

11 DURING THE NEXT WEEK Ben Cartwright seldom ventured more than a few blocks from the tall brick building that housed the Marye brokerage office. From under three hundred dollars a share, Hale and Norcross had risen to two thousand, nine hundred and twenty-five dollars a share in that brief span of time as both William Sharon and Ben Cartwright backed up their unconditional buy orders.

Now, suddenly, the price froze, and the stock-wise people of Virginia City started supplying their own versions of why it had happened. Someone was holding out a large bloc of shares. Someone had changed in his loyalty from Ben Cartwright to William Sharon, or the other way around. Ben Cartwright and William Sharon were really secretly in partnership . . .

It was all speculation. The real reason for the freeze was much more dramatic. There were only three uncommitted shares of Hale and Norcross stock outstanding, and no one could find the owner of those shares. At this moment, Ben Cartwright and William Sharon were in equal control. Those three missing shares would make the difference. Both Ben's and Sharon's brokers started a marathon, around-the-clock search for the identity of the owner of those three critical shares.

This was no simple task, Ben knew, and it was bound to take time. The owner of the shares was there on the corporation books, as big as life, but unfortunately no one had ever heard of him, and consequently no one had any idea where he might be found. Ben stared at that name—Thadeus Montgomery Smith. It meant absolutely nothing. The address was Placerville, California, and that was worthless. A thousand people a day passed through Placerville, and they often gave this freighting headquarters and major stage stop as an address. Added to this was the fact that some Comstockers changed names more often than they changed clothes. Quite often, shares were handed over as gifts for one reason or another and the changes of ownership were never recorded. For all anyone knew, Thadeus Montgomery Smith might have long ago fallen down a mine shaft in a drunken stupor and taken his three precious shares with him.

And so, until the identity of Thadeus Montgomery Smith was established, Ben Cartwright and William Sharon held equal control of the Hale and Norcross mine, and there it stood. It was as if Ben Cartwright and William Sharon were glaring at each other across a prize fight ring as they rested between rounds.

The entire town was in an uproar as it watched the battle of these two giants. This was something they could understand, and the average man didn't care who won. Some had sold a share or two far below its present asking price and these bitterly denounced either the Bank or Ben Cartwright, depending upon which had snatched up their particular shares. Many, like Beth Kelly, held onto their shares, but their votes were secure.

"Perhaps you ought to sell, Beth," Ben told her quietly when the stock hit a new top.

"What's the matter?" she asked, teasing. "Afraid I won't vote your way?"

"I could lose out, Beth," Ben said. "I think perhaps you

should take your profit while I've still got money to buy you out."

"Spend your money someplace else, Ben," she said. "Let's just say we're in this together."

He took both her hands and held them and looked deep into her eyes. "I'm very fond of you, do you know that?" he said.

"And very careful in your choice of words."

He held her close for a moment and brushed her cheek with his lips. "I'm a coward, Beth," he said simply.

"So am I, Ben," she said. "I'm just as afraid of being hurt again as you are."

He thought of her now as he rode out of Virginia City. When he was away from her he often dreamed of asking her to be his wife. When he was near her he thought of the tragedy that had struck three times: Adam's mother, Elizabeth; Inger—and each time he looked at his son Hoss he thought of her; and there on a promontory jutting into Lake Tahoe he had buried Little Joe's mother, Marie . . . He urged Buck into a jogging trot and rode on.

During these weeks, while he had fought the Hale and Norcross stock to a stalemate with Sharon, he had seen Hoss only once, when he came into town for supplies. He had not seen Little Joe at all.

He was now heading for a little ranch to the south, where he was experimenting with the first alfalfa ever grown in Nevada. He had purchased the seeds from a ship's captain, who had obtained them in Chile. He wanted to see how the crop had survived that first brief but savage snow. After that he would head immediately for the flume site, where he had made arrangements to meet Hoss and Little Joe. Buck seemed to sense the urgency in Ben and he quickened his pace.

*   *   *

"So you figure you're a top woods boss, do you?" Matt Vogel asked. He was standing spread-legged in the barnyard of one of his gigantic stables. He took a delight in using this place as an office.

"I'm the best," Neil Larson said. His lower lip was punched out by the constant ball of snuff. He spit a brown stream and added, "I used to have an outfit of my own."

"What happened?" Matt said. "Get caught?"

The muscles along Larson's jaw tightened momentarily, then relaxed and he started to grin. "You come right at a man, don't you?" he said.

"That's right," Vogel said. "There's a saying around I don't ask no man to do a job I can't do myself. Including my own fighting, if need be."

"I understand that kind of talk," Larson said.

Vogel looked steadily at the big man in front of him, measuring him, and measuring him accurately. This was a man who wouldn't back down from trouble, Vogel decided, and he was a man who would take orders blindly so long as he was treated in a manner he considered fair.

"What have you got against Ben Cartwright?" Vogel asked suddenly. He asked the question in such a manner that made it impossible to predict what sort of answer was expected.

"Personal," Larson said.

"He catch you logging on the Ponderosa?"

"That make any difference to you?"

"Come spring, my outfit will be logging on the Ponderosa," Vogel said. "A man that's worked that timber before might be valuable to me." He shrugged. "Of course, if you'd as soon stay out of the way of the Cartwrights . . ."

"I ain't dodgin' the Cartwrights," Larson said.

"Good," Vogel said. "Neither am I. You say you can get your old crew together?"

106

"In a day or so. Couple of 'em are in jail. Got to celebrating a little too much when I come back from down below."

Vogel took a slip of paper and a stub of pencil from his pocket. He scribbled down a name and address, shoved the paper at Larson.

"That's my lawyer," Vogel said. "Tell him I said get your crew out of jail."

"We got the job?"

"You got it," Vogel said.

He turned and walked off, his eyes expertly appraising a new bunch of mules he had just purchased. Vogel had never felt more expansive in his life, and, except for one nagging worry, this bright blue morning would have been perfection itself.

For three weeks now he had tried to figure out some way in which he could get Sharon obligated to him. He didn't own any Hale and Norcross stock, and as he watched the price soar he was sorry he didn't. He had even considered buying some, but he had rejected that idea, because although he could then vote it Sharon's way, he would actually be buying the stock out from under the Bank group. The stock market had never appealed greatly to Matt, anyway. He liked the smell of horses and harness and the creak of wagon wheels and the jangle of team bells. These were things he could touch and feel, and they were as real as the sluiced devastation of the hydraulic nozzles that had started him on his way to wealth.

He walked into the wagon yard where a dozen blacksmiths were at work on tires and couplings, and beyond them was a carpenter shop where four men, employed full time, carved singletrees and doubletrees and wagon tongues. At present, Matt Vogel bought his wagons in Sacramento and brought them loaded across the Sierra. He'd have his own wagon factory here soon, he decided.

He went to the dispatch office where a battery of clerks with green eyeshades perched on high stools at slant-top desks, working over manifests and orders and payrolls.

One of the clerks looked up and said, "Oh, Mr. Vogel. A boy just came by and left this note for you." He handed across an envelope.

Matt Vogel tore open the envelope and scowled down at the handwriting that was becoming increasingly familiar to him. William Sharon wanted to see him.

Again Matt felt that prick of resentment, that desire to tell Sharon to go to hell. But again he knew he would do whatever William Sharon wanted him to do. At this point, he was completely dependent on Sharon. If Sharon said "Frog," Matt Vogel had no choice but to jump.

He had to change that situation, Matt knew. Somehow, there was a way. He turned and left the freight yard and started up toward the Bank office at C and Taylor.

*   *   *

The canyon was steep and narrow and rock bound, an upheaval of desert tossed carelessly against the eastern slope of the Sierra. Ben Cartwright turned up the collar of his coat as the heatless sun buried itself in a mass of grey-black clouds rapidly blotting out the incredible blue of the Nevada sky. This was the time of year when the weather changed as rapidly as the price of mining stock. The peculiar chill and stillness that presaged snow settled into the depths of the treacherous gorge.

A semblance of roadway had been hacked out through the willows along the creek, and high on the cliff across the gorge surveyor's stakes marked the path the fifteen-mile-long flume would take from the summit down to the mills at Carson Valley. It was an incredible task, and if people hadn't scoffed at the practicality of it, Ben would have been surprised. Even his own son, Hoss, had been violently opposed to the expenditure at first, but now he was one of the flume's staunchest supporters.

For several years now the Comstock had known some way had to be developed to cut the transportation costs. The flume was Ben Cartwright's answer to one phase of that problem.

With a small head of water turned into the summit end of the flume, finished lumber, cord wood and even logs could be sent rushing down the planked trough at express-train speeds. If this flume proved successful—and Ben was sure it would—he intended to extend the network of these trestle-supported conveyors into the furthest reaches of the Ponderosa, where the vast groves of standing timber could not only sustain cutting but would actually benefit by it. Thus the flume fitted into his long-range conservation program and his dream of preserving the beauty of the Ponderosa, just as he had so carefully tended and preserved the splendid grove that sheltered the grave of Little Joe's mother.

The wind shifted, and now he could hear the ringing of hammers in the clear, thin air, and in time the shouts of mule skinners mingled with the slapping sounds of finished planks being unloaded from wagons. An impatience to see what progress had been made seized Ben, and along with it was the keen desire to see Hoss and Little Joe again. The past three weeks had been nerve-wracking; the time ahead would be worse, he knew.

Again his thoughts turned to finances and to the present price of Hale and Norcross. It was a safe bet, for two sound reasons, that the price of the stock would continue to spiral beyond the present twenty-nine hundred and twenty-five dollars. If the elusive Thadeus Montgomery Smith was ever found, he would be in a position to just sit back and let Ben and Sharon bid against each other for those three crucial shares. In the event he was not found, then Ben and Sharon would have no recourse except to keep bidding the stock up to an inevitable point where some erstwhile loyal supporter could no longer afford to be loyal.

Added to the drain of the proxy fight was the ten to fifteen thousand dollars per mile cost of the flume itself. The planks that formed the trough were two feet wide, one and a half inches thick and sixteen feet long. Each took two men to handle, and it would take thousands of planks to complete that entire fifteen miles. Added to this were the forests of support timbers, for the flume traveled over canyons on trestles as high as seventy-five feet, and it clung to cliffs and rounded the shoulders of hills, always maintaining a grade of four feet to the rod. Experiments had proved that a steeper pitch would toss the hurtling lumber out on curves and break it into match sticks. A lesser grade would make the movement of the lumber too sluggish to be practical.

It was a beautiful piece of engineering, and although he had kept in close touch with Adam on the progress, he often wished his oldest son had been able to stay and see the job to completion. He did have the consolation of knowing, however, that the head engineer and head surveyor on the project were classmates of Adam's and had been hand-picked by him before his departure for Europe.

The sounds were increasing now, clashing against the walls of the canyon, trampling upon each other until team bells, the rasp of saws, the ring of hammers and the crash of lumber all blended into an incongruous symphony that was picked up and tossed back and forth by the rising wind. He rode around a bend in the canyon, and there was the spiderwork trestling of the flume itself, stark against the darkening sky.

From here, the very air seemed filled with uprights and cross-braces fingering up toward emptiness, but as Ben rode further around the bend he saw the progress of the flume-laying crew and the V of new lumber curved gracefully around the shoulder of the mountain, back toward its beginning. At this, the near end, men swarmed along the two-foot wide catwalk, carrying lumber, putting it in place, laying the flume as the trestle-work progressed, in much the manner of a railroad gang laying track.

Under the progressing trestle-work was a movable blacksmith shop. A grindstone, operated by a foot pedal, spit sparks from the glistening bit of a broad axe. Kegs and kegs of square, iron nails were stacked there, and supplies were sent up to the crew working in the dizzying heights of the trestle by a system of blocks and tackle.

Several wagon loads of lumber were lined up, waiting to move up to the platform where they could unload. A derrick had been rigged here, and a blindfolded mule driven by a young boy had worn a deep rut in the ground from the constant pulling and backing that lifted the finished lumber up to the work crews on the flume.

The activity was moving at a feverish pitch, Ben was glad to note, and he rode in unnoticed by anyone save one of the teamsters. The teamster grinned and said, "If you're looking for Hoss and Little Joe they're yonder at the paymaster's shack."

Ben waved his thanks and rode on toward the jerry-built structure at the edge of a clearing. He noticed about a dozen men clustered around the shack and wondered why they would be here in the middle of the afternoon. He dismounted and tied Buck and moved over toward the makeshift office. Before he was there he saw Hoss come out and hold up his hands for silence. Ben held back.

"Boys," Hoss was saying, "I can't pay you off in cash because we just ain't got that much on hand. We bring the payroll up once a week from the bank in Virginia City and we didn't expect to do any more paying off until Saturday night."

Joe had moved out to stand beside his brother.

111

A man Ben didn't know, apparently a spokesman for the group, said, "You meet our price, we'll stay on."

"We meet your price we'll have to raise the wages of everybody working on the flume," Joe said. "We can't do it."

Ben moved on, still for the most part unnoticed, for over two-thirds of the workmen here were unknown to him. He thought he saw a flash of relief in the eyes of both Hoss and Little Joe when they saw him. He moved up alongside them, giving a casual glance inside the shack where the harried paymaster was wiping perspiration from his face in spite of the cold. Jim Willy sat tilted back in a chair, a rifle across his lap.

"What's this all about?" Ben asked quietly.

"Somebody's raiding our labor gang, Pa," Hoss said. "That fellow Bruce Cameron—you know the one—he's been hanging around here offering to hire our boys for a dollar a day more than we're paying."

"Is Cameron around here now?" Ben asked.

Little Joe got a peculiar grin on his face. He rubbed the knuckles of his left hand into the gloved palm of his right, then blew on them. "He decided to leave a while ago," he said.

Ben turned to the men.

"Gentlemen," he said, "I need your help and I need it badly, but an unsatisfied workman is of no use to me. If you'll step up orderly, one at a time, I'll have pay vouchers made out for you. You can take them to my bank in Virginia City and they will be honored without question."

The spokesman moved forward again. He spread his feet and spit across the center of his lips.

"We was promised our pay in silver when we come to work here," the man said.

"That's right, you were," Ben said. "Every Saturday night. So if that's what you want, come back Saturday

112

night and you'll be paid in silver. Now get out of here. You're on private land."

The workmen looked at each other and a muttering started to grow. Ben unbuckled his coat and the gun on his hip was starkly apparent. Silently, Jim Willy appeared in the doorway, the rifle held across his chest. A dozen men stood there facing the three Cartwrights and Jim Willy.

The spokesman for the men licked his lips. "We'll take your paper," he said.

*   *   *

The paymaster wiped the perspiration from his forehead with a trembling hand. "I'm glad that's over," he said. "I thought for a while they were going to move right in here."

"If they had of, there'd have been another Paiute War," Jim Willy said.

Ben said, "How long has this been going on?"

"Been a lot of talk for about a week," Hoss said. "This is the first bunch that's actually quit."

"I figure Matt Vogel's behind it," Little Joe said. "I was up at the north end of the Lake day before yesterday and he must have a hundred men in there."

"No attempt to move onto the Ponderosa?" Ben asked.

"He's staying clear just as if he wanted to," Joe said.

Ben turned to Jim Willy. "How's the wood cutting coming along?"

"We've got about five hundred cords moved over to the river," Jim said.

"A third of it," Ben mused. "How's the weather been up there?"

"I thought that last snow was going to move us out sure," Jim said.

"Looks to me like we can expect more of it tonight," Hoss said.

113

Jim Willy said, "Why don't you leave the weather predicting to the Indians? It's about all we got left."

"All right, go do a snow dance," Joe said.

Ben said, "I'll see if I can't get an injunction to keep Bruce Cameron away from here."

"Joe gave him a pretty good injunction," Hoss said. "Right on the point of the chin."

"I can't say I'm displeased," Ben said, "but that's about all we can expect—keep him away from here. We can't keep the man out of a public place and if he wants to go over to the saloon on the Placerville road where our boys hang out on payday there's not much we can do to stop him."

The three Cartwrights and Jim Willy had moved out of the paymaster's shack now and they were standing there, watching the work going on on the flume.

"How things been going with you, Pa?" Hoss asked finally.

Ben told them, as briefly as he could.

"Sharon's really pushing you right up against the wall, isn't he?" Joe said.

"He's trying it, Joseph," Ben said. "The devil of it is, I'm afraid this is only the beginning."

"Anything I can do, Mr. Cartwright?" Jim Willy asked.

"That crew of yours," Ben said. "Do you suppose there are any of them who would like to stay on after the woodcutting season?"

"I don't know," Jim Willy said. "Most of them just figure on say May to November."

"I wish you'd talk to them," Ben said. "We're going to need all the help we can get right here."

"I imagine I can get some of them to stay on," Jim said.

"The cattle will be down on the lower pastures by the end of the week," Joe said. "I talked to José just this morning."

114

"You boys have been doing a fine job," Ben said. "All three of you. I wish I could tell you to take some time off, but you're pretty much going to have to take care of things until this Hale and Norcross business is settled——"

He broke off as he noticed Hoss looking off down the canyon, his expression puzzled.

"Who in the devil could that be, ridin' up here this time of day?" Hoss asked.

They all turned and now they saw the rider, bundled against the increasing cold. He was just coming around the bend, riding as fast as the terrain would allow. Ben felt the bottom drop out of his stomach.

"You know him, Pa?" Joe asked.

"Yes," Ben said quietly. "I know him. He's from the Marye Brokerage office. I made arrangements for them to send a messenger if anything went wrong."

He caught the exchange of glances among Jim Willy, Hoss and Little Joe as he moved out to meet the messenger.

The lad was not used to hard riding and he slid out of his saddle with an obvious relief. "I got here soon as I could, Mr. Cartwright," he said, and he handed across an envelope. Ben ripped it open and scanned it quickly.

The note was brief and to the point. Sharon, in his effort to smoke out the by now almost legendary Thadeus Montgomery Smith and his three critical shares, had managed to bull the price of Hale and Norcross stock up to four thousand, one hundred dollars a share. And it seemed his strategy had worked. Thadeus Montgomery Smith himself had not put in an appearance, but someone who remembered him had.

Ben handed the note across to Hoss.

For a long moment Hoss looked at the message, then he looked up at his father. "I just don't believe it," he said. "I always thought his name was Holloway."

115

"They wouldn't have sent me this message if they hadn't been sure," Ben said.

"But old Bearpaw Holloway . . ."

The mysterious Thadeus Montgomery Smith was a bearded, old eccentric trapper who showed up in Virginia City once or twice a year. For the most part he lived as a hermit someplace up in the high Sierra.

Hoss looked steadily at his father. "You got to have those three shares, don't you?"

"Either that or lose to Sharon," Ben said simply.

"I know how to find old Bearpaw," Hoss said.

"So do I," Ben said. "But nobody would ever make it back into that high country with the weather what it is."

"Pa, you know as well as I do, if I don't make it up there, somebody else will," Hoss said. He dismissed it as an accomplished fact. "I'll saddle up. Still a couple of hours of daylight."

"Hoss," Ben said, "I can't let you do this."

"Why?" Hoss said. "Because you're in this all alone?" He didn't wait for an answer.

When Ben turned he saw Little Joe and Jim Willy watching him. They moved toward him and almost in unison they said, "Hoss is right. You just tell us what you want us to do."

12 THE DEVIL KNIFE WIND that drove down from the snow fields cut through Matt Vogel's bearskin teamster's coat and pounded Lunger Smith deeper into his saddle, but Matt didn't care. The roll of the horse between his knees as the animal lunged up the ever steepening trail was a lifting surge of power that ran through Vogel's frame and left him warm. If he had planned it all himself, fate couldn't have played into his hands any more completely. He looked across at the hunched-over figure of the hired gunman riding alongside him. "Looks like weather up ahead," Matt said.

"What do you call this?" Smith complained.

Vogel threw back his head and laughed. What was a little weather when he had William Sharon eating out of his hand?

This morning seemed an eternity ago. He had hired Neil Larson, and then the message had come that Sharon wanted to see him and he had felt that prick of resentment . . . now he was riding into the high country to pick up three shares of stock from a crazy old galoot and Bill Sharon had practically licked his hands thanking him because he, Vogel, had volunteered to make the trip. Sharon was a city man. He considered this trip a complete impossibility at this time of year and Vogel hadn't done one thing to change that viewpoint.

"Just remember I wouldn't even risk it for anyone except you, Bill," Vogel had said. "I'm doing it because I know what it means to you, and I wouldn't trust the job to any other man alive."

"Matt, I'll never forget it, not so long as I live," Sharon said. He handed a piece of paper across the desk. "This is a bank draft, signed, the amount left blank. I don't want any kick-back. Tell him the current offer—forty-one hundred dollars a share. Buy it for that if you can; go higher if you have to."

"Probably buy it for ten dollars," Vogel said. "Old Bearpaw wouldn't know any better."

He saw the sudden hardness in Sharon and decided not to push his luck.

"You pay the going price," Sharon said, "more if you

117

have to. I want those three shares of stock and I want them clean."

It was late afternoon now, and in the past hour or so Vogel had let a dozen ideas run through his head and had reluctantly rejected them all. He still believed he could buy that stock from the eccentric old trapper for any price and then tell Sharon he had paid five thousand a share or more. It was tempting, but it was small thinking, Vogel decided. A few months back, perhaps he would have tried it, but now he was part of big business and he was going to be a lot bigger.

The pale-eyed gunman said, "I still can't figure why you wanted me along."

"Because I pay you to do what I say," Matt Vogel said.

"You got any complaints, say so," Smith said. "I asked you why you brought me along."

Matt looked across at the gunman and let a grin touch his lips. A man like Lunger Smith could be touchy. Matt didn't want him touchy now.

"I told you what these three shares of stock mean to me, didn't I?" Matt asked.

"You told me what they meant to Sharon."

"Same thing," Vogel said. "Me and Sharon. We're one and the same from here on."

"You gonna answer my question?"

"These three shares ain't no secret," Vogel said. "Ben Cartwright will find out about them. He'll send somebody after them." He paused and looked intently at the gunman. "I don't want that somebody to get through."

"I guess that answers my question."

"Any objection?"

"Why?" Smith said. "Like you said, you pay me to do what you say."

They reined up then to let their horses blow and Vogel turned in his saddle and looked back. Far below, the forest stretched into a gathering darkness. There was no sign of anyone on the trail.

"Let's make camp," Vogel said. "I want to get an early start in the morning."

Lunger Smith wearily swung out of his saddle. He took off his right glove and drew the rifle from the saddle scabbard and checked it carefully.

"I best keep this by the fire," he said. "Gets too cold, it might gum up."

Matt Vogel watched the thin, professional gunman. He could understand a man like this. Pay him his wages and he would do you a job. When you were through with him, get rid of him.

"I'll build a fire," Matt said.

* * *

When Hoss left the flume camp, he was approximately two hours behind Matt Vogel and Lunger Smith. Ben had hurried directly back to Virginia City after leaving Jim Willy in full charge of the flume crew. He had sent Little Joe down to join José Bettencort, for with the threatening weather, he wanted to make sure the cattle were in a position where they could be fed if that became necessary.

Hoss reached down and patted Chub's neck. There was a long ride ahead and a hard one and he intended to push the horse just as fast as he dared. The big, white-stockinged black responded and moved into a mile-eating jog.

No one knew this country any better than Hoss Cartwright, and he mentally calculated certain short-cuts he could take that might equalize the time differential between his departure time and the departure time of whoever had left from Virginia City earlier in the day. Common sense said someone had. He had a race on his hands and he knew it.

He would ride as late as he dared tonight, he decided,

119

for he would be mostly in timber and ridge country. To-morrow he would start the climb over the backbone of the Sierra. He glanced at the sky from old habit and knew that time was not the only thing he would have to battle. Another thousand feet of elevation and he would be in snow.

Darkness dropped like a blanket and still he pushed on, sensing his way from an old knowledge of the country, cutting finally into the abandoned logging road that would lead him to the area where Ben had first encountered Neil Larson and his crew cutting Ponderosa timber. Hoss knew the area well, and he remembered a lightning-splintered pitch-pine stump that would give him quick kindling for a fire. Chub took advantage of the semi-cleared and hastily constructed logging road and quickened his pace.

They pushed on then for an hour more and Hoss sensed, rather than saw, when he was into the logged-off area. He pulled Chub in and let him pick his own way through the residual of slashings and bark that remained from the uncontrolled cutting of Neil Larson and his crew.

Even in this darkness the wanton devastation was apparent and Hoss felt the anger rising inside him, for to Hoss, as to Ben, a tree was a personal, living thing and he and his father had spent many a night pouring over writings on conservation and advanced logging methods. They had developed a great number of such methods themselves.

As he moved deeper into the clearing the night lightened to some extent, and soon he found the place he was seeking. He dismounted and, taking a hand axe from his saddle, found the stump and sliced off several long splinters of the pitch impregnated pine. When he applied a match the pitch flared into a yellow flame, and a long trailer of black smoke stained the kindling and his fingers as he carefully laid a fire. He unsaddled and unpacked by the glow of it.

He fed Chub from the oats he had brought along and put him on a short picket rope, and by then his coffee was brewing and the thick slabs of bacon were sizzling and crackling in the black iron skillet and the aroma of it was stronger than the smell of dampness and of crushed and broken pine.

He ate and washed his dishes in the only clear pool he could find on the small stream that had always wandered through the meadow. It was impossibly choked with scraps of bark and other debris, dammed off where logs had been dragged across it. This had once been a fine trout stream. It never would be again.

He took down his bedroll and spread a ground sheet and blankets and turned in, fully clothed. He heard the stirring of the high wind in the trees around the clearing and he thought of Matt Vogel and his threat to log off the Ponderosa. The thought haunted him as he drifted off to sleep.

When he awoke in the morning the ground was white with snow. He looked up the slopes and into a grey wall of darkness. High above his head, the wind howled a dirge.

* * *

Matt Vogel and Lunger Smith worked in the bone chilling darkness of the blizzard as they tried to saddle their mounts. The wind was a constant scream and the snow came at a level slant that burned a man's eyes. Lunger Smith fumbled at his cinch, then turned quickly, colliding with Matt Vogel.

"We're fools to try it!" Smith shouted. "Camp here until it's over!"

"Can't afford the time," Vogel shouted back.

"What good's that stock to you if you're dead?"

"Know the trail," Vogel said. "Taken a pack train through here a dozen times. I'm going on. Stay here if you want."

"You've got the food and the blankets!"

"That's right," Vogel said. "Remember it."

He moved no more than six feet before he was momentarily lost to sight in the powdery snow that swirled as if someone had tossed it with a shovel. Smith turned back to his horse, leaning against the animal's side, grateful for the warmth that seeped into his emaciated frame. He fastened his cinch and somehow managed to get into the saddle. Vogel, mounted, loomed out of the white darkness only a few feet away. He shouted, but Smith couldn't hear. Vogel cupped his hands around his mouth.

"Stay close!" Vogel said. "You get lost I ain't gonna stick around looking for you."

"You walk out on me I'll kill you," Smith said.

Vogel had already ridden off and Smith knew he hadn't heard that last remark. This was no time to follow up his threat. This was a matter of survival. He turned his horse and rode to catch up with Vogel and now he rode with his stirrup touching Vogel's stirrup. In time the trail narrowed and he could no longer ride in that manner. He fell behind, but he kept close enough to see the rider in front of him.

He didn't know how long he rode this way. He was too cold to think in increments of time. He only knew that the wind had increased and the trail had steepened and the visibility had dropped to zero. He kicked his horse forward and a blast of wind nearly knocked him from the saddle. The sound of Matt Vogel's voice startled him with its nearness.

"Get off and lead 'em," Vogel shouted.

Numbly, not much caring, Lunger Smith did as he was told. His feet were so cold his legs nearly buckled under him. He fumbled for his reins and wasn't sure if he had both of them or not. He knew Vogel's horse was moving on up the trail and he started after it, stumbling along blindly, tugging at his own horse.

It was some sixth sense that first warned him that

he was lagging behind. He tried to hurry up, but the horse kept holding back and now he remembered a recurring dream in which he wanted to run away from some terror but his feet were leaden and wouldn't move as fast as his brain told them to move . . . He started to panic and he remembered someone, a long time ago, telling him not to panic, but he had been in water that time and this was not water—or was it? He couldn't tell. It was liquid and swirling and a man couldn't see six inches ahead of his face.

The panic in Lunger Smith became real. He stopped and shouted into the wind and the wind tore the words from his throat and spit them out into the blinding whiteness. He listened for some answer and got only the howl of the blizzard. Something close to a sob caught in the throat of the amber-eyed killer. He floundered on, tugging at the reins of his reluctant horse, his only contact with reality. The horrible suspicion that he was alone became a crushing reality.

He tried to mutter some sort of prayer and discovered he didn't know how and that sent a chill of fear through him that was as real as the snow cold. He floundered on and stumbled and felt the reins jerk free of his grip. He tried to get to his feet and was up to his armpits in snow and he felt the forefeet of his horse smash against his shoulder as the animal struggled for footing that wasn't there.

Pain slashed wickedly down his side—almost a relief to the chilled numbness that had stunned his body for the past hour. He tried to move and found he could, and he started the laborious climb out of the small crevasse into which he had fallen.

He forgot the horse, for his pain and his cold-benumbed brain kept shouting at him to survive and abandon all else. He cursed the day he had ever gone to work for Matt Vogel . . .

He clutched for some support to pull himself upward.

His hand found emptiness. He felt himself sliding, then he was falling and he landed on his left shoulder and the pain was a searing light stabbing through his brain.

In a moment of delirium he thought he saw Matt Vogel standing revealed in that shaft of light.

"Matt?" Lunger Smith said. There was no answer. "Matt?" He was shouting now but could not hear his own voice. He felt hysteria that was sharper than the pain in his crushed shoulder.

He started to cry and he couldn't remember if he had ever cried before in his life.

In the moment before he lost consciousness Lunger Smith knew there was to be no escape. Not one soul with the exception of Matt Vogel knew he was up here on this accursed mountain. And Matt Vogel wasn't going to come back and look for him. Matt Vogel didn't care.

* * *

The blizzard smashed against Hoss Cartwright with sledge hammer blows, and still he refused to turn away from it. So long as he headed straight into the eye of the storm he knew where he was. Compromise for as much as five minutes and even he could become hopelessly lost.

The muffler across his mouth was stiff with ice where his breath had seeped through, and his eyebrows were white hummocks of snow, picked up on the rare occasions when he glanced up from under the brim of the tremendously high-crowned hat that had become so much a part of him. He was still riding, but he knew his horse couldn't last much longer. The wind shifted and he reined up hard. He could have sworn he had heard a cry for help. He lowered his head and rode on, knowing the tricks a wind like this could play on a man.

He felt Chub lunge into a drift and he slid from the saddle and took the cheek strap of the bridle. He spoke soothingly, his mouth against Chub's ear. The horse threshed at the snow and got its feet back under itself.

124

"It's all right, boy," Hoss said. "It's all right now."

He moved on, cautiously, leading his horse. The wail of the wind was like the cry of a man in pain and then suddenly there was a deathly stillness. The wind stopped blowing so unexpectedly it was almost like being thrust into a vacuum, and Hoss found himself sucking in a great gulp of air so cold it stung to the very bottom of his lungs.

The deathly quiet crawled up the mountain and lingered here on this ledge, but above him, up on the summit, the wind still threshed and battled, stripping the snow from the granite ridges.

He realized then that he was under the shelter of the summit rocks themselves and that this was only a temporary respite. He took time to get his bearings and knew he had not lost the trail. He patted Chub's neck and started on.

It was Chub who tugged back on the reins and threw up his head. Hoss turned quickly, sensing something wrong.

He saw it, then, down below the trail, struggling in a drift. It was a saddled horse.

There was no human in sight.

13 FOR JUST A MOMENT the wind swirled back around the point of the mountain and a blinding streamer of snow curtained what could have been an apparition, but now the wind was gone again and there was no doubt in Hoss Cartwright's mind that someone else was battling through this blizzard.

With characteristic directness, he knew that the only ones who could possibly be in this area in this kind of weather would be Bearpaw Holloway himself or the person who had been sent from William Sharon's office to beat him to those three shares of stock. It made no difference to Hoss which it might be. He left his horse and went plunging down the slope toward the foundering horse.

The lull in the wind continued to hold and one quick, expert glance told Hoss that he was too late so far as the animal was concerned. The left front leg was shattered below the knee and the pitiful struggling of the beast sent a stab of pain through the big man.

He took off his right mitten, unbuckled his coat and drew his gun. He rolled the cylinder to a full chamber and thumbed back the hammer. As well as he knew that this had to be done, the hatred of it was still there. He leveled the gun carefully, knowing the most important thing now was to not miss a vital spot. When he squeezed the trigger the buck of the gun against the palm of his hand was like a sickness that ran through his gigantic frame. He saw the startled pain in those trusting eyes and it was as if they were saying, "Thank God, help has come!"

The eyes glazed over. Yes, help had come. Help had been death.

Hoss Cartwright, who loved life so well, often wondered how it could be made up of so many small moments that a man could hate.

Someone had ridden that horse, obviously, so now he ground-tied his own animal and started walking around in circles. The rider could have fallen as far as a mile back. He had no way of judging. He only knew that someplace near here was either a dead man or a man who needed help.

He checked the path he had made through the snow and then he moved out three feet and started a wider circle. It was on the tenth circle that he almost fell on the body of Lunger Smith.

He slid down into the crevasse that would not have presented a particular hazard to a man with good health and with knowledge of what he was doing. Lunger Smith had had neither. He was an emaciated man with a strength-consuming disease, and at the moment he had slipped, he had been in a state of acute panic. In addition, his horse had accidentally struck him on the shoulder.

Hoss had no way of knowing these things, but he had an instinctive feeling for the hurt and wounded and it didn't make much difference whether it was a flower, a bird, an animal or a human being.

He lifted the head of the amber-eyed gunman and his ungloved fingers sought the man's pulse. There was life there. Not much, but it was there.

Slowly, carefully, by calling upon almost superhuman strength, Hoss Cartwright dragged the lanky form of one of Virginia City's most notorious gunmen out of that clutching pit and up onto the lip of the granite supported snow above.

Looking back down into the crumbling crevasse, Hoss thought of the time, years and years ago, out on a wild stretch of prairie, when he had first learned about doodle bugs. Ant bears, some people called them. They were small insects with lobster-like claws, and they dug pits in the sandy soil and waited there until an unwary ant lost his footing and fell to the bottom of that conical pit. And then those claws would reach up and the ant would sink out of sight and be gone forever.

Hoss Cartwright remembered the day his mother had died. They had explained it to him; they had told him about it. But he had never really known until he had lain there alone on the warm and vibrant grass, with the smell of the earth in his nostrils, and had looked down into the cone of an ant bear's pit and an ant had slipped and the claws had shown and the ant was gone. It was out of sight, forever and forever. And then Hoss Cartwright had known that his mother was dead. He turned and

127

looked down into the cold, grey face of the man he held in his arms.

Hoss was exhausted, beyond belief, but the man was alive and when the knife that cuts the final thread of life is this close, no one stops to wonder if this one stays and this one goes. He got up from his knees and lifted the man and carried him in his arms.

He went to his horse then and he draped the body of Lunger Smith across the saddle and he picked up the reins and started walking, slowly, slogging toward the summit of the Sierra.

*   *   *

God was kind up there on top, for the snow had ceased. On the other side, the snow still fell, but it fell gently, and the howling hell that swept down the eastern slopes and became the terrifying Washoe Zephyrs in the spring and fall no longer existed. There was a quiet hush, as the snow built its temporal monuments upon the needles of the sugar pines and the fan-like bows of the firs. The clumps of bear clover were noncommittal shrugs on the undulating white hillside. Where tricks of wind had chosen to toy with the grey green manzanita, small snatches of red bark blushed through like the cheek of a maiden behind the white of a wedding veil.

There were tantalizing and fleeting glances of blue through the grey pallor above, sure signs that the storm was breaking. Hoss Cartwright moved on, in spite of his own fatigue, leading the horse that carried the body of a worthless man who had killed perhaps twenty times, but who was incapable of stopping the death hand that was reaching out for him now.

They came to a stream, and here icicles had formed, and the glitter of cold coated the leaves of the ferns with stiff fingers of death. He had been here in summer once, and it had been a place of love and greenery and quiet.

128

Hoss Cartwright pushed on through the brittle, ice-sheathed limbs of the hazel nut and up through the naked aspen and down through a valley, and beyond was utter whiteness and then, at the head of a box canyon, was a column of blue smoke.

He had not lost his way. That was the cabin of Bearpaw Holloway. And until this moment, Hoss had forgotten why he was coming here. He only knew that a fellow creature, draped across that saddle, had needed help.

Hoss didn't raise his eyes. He didn't say a prayer. He had long ago made his own covenant with God. The outdoors was his church. He felt he understood what was right and he felt that his God should understand this, too. He led the horse forward.

He hardly knew when he reached the door of the cabin. The bearded face that greeted him was familiar, but it was out of a past that seemed so long ago he could not immediately identify it.

The eyes were glittering and bright, but they were intelligent, and no one could have told this old man's age. Hoss shook his head to bring himself back to reality and still he could not remember why he was here. He said, "Bearpaw, you remember me? I'm Hoss Cartwright."

The bearded face said, "I remember you, Hoss. We'll talk later. You got troubles."

"He's frozen," Hoss said.

"Maybe," the old man in the doorway said. "Bring him in."

The body of Lunger Smith felt light in Hoss's arms as he packed him into the room and put him there on a bunk, and old Bearpaw Holloway leaned over him and put his ear to the man's chest and then he looked up at Hoss. The glittering eyes lost some of their brightness as he said, "His chest is rattlin' like a snake's tail. It ain't too good. I got manzanita tea. You take them blankets and warm 'em by the fireplace there."

They worked furiously, the two of them, and they did not consider whether this was a life worth saving. They knew only that this was a life.

"Breathin' better," old Bearpaw Holloway said finally. "Maybe if he can sleep . . ."

In spite of the gigantic isolation that sprawled outside and spilled around them, there was no particular privacy here in the cabin, for the room was small. But the fire in the fireplace was a good fire and the warmth it spread was as fine as if it had been the warmth that permeated one of the finest mansions in Virginia City, and the home-made pine table was an elegant table and the bench on which Hoss Cartwright collapsed was as magnificent as a tufted velvet settee in the Washoe Club above the Crystal Saloon.

Hoss slowly raised his head, and for the first time he became fully aware that Matt Vogel was sitting there, looking at him. There was a wide grin on Matt Vogel's lips.

Reality was back now and immediately Hoss knew why Matt Vogel was here. He turned slowly and looked at Bearpaw Holloway.

He was talking to a blank wall and he knew it before he ever opened his mouth and there was no conviction whatsoever in what he said. "Bearpaw," Hoss started. "As long as Lunger is sleeping there was something I wanted to talk to you about—"

"This, maybe?" Matt Vogel said. He held up some gilt-edged certificates; and Hoss didn't have to glance at them a second time. They were the three shares of Hale and Norcross stock.

"I'll buy them from you," Hoss said.

"I suppose you would," Vogel said.

The heat of the fireplace was reaching through and some of the numbness and pain was running out of Hoss's massive frame. He stared at Vogel and said, "You got here in a hurry."

"That's right," Vogel said. "I was on a business trip. I don't stop and waste time."

"Not even long enough to save a man's life?" Hoss asked.

Vogel looked at him intently. "If I was you," he said, "I'd think a long time before I talked that way in town." He moved over to the door, opened it and peered out. "I'll feed the horses," he said, and he went outside.

For a long moment the old man sat there, his eyes downcast, then he forced himself to look at Hoss. "You wanted that stock, didn't you?" he said.

"Yeah, Bearpaw," Hoss said. "I wanted it pretty bad."

"I guess I should have known," Bearpaw said. "Matt Vogel ridin' out of a storm like that, offering me that kind of money—"

"I'm not blaming you, Bearpaw," Hoss said.

"Twelve thousand three hundred dollars," the old man said. "I never knew there was that much money, Hoss."

"Sure. I said I understood."

"No, I don't reckon you do," Bearpaw said. "You see, I know how folks talk about me. They say I'm queer in the head, livin' up here in these hills this way."

"A man's got a right to live where he wants," Hoss said.

"I just never did learn how to get along with folks," the old man said. "That don't mean I don't get lonesome. I get lonesome just like anybody else." His eyes brightened. "Remember the time you come to see me, Hoss?"

"I guess I wasn't such good company that time," Hoss said.

"Yes you was," the old man said. "You was all broke up because that girl you was in love with had died and the first thing you thought of was that you needed to be alone." He stopped and shook his head. "I know that feeling, but it ain't really so, neither. You really want to be around someone but it's got to be someone who won't

131

pester you none—somebody who'll let you think your own thoughts. I reckon you got to be alone with the hurt that's in you if it's big enough, but that don't mean other folks can't be around."

Hoss nodded. "Yeah, I guess you're right, Bearpaw." He had the distinct feeling that this was the most talking the old man had done in many years. It seemed as if suddenly there were so many things that had to be said.

"A man gets to wishing he could do things over," Bearpaw said. "I wish I hadn't sold that stock to Vogel. I wish I had kept it for you. But I signed my name and I took his money and I can't undo it."

"I just got here too late, that's all," Hoss said.

"Sometimes I get to figgerin' I'd like to undo my whole life," the trapper said, and now he was talking to himself and it was as if Hoss had ceased to exist. "A lot of money," he said. "More than I'll likely be able to spend. I'll get me a haircut and a shave and new clothes and I'll mix right in with folks. I'm gonna undo it all and start over." He looked up and met Hoss's eyes. "I get lonesome too, Hoss," he said.

Hoss nodded. Outside he could hear Matt Vogel scraping the snow from his boots and then the door opened, letting in a blast of cold air. Vogel came back into the cabin.

"It's clearing," Vogel said. "I'm leaving. I'll need some grub, old man."

Bearpaw stood up slowly. "You tricked me out of my stock," he said. "I figger Cartwright here would of give me more."

"So would I if you'd asked for it," Vogel said. "I made you an offer and you took it. That's the way I do business. How about some grub?"

"How about two hundred dollars?" Bearpaw said. "That's how I do business."

"You can go to hell," Vogel said. "I'm not that hungry." He turned to leave.

Hoss said, "What about Smith?"

"What about him?" Vogel said. "I'm no doctor. I can't do him no good."

"I thought maybe he was a friend of yours," Hoss said.

"You thought wrong," Vogel said. He slammed the door as he left the cabin.

The two men stood there by the fire, looking at the closed door. They turned simultaneously at the sound from the couch in the corner. Lunger Smith had turned under his blankets and his eyes were open, bright and staring.

"He left me," Smith said. "I'll kill him for that."

Hoss moved across and kneeled down by the couch. He motioned for Bearpaw to bring him a dipper of water. He lifted the gunman's head and forced a little of the water across the feverish lips. The gunman's amber eyes moved slowly from the face of Hoss to the bearded face of Bearpaw then back to Hoss again.

"You're one of the Cartwrights," Lunger said.

"That's right," Hoss said. "Don't try to talk."

"I was supposed to kill you," Lunger said. "That's what I was hired for."

"You didn't," Hoss said, "so forget it."

"Vogel won't quit," the gunman said. "He's got other hired guns. Pete Wilson—the kid."

"What about Pete Wilson?" Hoss asked.

Lunger's voice was fading fast. "Wants a reputation . . . look out for him . . . I know his kind . . . Pete Wilson . . ." The voice trailed off and the gunman's head snapped back.

Hoss stood up and gently pulled a blanket up over the face of Lunger Smith.

"What kind of a man would hire out to kill?" Bearpaw asked. "What kind of a man was he, Hoss?"

"It don't really make much difference now, does it?" Hoss said.

Bearpaw stood there staring down at the shape on the

couch. "I don't get along good with folks, Hoss," the old man said. "Them things I said—I didn't really mean it. I couldn't get along where folks hire out to kill. I ain't goin' down below, Hoss. I'm gonna stay right here."

Hoss went outside. The air was cold, but the wind had quit and the skies were clearing. Across the otherwise unblemished expanse of snow he saw the tracks left by Matt Vogel's horse.

He tried to think of Pete Wilson as a killer and he couldn't. He could only think of the fact that he had failed.

14 IN SPITE of the pressure of the past few days, Pete Wilson had rarely been out of Joe Cartwright's mind since that encounter up on the shoulder of Mt. Rose.

They had been friends once—good friends—and to Joe that meant you tried to understand each other. He thought of Ellen then, and knew he could never completely forget that he had been in love with her and he realized Pete knew that, too. That was between them, it always would be, and knowing Pete as well as he did, Joe knew it was a festering sore. Joe had hoped it would disappear and he knew that Ellen worked constantly to bolster Pete's ego. He had no way of knowing how successful she had been.

The cattle were all down on the winter pasture now, and Joe had let most of the crew go, for José Bettencort and a half dozen of his vaqueros could handle the winter feeding chores. He saw the roofed-over stacks of meadow hay as he rode across the flats toward Washoe Lake. He was going to Virginia City to report to his father, and beyond that he was hopefully going to have himself a night on the town.

He hadn't really planned to stop, but when he came to the road that led down the valley a short distance to Pete Wilson's place, he turned Cochise that way. He had no idea whether or not Pete was still working for Matt Vogel and therefore he had no idea if Pete would be home. If he wasn't, he would just say a casual hello to Ellen and ride on.

He came to the gate at the end of the lane and without dismounting reached down and unfastened it and rode through, turned the horse, and still in the saddle, fastened the gate. He wondered how many hundred times he had been through that same gate. This little ranch had once been part of the Ponderosa. It had been given to Ellen's father as a gift for his long years of service as foreman to the Cartwrights.

Again Joe's thoughts went to Pete, and he knew that Pete resented the fact that he was living on his wife's land, left to her when her father was killed in a logging accident just two years ago this month.

He had just finished closing the gate when he heard the gunshots—sharp, snarling, whiplashes of sound in the thin, clear air. He wheeled Cochise so abruptly the animal reared. Grazing cattle, startled by the sounds, threw tails to the wind and ran and stopped and turned and stood stiff-legged as they looked back. The gunshots slapped against the wall of the mountain and echoed back across the valley.

The shots had come from the direction of Pete Wilson's house and a premonition of trouble gripped the pit of Joe's stomach. He unbuttoned his coat and pushed it back to reveal the holstered gun he wore on his left side. He rode slowly down the lane, alert to every sound.

Again gunshots smashed the air and then he saw Pete Wilson, standing there in a clearing, feet spread, half crouched, and he saw the riddled tin cans that had been Pete Wilson's targets. Joe felt a surge of relief and there was a big grin on his face as he rode up behind Pete, unnoticed. He put both hands on the saddle horn, leaned forward and said, "Have any of 'em shot back yet?"

Pete Wilson whirled so suddenly it was obvious that every nerve in his body was as taut as a fiddle string. He tried to conceal it, tried to appear relaxed, but it didn't come off so well.

"Target practice," Pete said.

Joe gestured to the tied-down holster.

"A little fast draw practice too?"

Pete bristled noticeably.

"Any objection?" he said. "You practice."

"No objection," Joe said. "You still working for Vogel?"

Pete's features hardened. "I suppose you're going to tell me to quit, too. I've heard nothing else from my wife."

"Look, Pete," Joe said. "Remember me? I'm Joe Cartwright. If you're worried about that thing up on the mountain, forget it and so will I. You were hired to do a job—you had no way of knowing it was me——"

"Yeah," Pete said. "That's how it was."

Joe was looking around. "Place looks good," he said.

"Meaning Ellen takes better care of it while I'm away than I do when I'm here, is that it?"

"Look, boy," Joe said, "you're getting touchy as a teased snake, ain't you?"

"I'm sick of people breathing on the back of my neck," Pete said. "I'm sick of being reminded that this land was once Cartwright land—that it was the Cartwrights who took care of my wife's father. I'm sick of you being held up to me as a shining example." The bitterness was in his voice. "I'm getting pretty sick of the name Cartwright."

136

"What's eating on you, Pete?" Joe asked quietly.

"I thought I just said it pretty plain," Pete Wilson said.

"Plain enough," Joe said. "Except I don't believe that's all of it."

The anger on Pete Wilson's face was deepening. "You ever stop to figure how damn smug you are?" he said. "You and your big ranch and all your money. Anything you want any time you want it. Just sign your name. Cartwright. That's magic. You think I wouldn't like that? You damn right I would and I'm gonna have it! I'm working for a man who's gonna be a lot bigger than any Cartwright this country ever saw and I'm gonna get big right alongside him."

Joe looked at this man he thought he knew so well and realized he had never known him at all. He said, "Good for you, Pete. If that's the way you want it. I just hope you and I don't wind up on opposite sides of the fence."

"I figger we already have, Joe," Pete Wilson said quietly.

Joe shook his head. "Not unless you want it that way."

"You forced me to say this, Joe," Pete Wilson said. "I don't want you hanging around here. Not while I'm gone."

Joe felt an anger he couldn't control. "You make that plain enough," Joe said. He tightened his grip on his reins. "Don't let the feel of that gun get into your blood," Joe said softly. "They tell me it does with some."

He wheeled his horse and rode away from the man who had once been his friend. He felt as if he needed a bath.

* * *

Before stabling his horse in Virginia City, Joe checked the stock dial on the Marye Building and gave a whistle of disbelief. In the past two days Hale and Norcross had jumped three thousand dollars a share and the bid price was now seven thousand one hundred dollars.

Joe went to the stable and from there directly to the

137

Marye office, throbbing with its usual activity. He saw his father, James Fair and John Mackay seated together, talking quietly, their voices obscured by the room's hubbub.

He went across and joined them, exchanging brief greetings with Fair and Mackay.

The appearance of his father startled him. Ben was haggard and drawn. There were dark circles under his eyes and a stubble of beard covered his cheeks. His clothes were rumpled and he looked as if he hadn't slept in several nights.

"Thought you'd want to know the cattle are all set for the winter," Joe said.

"Thank you, son," Ben said. "Glad to have *some* good news."

"You haven't lost out yet, Ben," John Mackay said. "If Hoss got those three shares . . ."

"Pretty obvious Sharon figures those three shares are still in the running," Joe said.

"He sent Matt Vogel himself after them," Ben said. He switched the subject abruptly. "How's Jim Willy doing?"

"He could only get ten of the Indians to stay on the flume," Joe said. "No more men have quit so far."

"I wish I knew them all better," Ben said. "I wish they were all old Ponderosa hands and then maybe they'd understand if I had to skip a payroll or two."

"Getting that bad, Pa?" Joe asked quietly.

"It could be," Ben said. He looked up then and he was talking to Little Joe and to Little Joe alone. "I shouldn't have let Hoss go."

"You couldn't have stopped him, Pa." He put a hand on his father's shoulder. "Look, if there's anything else you want me to do—if you want me to ride out and meet Hoss . . ."

"Maybe tomorrow morning, if he isn't back," Ben said. "Get yourself a little relaxation. You haven't had a day off in two months."

"Any chance of meeting me down at the Bucket of Blood a little later? You look like you could do with some relaxation yourself."

"I guess I could," Ben said. He turned back to the big board where the clerk was chalking up new figures. Hale and Norcross hadn't moved.

It was just as Ben and Fair and Mackay had figured. Those three shares of Bearpaw Holloway's would swing the election.

Joe Cartwright walked out into the wildly swirling excitement of Virginia City, but it was an excitement that could no longer touch him. It was the first time in his life he had ever seen his father so thoroughly stamped with the mark of defeat, and it was a sight he didn't relish.

He thought of his brother Hoss, up there in those mountains, and of Matt Vogel and he felt genuine fear. He knew then what his father was feeling. As important as those three shares of stock had become, there was an even greater concern.

Ben, like Little Joe, was wondering how far Matt Vogel would go to procure those shares. Men had been killed for a lot less.

He went down to C Street with its constant snarl of wagons and buckboards and buggies and horses and Chinese wood peddlers, and he pushed his way through the throng down toward Don McBride's Bucket of Blood Saloon.

The Bucket of Blood was not as elegant as the Crystal Saloon, but it was an easy-going place that accurately reflected the attitude of its proprietor. Don McBride himself was behind the bar and everyone in the place seemed to be having a good time, if noise was any indication.

McBride spotted Joe immediately and came hurrying down the bar to greet him. He was a bustling, stocky man with a big grin as brilliant as the red sleeve garters he wore.

"Joe Cartwright!" McBride boomed. "Been a long

time, boy!" He shook hands warmly and the grin on Joe's face started to fade as he realized he was standing in a pool of silence. He looked around, sensing something wrong.

A man just up the bar from him turned and faced Little Joe. The man was smiling, a not unhandsome smile. He was dressed in range garb, his high-crown hat pushed up on his forehead.

"Stevens, you said they call you, that right?" Joe asked.

"You got a good memory," Stevens said.

"Yeah. Especially for somebody who holds a rifle on me."

People were starting to move back, doing their best to pretend they hadn't heard. A few drifted out onto the sidewalk. Don McBride mopped the bar furiously.

"How about a beer, Little Joe? On the house." McBride's voice was booming.

There were four other men with Stevens, but Joe did not recognize any of them. One, the largest of the bunch, pushed the others aside and took a stance directly in front of Little Joe.

"So you're a Cartwright, are you?" the big man said. From his clothes, Joe picked him as a logger.

"Something wrong with that?" Joe asked.

Don McBride was starting to sweat. He moved up and said heartily, "Joe, meet Neil Larson. Fairly new around here."

"I met your father," Neil Larson said. "I don't like him."

"I doubt he's losing any sleep over it," Joe said.

"I don't like smart kids, either," Larson said.

"Sounds to me like you have trouble getting along," Joe said.

A grin lifted one corner of Larson's mouth. He glanced around and was flanked by two of his men.

Stevens still lounged against the bar, that grin on his face. He was the only one of the group who was armed.

Larson moved forward suddenly and made a move toward Joe's gun. Joe sidestepped, and now Stevens had moved out from the bar, tense.

"All you Cartwrights carry guns?" Larson asked.

Joe's voice was deadly. "You can get yourself killed reaching for a man's gun like that."

"He's right, Larson," Stevens said softly.

"Boys," Larson said, "he just threatened to kill me."

"Now, Larson," McBride pleaded. "He didn't mean it that way.

"I think he did," Larson said. "Don't you boys?"

"We think so," one of them said. He reached out and shoved Joe hard.

As Joe stepped back, the second man caught him and shoved him forward. Larson was waiting for him. He drove a fist right into the center of Joe's face. Stevens turned back to the bar.

"Give me a beer, bartender," Stevens said.

Joe turned, swinging with all his might, and his fist found a target, but now the plan was all too plain. He was fighting three men and they weren't going to let up on him. He felt himself being grabbed from behind, his arms pinioned behind him, and Larson took his time, measured his blows and systematically started beating Joe's face into a pulp.

Through a film of blood, Joe saw Don McBride come out from behind the bar, but he couldn't see what happened to him. He felt his head being rocked back, time and time again, felt a fist sink into the pit of his stomach. Suddenly the two men holding him let go and he fell to the floor. He tried to roll, and he felt the toe of a man's boot crash into his ribs.

The room was spinning and he was violently sick to his stomach but Larson had no intention of letting up. Joe

141

crawled to a table, clung to it, tried to pull himself erect. Somebody smashed his clutching fingers with a chair leg.

He fell flat on his face and a boot stomped into the small of his back and then all hell seemed to break loose around him and all he could see was a tangle of legs and he heard Roy Coffee's voice yelling, "Ben! Stop it!"

Slowly Joe's vision cleared and now he saw James Fair and John Mackay holding Ben who was struggling against them. He had never seen such savage anger on his father's face and he knew in that instant if Ben were turned loose he would kill Neil Larson with his bare hands. He dragged himself to his feet and Don McBride came across to help him to a chair.

"I'll get you a shot of whiskey," McBride said.

Sheriff Roy Coffee had a gun in his hand and he was herding Larson and the others toward the door. Three helmeted and long-coated city policemen, carrying night sticks, had moved up to help Roy. Stevens still stood at the bar, sipping his beer as if nothing had happened. McBride indicated him to Roy.

"He came in with them," McBride said.

"You part of it?" Roy Coffee asked.

"Ask him," Stevens said, indicating Joe.

Joe shook his head. "He wasn't any help, but he wasn't mixed up in it."

"Come on," Roy Coffee said. "You're gonna cool off."

"Don't worry, boys," Neil Larson said. "If Bruce Cameron don't come around to bail us out Matt Vogel himself will."

As soon as Roy had herded his prisoners out Fair and Mackay released the still quivering Ben Cartwright. Ben moved swiftly across to Joe and kneeled down by him. "I'll get you a doctor," he said.

Joe tried to grin. "I'll take that drink Don offered me first." Don brought it and Joe tossed it down. "Larson

142

said he didn't like you, Pa," Joe said wryly. "I believe him."

He looked up suddenly. Dan de Quille was standing there, looking down at him. "I wish you had saved this until I was short of news," the reporter said. He turned to Ben. "Matt Vogel just rode in."

Ben stood up slowly. "What did he say about Hoss?"

"Hoss was up at Bearpaw's cabin the last Matt saw of him." De Quille's voice was softer. "I don't think he's lying. Hoss is all right." He paused, tried to meet Ben's eyes and couldn't. "No need for Matt to lie, Ben."

For a long moment Ben stood there staring at Dan de Quille, James G. Fair and John W. Mackay.

"We lost, didn't we?" he asked quietly.

"Yes, Ben," Dan said. "You lost. Sharon is already calling for a special meeting to elect himself and his own directors."

Ben Cartwright sat down heavily. He remembered that first meeting so clearly in this moment. The Hale and Norcross first, William Sharon had said. After that, the Ponderosa.

15 WINTER, in Nevada, presented a variety of weather, and this year was no exception. There were times when the skies were brilliantly clear, the days comparatively warm, the nights plunging to below freezing. There were days of sudden snowstorms, swirling down from the Sierra, and there were days of the Indian pogonip freezes when the entire world seemed a sheath of white ice. During one of these ice storms, a stagecoach was blown off the Geiger Grade and the driver and three passengers were killed. To Ben Cartwright, it seemed the longest winter he had ever experienced in his life.

Today the deceit of false spring was everywhere, the air soft and warm and scented. Out at the side of the house the first shoots of the "China Lilies" were thrusting their way through the ground so recently frozen, confident and proudly erect. Ben leaned forward in his saddle and breathed deeply. For just a moment he let himself forget that spring would be the beginning of his real trouble. For just one moment he let himself enjoy the Ponderosa and the magnificence of a nature that was a perfumed woman awakening from refreshing slumber.

Down the slope he could see the glittering, blue expanse of Washoe Lake, spoiled only by the pillar of smoke from the sawmill at Washoe City and the thin, acrid, yellow plume from the thudding stamp mill at the town of Ophir. He was no more than two miles from the Ponderosa ranchhouse but he had left its sanctuary. There before him was the evidence of the encroachment of the Comstock.

He rode on down toward the meadows that were starting to green under their mulch of snow-flattened and frost-browned meadow hay, and he saw the stacks that had fed his cattle during the long winter. They were chewed out around the bases and looked like huge mushrooms standing there against the incredibly blue sky. He filled his lungs with the goodness of the air, then caught his breath and expelled it. Fumes of sulphur and bluestone drifted across from the mill at Ophir.

On a day such as this, it was hard to remember the savagery of winter, but a glance around at the mountain peaks at his back drove the reminder home to Ben. The peaks were still packed with snow, and here and there,

silhouetted in the thin, clear air, stood pines stripped of
needles and of bark and of life itself. For years they had
dug their roots into the ice-cracked granite, digging in
a verdant and vibrant attempt to stand against nature.
They stood there now as monuments to their failure.

Ben rode on, fighting to avoid a spell of melancholy that
had been with him most of the winter. A man had to think
of what he had accomplished, not of what he had lost.
Wind, snow, drought, freezes, hail and flood had all been
known to the Ponderosa. The Ponderosa had survived because of planning—because of methods to conserve its
forests—because of check dams and drainage ditches
. . . and because of a determination to survive.

Ben's jaws set. That determination to survive was still
there, as strong as ever. Time and again on the long
nights before the log fire in the big house he and Hoss
and Little Joe had gone over the threat that was shaping
against them. Never had any one of them suggested backing down from it. They had all three assumed they would
meet it head on, fight it and win it together. Together
. . . Ben wondered if his sons had moments of misgivings
when they were alone. He decided they would not be very
normal men if they did not have such moments, for he
himself did.

A faint twinge of woodsmoke in the air caught his
nostrils and a pinprick of nostalgia found a particular
part of his being. It was a moment on the prairie with
Hoss's mother, a long time ago . . . not this wood, not
this smoke, but for just this fleeting moment a small part
of someone loved. As he rode down closer to the lake, the
ever-present swarm of sea gulls swirled overhead, and his
lips set firmly. He remembered a clipper ship and the
long nights with Captain Stoddard, stern, demanding, and
Captain Stoddard's daughter, Elizabeth, waiting there
in Boston . . . Ben Cartwright shook himself from his
reverie.

He spent a pleasant hour with José Bettencort, going over the cow count, pleased with the condition of the cattle themselves. Here in this valley were the cows that would start calving any time now. The steer herds—the two and three year olds that would soon be driven up to Virginia City for slaughter—were kept further down toward Carson City.

When he left José he did not have any real destination in mind. He stopped in the little community of Franktown and had a beer, not because he wanted one but because he needed something to do. Beyond here he paused to look at the towering elegance of the mansion that Mr. and Mrs. Sandy Bowers had erected to their success in the Comstock and he found it depressing. He had nothing against Ellie and Sandy Bowers, but this was not the Ponderosa. That mansion was a transitory symbol to blind luck.

He went on through the town of Ophir and idly watched the continuing line of ore wagons crossing the causeway on their way to the mill, and the sight of it depressed him more, for those were Matt Vogel's wagons and that was one of William Sharon's mills. Sharon had made good on his boast that the Union Mill and Mining Company was not an idle dream. Nothing could have been more real.

It had only been a few short months since Sharon and his people had taken over the Hale and Norcross, but the change on the Comstock was already apparent.

The syndicate had started with seven mills, which the bank had obtained by foreclosure, and this while there was not enough ore coming out of the mines to keep one-fourth of the mills of the district busy. Sharon wielded the whip of the bank's financial power without mercy. "Either give us your mill business," he told the struggling mines, "or we shut down on your credit." The ultimatum never failed to bring results. The syndicate mills ran night and day, while scores of independents

146

rusted in idleness. As these mills failed, Union Mill and Mining picked them up on foreclosures. At the rate it was going, Ben figured, it wouldn't take more than two years for the syndicate to own every mill on the Comstock.

There seemed to be no way to stop them and no way they could lose. If the mines produced, the syndicate mills would work their ore. If the mines did not produce, the syndicate would assess the stockholders and continue to support the general business of the community—and that especially meant Matt Vogel's freight lines. Every time a new body of ore was opened in an assessment mine, the price of the stock soared on the San Francisco market. If the amount of ore was large and the grade high, the mill company took a large profit in the working of it. If the ore body was limited and poor, the speculative stock buyers—not the monopoly—stood the loss.

During the winter, Ben had had more than a dozen meetings with good friends who had given him their proxies in the now famous fight for the control of the Hale and Norcross Mine. They would stay with him, they said, but in each one of them Ben detected the first gnawings of worry and fear. The Bank of California was a big one to fight. His friends were starting to ask Ben Cartwright what they should do, and Ben knew he could not stall the answer forever.

He was not a man who knew how to feel sorry for himself, but he did believe in examining whatever he was up against from all angles. One quick look at his bank account told him he had taken a good beating on the Hale and Norcross affair. A bit of projection told him he would be facing Matt Vogel's lumber crews swarming over the Ponderosa just as soon as the ground in the high country was dry enough for logging.

Beyond that, Ben knew that Sharon would never stop putting pressure on him and on those who supported him. Ben still owned enough stock to be a serious threat to the management Sharon had set up. But Sharon's fight now was not against a bloc of stock; it was a personal thing, directed against Ben Cartwright himself. Control of the Hale and Norcross was only a step in the scheme of things. The real goal was the Ponderosa and its timber. The devil of it was, the Bank crowd could well afford to close down the Hale and Norcross and just wait it out.

The question was, then, could Ben's supporters, who had so loyally pledged their proxies, afford this sort of prolonged battle? And, from a purely personal angle, could Ben himself afford it so far as his over-all dream of the Ponderosa and its legacy to his sons was concerned. Ben Cartwright had spent an entire winter thinking about those questions. The time had come now to give them an answer.

He felt a sudden urge to go on up to Virginia City and talk with Fair and Mackay and Dan de Quille and even Roy Coffee and—why not admit it?—he wanted to see Beth. He hadn't seen her since Christmas. His thoughts drifted back to that day as the big buckskin turned toward the Geiger Grade.

* * *

Christmas Day had dawned frosty and bright, and the snow on the trees and on the ground sparkled with a million diamonds of light. Hop Sing had been up for hours and the big house was alive with delicious aromas of good things to eat.

Ben, fully dressed, was the first one downstairs. For a long time he stood on the stair landing, looking at the silver-tip fir that nearly touched the ceiling, feeling the warmth of the great fireplace. For this moment, standing there alone, he wanted to capture the memories of other Christmas mornings.

He had felt that blending of sadness and joy that are the ingredients of memory, then he came on into the room, bellowing now, "Hop Sing! Is that coffee I smell?"

Hop Sing came out of the kitchen, the coffeepot in his hand. "Better you drink tea," he said. "Better for you."

For a moment the two men stood there scowling at each other, then Hop Sing's features broke into that sunrise grin of his. "Melly Clistmas, Mister Cartlight," he said.

Ben moved forward and put an arm around Hop Sing's shoulder. "Merry Christmas, Hop Sing," Ben said. "And thanks for a million favors."

Hop Sing scurried back into the kitchen, a man who did not dally long with sentiment. Ben sat down at the table and hurriedly drank his coffee. He had an errand to run this morning. One he had run every Christmas morning for eighteen years now.

He put on his bearskin greatcoat and the fur hat with the ear flaps and started toward the door.

"You supposed to eat breakfast before you go get Miss Ellen," Hop Sing said.

"I am not," Ben said. "She always has something waiting for me at her house." He went on out the door.

Old Kirk had hitched up the sleigh and had it ready. He sniffed deeply and thrust a package into Ben's hands. "Ain't fer you," Kirk said, "Fer Miss Ellen."

"Why don't you give it to her when she gets here, Kirk?" Ben asked.

"Because I don't like her fussin' over me, that's why!" Kirk said and he went storming off. Ben got into the sleigh, chuckling, as happy as he had been that first Christmas morning when he had gone to pick up the infant Ellen Mansfield and her mother and father. Two years later the mother was dead and now George Mansfield was gone too . . . and Ellen Mansfield was Ellen Wilson now.

That had been a disappointment, Ben admitted secretly. He had always just taken it for granted that Ellen would be his daughter-in-law. *That's what a man gets for taking affairs of the heart for granted,* he thought. He drove swiftly down toward the valley, the sleigh bells jingling merrily in the frosty air.

Thin smoke trailed from the stove pipe of the kitchen side of Pete Wilson's house, but there was no indication of a fire in the fireplace. Since they had been invited to spend the whole day and the night at the Ponderosa they probably figured they didn't need one, Ben thought. He went to the door and pounded on it.

"Open up! It's Santa Claus!" he shouted.

He heard her moving around inside the house and then the door opened. She had a shawl around her shoulders and she looked like a little old lady.

"Ellen! Are you ill?" he asked.

She just shook her head and moved aside so that he could enter the room and immediately he knew she had been crying. Her eyes were swollen and she had tried hurriedly to wipe away the tear streaks from her cheeks but she had not been successful. He reached out and put a hand under her chin and tilted her face up.

"All right, honey," he said softly. "Tell me."

"Uncle Ben I can't spend Christmas with you!" she blurted.

"Well, I'm flattered that you'd be this disappointed and I don't mind saying I'm plenty disappointed myself, but it's really not quite the end of the world." He looked around. "Where's Pete? Not through with chores yet?"

"He isn't here," she said.

"Oh? Where is he?"

"He had to work."

"On Christmas Day?"

She ran into his arms and clung to him and her sobs were wracking, dry sounds of pain. "Oh, Uncle Ben," she said. "I'm so miserable. So miserable."

"Is there anything I can do?"

"No," she said. "Nothing." She looked up, the tears

150

brimming in her eyes. "You see, Uncle Ben, I love him," she said. "Regardless of what he does, I love him."

Ben Cartwright had driven slowly back to the ranch, deep in thought. Something fine had gone out of the day for him but he wouldn't let it be spoiled for the others. He thought of Little Joe and knew he couldn't tell him what had happened there this morning. He remembered when Pete Wilson had first announced that he and Ellen were getting married. He remembered so clearly his son Joe standing there, stunned, then getting control of himself.

"If you ever hurt her I'll kill you, Pete," Joe Cartwright had said.

It had sounded like a childish, age-old cliché, a mere figure of speech. It hadn't been. Ben Cartwright knew his son.

He went back to the ranch and made an excuse he could not even remember, and then there was no time to think about it for the guests were arriving. John Mackay was there and several of the neighbors with their children and some of the employees with theirs.

Later, James Fair and his wife Theresa arrived in a sleigh, bringing Beth Kelly and Roy Coffee with them. Fair had met and married Theresa during his stay in Angels Camp over in California, where the pretty, dark-eyed widow had conducted a rooming house in the neighboring town of Carson Hills. She was Beth Kelly's closest friend.

Roy Coffee was starting to assist Beth out of the sleigh when Ben came across to him.

"I believe I can handle that very pleasant chore," Ben said.

"Don't start picking on me or I won't give you your Christmas present," Roy said.

Ben had lifted Beth from the sleigh and he was momentarily holding her free of the ground.

"I don't care," he said against Beth's cheek. "I've got my present."

* * *

Ben Cartwright rode up the Geiger Grade toward Virginia City. He was whistling for the first time in two months.

He came around the bend at the north end of town and there were quite a few lights twinkling, although it was only three o'clock in the afternoon.

The winter sun had already dropped behind Mt. Davidson.

16 DEEP MUD from the recent thaw made the streets more impassable than ever. Added to this was the fact that the afternoon shift was on its way to work. Smoke from the mills and the hoisting works hung low in the quickly chilling air as the shadows fell on the town. Eastward, in the distance, the bright sunlight still reflected from the snow-capped peaks across the desert.

Ben let his horse pick its own way through the throng and when he was opposite the Crystal Saloon he almost ran into Sheriff Roy Coffee who was coming out, obviously headed for his saddled horse which was tied to the hitch rail.

Roy looked up quickly, annoyance written all over his features, but before he could say anything Ben said, "Why don't you watch where you're going? You want to bruise my horse?"

"I ought to bruise you," Roy said, and the old, familiar grin wrinkled his face. "Dog gone if you ain't just like an old bear," he said. "Hibernate all winter and come out the first day the sun shines."

Ben was swinging out of his saddle. He looked at the heavy sheepskin-lined coat Roy wore, the rifle in the saddle scabbard, the poncho rolled behind the saddle.

"What are you up to?" Ben asked. "Going on a man hunt?"

"Matter of fact, I am," Roy said. "Got time for a drink, though."

"You buying or asking?" Ben asked.

"Can't let you buy," Roy said. "Somebody might decide you were bribing an officer of the law."

Ben tied his horse and the two men went into the saloon. Quincy Malloy was behind the bar and his ears perked up as he sensed the chance to overhear some gossip. He moved over to the two men, wiping the bar vigorously as he moved.

"Thought you just left here, Sheriff," Quincy said.

"That was yesterday, Quincy," Roy Coffee said. "Time sure gets away from a man, don't it?"

"Good to see you, Mr. Cartwright," Quincy said. "You ain't been in for a long time. Cold enough for whiskey?"

"Cold enough," Ben said.

Quincy slid out the bottle and two glasses and Ben and Roy poured their own. As Ben lifted his glass he said, "Did you mean it about going on a man hunt?"

"Yep," Roy said, downing his drink. "I meant it. Some playmates of yours."

"What do you mean by that?"

"Remember Neil Larson?"

Ben felt an old surge of anger as he thought of Little Joe lying there on the floor, half dead from the beating he had taken. "I'm not likely to forget him," Ben said. "Who did he kill?"

"Nobody," Roy said. "I'm after one of his crew."

"What happened?"

"They been holed up in a shack over in Six Mile Canyon all winter," Roy said. "I guess Matt Vogel's paying their wages, because they sure got money for whiskey. Way I hear it, the bunch of 'em got drunk and started whittlin' on each other. Got one of 'em over in the Sisters of Mercy Hospital minus an ear and another one with his belly ripped open that ain't apt to make it to morning. He's the one told who it was had the longest knife."

"Nice people," Ben said.

"Town's full of 'em," Roy said. "The Chief had to put on ten extra policemen and I'm askin' the Board of Supervisors for three more deputies." He shook his head as Ben started to pour him another drink. "Never mind my problems," he said. "What do you think of Hale and Norcross?"

"What do you mean?" Ben asked.

"You ain't heard?" Roy said, surprised. "I figured that was why you were in town."

"Just wanted to get out for a day or so," Ben said. "I was getting cabin fever. What about Hale and Norcross?"

"Thought you knew or I would have told you right off," Roy said. "They got twenty-five men down at the thousand-foot level. Been sending 'em down champagne, oysters, steaks. Can't get a word out of anybody. Even Dan de Quille can't find out what's going on."

"They've either hit a horse or a bonanza and Sharon wants to keep it secret until he can juggle the stock to his advantage," Ben said.

"Sure, everybody knows that," Roy said. "But which is it?"

"What's the stock been doing?"

"Jumpin' around like a grasshopper on a hot skillet. Up one day, down the next. All kinds of talk floatin' around, but when you chase it down that's all it is—talk.

Couple days ago there was word out they'd hit a ten-foot-wide vein of solid silver. Yesterday the word was the mine was flooding and never would be able to be worked again."

"How many times have we heard that kind of talk, Roy?"

"Ever since old Pancake Comstock and Old Virginny and McLaughlin and the rest of 'em got wise to the fact the blue stuff they were throwin' away was silver, I reckon," Roy said. He tugged on his gloves. "Guess I better get about my business."

"You going after a killer alone?" Ben asked.

Roy squinted his eye in that characteristic way he had. "Don't tell on me, Ben," he said, "but that killer will be passed out cold by the time I get there."

"How can you be sure?" Ben asked.

"I sent him two quarts of whiskey," Roy Coffee said.

Ben looked after the departing form of the Sheriff of Storey County and started to chuckle. He knew Roy well enough to realize that the Sheriff had no doubt done exactly what he said he had done. He paid Quincy for the drinks and went outside.

The temperature had dropped rapidly and traffic was beginning to thin on the street. He mounted Buck and rode to where he could get a look at the stock dial on the Marye Building. It told him nothing.

Hale and Norcross, at its impossibly inflated price of seven thousand one hundred dollars a share, had dropped rapidly after William Sharon's Union Mill and Mining monopoly had taken over the operation. This had been a surprise to no one. There was some profit taking among holders of individual shares, but the mine had hit a small bonanza and the price had firmed out at a little over four hundred dollars and the stock was paying a dividend. It was up about ten dollars at the moment, but such fluctuations were to be expected when a mine suddenly clamped an air-tight secrecy on its operation. As Roy Coffee had pointed out, the stock reacted to every bit of gossip and would continue to do so until the truth of the condition of the mine was known.

Ben had always had faith in Hale and Norcross, and that faith had been bolstered by James G. Fair, who had served briefly as the mine's Superintendent. Perhaps they had hit a real bonanza. If this were so, Sharon and his Superintendent would want to keep it quiet until they could notify their directors in San Francisco to corner as much stock as possible. On the other hand, Ben realized, the mine could just as well have hit borrasca, and in this case, Sharon would have notified San Francisco to start quietly selling out. Such manipulations were the rule rather than the exception, and elaborate telegraphic codes had been worked out to guard the secrets. A young friend of Little Joe who worked in the telegraph office had made himself independently wealthy by breaking a code and buying accordingly. Ben rode on up toward the stable and put up his horse.

The hoisting works of the Hale and Norcross stood at the south end of Virginia City between the huge pile of the ore dump of the Chollar Potosi and the impressive buildings of the Savage. Standing in front of the stable Ben could look down on the activity below, and even if Roy hadn't told him, he would have known that something unusual was going on.

There was a big crowd gathered in front of the hoisting works building and a spring wagon, the bed covered with a canvas, was inching its way through the crowd. It stopped at the main entrance of the building and the driver hopped down, ran around his wagon and threw back the canvas. Ben could hear the shout go up from the crowd.

From here it was impossible to identify the individual items, but he saw the ice, the bottles, and the white linen covered platters. "Secret shifts," as they were called, were always treated well as compensation for their silence and their long stays under ground.

It was like a picnic down there, everyone hooting and yelling, and now volunteers were helping pack the food into the main building where it would be put on the cage and lowered down the shaft to the men below. *A picnic,* Ben thought. *To them, maybe, but to a lot of others, it could well be tragedy.*

There was no way of telling which way to move at a time like this, and that was the way Sharon intended it. A man could sell and turn out to be a fool or he could hold and find himself wiped out. Ben had already taken a beating on the Hale and Norcross stock he still held; the question was, then, should he gamble on making back some of his loss or sell and hedge against a future loss?

He thought of the Ponderosa and of Hoss and Little Joe and his obligation to them. The flume was eating up money faster than it was coming in, and the opening of the logging season was only weeks away.

He looked at his watch and realized Beth Kelly would at this moment be overseeing things in the kitchen. She had three Chinese helping her and she had ten hungry men to feed. Most of the men who boarded at her place had known her husband before his suicide and they were all intensely loyal to Beth. As with many other boarding houses in Virginia City, Beth's place was a sort of home away from home for the Washoe widowers. In running it, Beth had found a way to an independence she could not have had otherwise, and she clung to it fiercely.

This would be no time to visit her, Ben knew. He decided to wander on down to the Washoe Club in the hopes he might run into Jim Fair or John Mackay. He would ask them their opinion about Hale and Norcross, even though he knew their answer. Both were incurable optimists, so far as the Comstock was concerned. *But I have to have more than mere optimism,* Ben thought to himself. He had almost made up his mind, but it was a big

157

decision—and once it was made there would be no turning back.

He went down the hill, feeling strangely alone.

*   *   *

It was almost eight o'clock when Ben arrived at Beth Kelly's. She opened the door and stood there smiling up at him. There were little crinkles under her eyes and with her chin lifted this way she looked particularly lovely. He made a great show of peering around, then said in a stage whisper, "Are you alone?"

"Why?" she said. "Have you done something criminal?"

"Yes," he said, taking her into his arms. "I haven't kissed you in two months."

"Ben," she protested. "You could at least come inside and close the door! Do you want the neighbors talking?"

"Do you have reason to believe they aren't already talking?" Ben asked.

They went inside. He put his hat on the hall tree and she helped him with his coat and without looking at her he said, "Quite a bit of excitement."

She took his coat and hung it up. "Honestly, Ben, I haven't seen anything like it since Kevin was alive. Wouldn't he have loved every minute of it?"

"He would have been right in the middle of it, all right," Ben said. He turned toward her. "You look lovely, Beth."

"Thank you, Ben," she said softly.

For a moment they stood there, looking at each other, and then, as it always was when they were completely alone, a wall of caution seemed to build between them. She moved away from him, her hands making small, nervous gestures.

"Why don't you take your favorite chair?" she said. "I'll get us some coffee."

She didn't wait for his objection but went down the

hall and into the kitchen. Ben raised his eyes to the portrait of the handsome Black Irishman who had broken every code of his religion by taking his own life. He seemed to be here in this room, always. He took his eyes away and called out. "Have you seen Ellen Wilson?"

"Yes," she answered from the kitchen. "Just the other day. When I was marketing."

She came back into the room with the familiar coffee service, pausing momentarily as she noted that Ben was standing beneath her husband's portrait. She set the coffee down carefully.

"Did she seem all right?" Ben asked.

"What? Oh, Ellen." She fussed with the cups and saucers and poured cream for herself. She looked up then and met Ben's eyes. "There's something wrong between her and Pete, isn't there?"

"I was hoping you'd be able to tell me," Ben said.

"I sensed it when she wasn't with us on Christmas day. I thought if you wanted to talk about it then you would, and when you didn't I tried to put it out of my mind."

Ben sat down and took the coffee she offered him. "Pete's a highly ambitious kid," Ben said. "That's why he keeps hopping from one thing to another—trying to find a shortcut."

"Roy Coffee tells me Pete's running around with the worst element in this town. He's drinking quite a bit, sometimes doesn't go home at night."

"What should I do, Beth?" Ben said. "Talk to him? Talk to Ellen?"

"I doubt Pete is going to listen to you," she said, "and he'll just resent anything you try to do for Ellen."

"Beth, Ellen is like my own daughter!"

"If she *were* your own daughter, Ben, I'd have to give you the same advice."

"Don't mention any of this to Little Joe, will you?" Ben said.

"No, Ben. I think I'd know better than that without being told."

They sipped their coffee and enjoyed each other's silence, and in time Ben said, "I think you ought to get rid of your Hale and Norcross."

Beth looked at him, surprised.

"Why?" she asked. "It's still worth five times what Kevin paid for it."

"Don't you think you ought to get rid of it while the price is still reasonably firm?"

"I really hadn't given it any thought," she said. "Hale and Norcross is a sound mine."

"Well look who's suddenly become a mining expert!" Ben said. "Don't you realize Sharon can manipulate the price?"

"I know what can happen. I've been around mines and mining just as long as you have, Mr. Cartwright."

"Then use your head and sell out!"

"What do you have, a crystal ball or something? I'm going to hang on."

"Confound it, Beth," Ben said, his voice rising, "why do you always have to be so darned bullheaded?"

"Bullheaded? Me bullheaded? Did you ever listen to yourself? You've been barking orders at your sons for so long you think you can do it with everyone! Well don't try it with me!"

"Keep your stock! Go ahead and lose every dollar you've got! I'm just trying to help you!"

"Who says I'm going to lose? I didn't pay any seven thousand one hundred dollars a share like some I could name!"

"I was trying to protect you and a lot of people like you!"

"I didn't ask you to!"

She stopped suddenly and bit her lip. She got up, came across and put a hand on Ben's arm.

"Ben, I didn't mean that."

He put his hand over her hand.

"I'm a little edgy I guess, Beth. Been cooped up too long."

"Jim Fair has a lot of faith in Hale and Norcross," Beth said. "I talked to him just last night. He thinks the main vein hasn't even been touched."

"Ask him about almost any mine on the lode and he'll give you the same answer."

"He's been right a lot more often than he's been wrong."

Ben nodded. He had to admit that was right. He took a deep breath.

"I've figured it and refigured it a hundred times, Beth. I've got a lot of money tied up in that stock. It's money I could well use to a much better advantage. In time— two or three years, perhaps—I could beat Sharon and his supporters to the wall." He looked at her and was glad to have someone to whom he could talk. "Beth, I can't afford it. I have to sell out. I just wanted to warn my friends, because I didn't want to see anyone hurt."

She gave him the compliment of remaining silent, and in that moment he recaptured the luxury of the tender companionship that can exist between a man and a woman.

He smiled softly.

"I'm sorry I shouted at you," he said.

She laid her head against his knee. "You know something?" she said. "It seems good to have somebody shout at me once in a while."

*   *   *

A business loss was nothing new to Ben Cartwright. He didn't like losses, but he had long ago learned that brooding about a loss was worse than a loss itself. He was now faced with a strictly business proposition—how best to utilize cash.

He went to everyone in town he knew who held Hale

161

and Norcross stock and who had supported him in his proxy battle against William Sharon. Some laughed in his face and told him he was a fool to sell. Some nodded their agreement. They held to the bird in the hand theory. He sent some telegrams to San Francisco, and then he headed for the Marye building. He sold his stock at four hundred and thirty dollars a share, perfectly aware that he, himself, had this day helped depress the price. He had, insofar as possible, tried to repay a debt of loyalty.

Once it was done, for all intents and purposes, he had put it out of his mind. If there were inner scars—and there were—the outside world would never know it. He had converted his stock into cash, simply because he thought the flume was a better long range investment. Had Hale and Norcross gone the other way, that would have been a different thing. It hadn't gone that way.

Suddenly he felt relieved of a great burden. He hadn't really thought of it, but he now realized that what he had done was put the Ponderosa before anything else.

He was whistling when he walked back toward the small hotel where he always stayed. He was half way there when he heard the shrill of the Hale and Norcross whistle. He saw men pause, then turn and run toward the hoisting works, and now there were torches being lighted and people were shouting.

Ben turned and hurried that way, knowing what it meant. The secret shift had been brought up from down below.

In a matter of hours now the world would know if Hale and Norcross was in borrasca or bonanza. To Ben it would make little difference, and somehow that didn't seem so important.

17 THERE WAS A GOOD-SIZED GROUP gathered in the building of the main hoisting works and Ben saw at once that William Sharon himself was there. He was somewhat surprised to see Jim Fair and John Mackay, for the breach between these two and Sharon had widened steadily in the past few months. Sharon had publicly referred to them as "those Irishmen" and "a couple of muckers"—a reference to their beginnings as plain miners. His irritation arose solely from the fact that Fair and Mackay refused to get caught up in the Bank of California web. Sharon was talking to Dan de Quille and Dan was busy taking notes. Ben looked over the crowd and didn't need to be told. There was gloom on the faces of all of them. Ben walked over toward the mouth of the shaft to join Fair and Mackay.

Warm, moist air from deep in the mine coming into contact with the cold air on the surface sent steam gushing from the opening of the shaft and billowing against the high ceiling. Several miners and shift bosses stood glumly by. The engineer sat on his raised platform behind his hoisting winch, his signal bell silent. Fair and Mackay nodded to Ben.

"Looks like a funeral," Ben said.

"According to Sharon, it is," Fair growled.

"You think it's real borrasca?" Ben asked.

"A lot of people would like to have the answer to that question," Mackay said. "Have you checked the stock?"

"Starting to drop fast," Ben said. "Looks like the syndicate dumped everything they had."

163

"I feel sorry for the poor devils who bought on margin," Mackay said. "When those brokers start calling for more mud in the morning and the shareholders don't have the money to cover——"

"I tried to talk Beth Kelly into selling," Ben said. "Thank goodness she owns hers outright."

"How bad will this hurt you, Ben?" Fair asked.

"I took my hurt up front," Ben said. "The loss I took this afternoon will be more like a bruise."

"You sold?" Mackay said.

"That's right."

"Maybe it was smart, maybe it wasn't," Fair grumbled. "I still say this mine hasn't been scratched." He stopped as Sharon and Dan de Quille approached.

"I'm sorry if you got hurt on your stock, Cartwright," Sharon said, "but as I think you'd be the first to say, business is business. Naturally I had to protect the Bank and its depositors."

"Naturally," Ben said. Actually, no one could criticize Sharon for what he had done. It was, as he said, simply good business.

"I want to go down and take a look at it for myself," Fair said with typical bluntness.

It was a well established custom on the Comstock that the Superintendent of one mine was always extended the courtesy of visiting another mine, unless that mine had a secret shift below. Since Sharon had already released the shift, Fair's demand was a legitimate one. On the other hand, it was the same as saying he doubted Sharon's story.

Ben saw Sharon flush, but he knew he didn't dare refuse Fair's request, for to do so would be to admit that the so-called borrasca was in fact no more than a stock manipulation. Ben saw Dan de Quille's nostrils twitch.

"I'll be happy to extend you the courtesy, Mr. Fair," Sharon said. "Take Cartwright and Mackay with you if you want." He turned abruptly to Dan de Quille. "If you'll

164

come on up to the office I'll show you those figures you were asking about." He moved off without looking back and Dan went with him.

Fair looked at Ben and Mackay. "There's room on the cage," he said. "Come along or don't. Suit yourselves." He moved off toward the dressing room to change his clothes.

"You going down?" Mackay asked Ben.

"Wouldn't miss it," Ben said.

The men all looked strangely alike when they came out of the dressing room, attired identically as they were in blue flannel pants, blue woolen shirts, heavy brogans and narrow-brimmed felt hats. The heat down below in most of the mines was so intense a person soon became drenched with perspiration, and a change of clothing was always provided for visitors. A shift foreman spoke to the engineer, then came across to join Fair, Mackay and Ben on the platform of the cage. The foreman lifted his hand in a signal to the engineer and immediately the cage dropped through the steam and into the depth and darkness of the shaft.

The steam, which had seemed terrifyingly formidable from above, was almost immediately gone, for it was nothing more than the same condensation that takes place on the surface of a lake and was as harmless as the steaming breath of a horse on a frosty morning.

The cage flashed past the stations of the upper levels. These were rooms of considerable size. Usually, they were brightly lighted, peopled by half-naked miners with candles or lanterns in their hands, noisy with voices and the clank of machinery. The stations, about a hundred feet apart, were still lighted, flashing by the plunging car like railroad stations in the night, but now they were abandoned. Ben felt the spring of the cable as they approached the thousand-foot level.

That "spring" was something he was never able to get used to. The cage had the same action as a toy ball suspended from a rubber string. Every time he felt it he caught himself wondering about just how much stretch there was to that flat-woven, steel wire cable. He was glad when the cage began to slow and came to a stop exactly on a level with the floor of the thousand-foot station.

Four coal oil lamps, mounted in brackets on the walls, gave the landing a cheerful enough look, but the idle ore cars, the lack of clothing hanging on the nails driven into the walls, reminded one at once that this mine was shut down. There was an eerie silence and the sound of the men's boots thudding hollowly as they moved to take the candles the foreman offered them. The boxes of candles, coils of fuse, picks, shovels and other mining equipment stood idly along the walls. The dipper hung from a nail and the cask of ice water was full.

The men followed the foreman down the main north and south drift, down the car track, past the prospect crosscuts that bisected the main drift at intervals and into the forest of timbers that made up the square sets.

The square sets, invented by Philip Deidesheimer, who had been a particularly close friend of Adam, were unique to the Comstock Lode and they never ceased to fascinate Ben, just as they never ceased to remind him of the deforestation and devastation that were blighting the Sierra.

The timbers used for these mine supports were from twelve to fourteen inches square. The posts were six feet, the caps five feet in length. The upper ends of the posts were framed so that the ends of four caps could rest upon each, with a mortise in the center in which to insert the tenon of the post of the next square set. Deidesheimer always claimed he got the idea from watching bees work, and the square sets, when assembled, did indeed closely resemble a giant honeycomb.

James Fair stopped and picked up a piece of rock from the floor of one of the sets. He barely glanced at it, then tossed it aside. They moved on.

166

The temperature here was about one hundred and twenty degrees and all the men were sweating profusely. Ben thought of the bath that would be awaiting them back at the dressing room. He saw Fair and Mackay examining the walls of one of the crosscuts, saw them exchange glances. Neither man spoke a word.

They had been below perhaps an hour when Fair said, "I'm satisfied."

"Petered out?" Ben asked.

"Nothing here but porphyry and other barren rock," Fair said. "Not a sign of sulphuret or chloride."

"We might as well go back up," Mackay said.

"I never object to that," Ben said.

Mackay grinned. "What's the matter, Ben? Prefer the Ponderosa to mining, do you?"

"Just seems to me there's a little more elbow room up on top," Ben said.

The foreman pulled the signal rope as soon as the men were in place and the cage went shooting to the top at a dizzying rate of speed.

Sharon was waiting for them at the top of the shaft. "Well?" he said.

"Tough luck, Sharon," Mackay said.

When they had had their baths and were changed back into their street clothes, Ben, Fair and Mackay went down to the Crystal Saloon. Quincy Malloy set out a bottle and said, "Hear you three been down in the Hale and Norcross."

"You hear a lot," Fair said.

"I try to keep up with things," Quincy said. He leaned forward, suddenly confidential. "Is it borrasca or a cover up?" he whispered.

Fair looked him straight in the eye. "If anybody asks you," Fair said, "you tell 'em Jim Fair says he never saw a more worthless pile of rock in his life."

Quincy Malloy hurried up and down the bar. Before

morning, every man, woman and child in Virginia City would know of James Fair's appraisal of the mine.

The three men went outside and said goodnight. As Ben started to leave, Fair stopped him.

"I may be in touch with you in a few days, Ben," he said.

"I'm not sure when I'll be back in town," Ben said.

"I don't want to see you in town," Fair said. "Mackay and I will come out to the ranch. If you're not there, we'll wait for you."

Ben caught a faint hint of excitement in Fair's voice.

"What's this all about?" Ben said.

"I'm not sure yet myself," Fair said. "But when I am sure, you'll be the first to know." He moved off up the street.

Ben looked at Mackay. "You know what he's talking about?"

"Not for sure," Mackay said, "but I can tell you this. He was telling Quincy Malloy the absolute truth when he said that pile of rock was worthless." He offered his hand. "Goodnight, Ben," he said.

Ben stood there a moment, watching him go. He shrugged. He had learned from long experience that there was no use pushing James G. Fair. When he had something to say, he'd say it. Ben went on to his hotel and went to bed.

When he awoke in the morning he checked Hale and Norcross stock. Quincy Malloy had obviously spread the word. The stock was selling for forty-two dollars a share.

18 REGARDLESS of what anyone said about William Sharon, he was a shrewd businessman with a fierce loyalty for William Ralston, his employer, and for the Bank of California which he represented. The failure of Hale and Norcross was the first thing that had gone amiss in his carefully laid plans, and he had worked through most of the night going over papers, looking for ways to correct this temporary setback.

He had gone down to his office at C and Taylor at an hour when most men were still having breakfast and now, at nine o'clock, he had already put in half a day's work. He had just been interrupted by the arrival of Matt Vogel, and there was irritation in his expression and in his voice when he said, "Matt, I wish you'd come back later."

"This won't take any time, Bill," Matt Vogel said.

Sharon threw down a pencil and expelled his breath, "All right," he said, "get to the point then."

"I need fifty thousand dollars," Matt Vogel said.

For a long moment Sharon stared at the man. "Haven't you any idea of what's been going on?" Sharon asked.

"Look, Bill," Vogel chuckled. "We're alone. You can drop the act."

"What act?" Sharon said.

Vogel winked and Sharon found that, too, irritating. "You ain't fooling me," Vogel said. "I know what you're doing."

"Really?" Sharon said. "Just what am I doing?"

"Playin' around with the stock," Vogel said. He was

169

smug and sure and now Sharon caught the sour smell of stale cigars and too much drinking.

Sharon leaned forward in his chair. "You told me once you didn't know much about stocks and didn't want to know," Sharon said.

"That's right," Vogel said.

"Then don't start pretending to know what you're talking about now," Sharon said, "because you're completely wrong."

"You mean it's a real borrasca?" Vogel said.

"Yes, that's what I mean." He went back to his paper work.

For a long moment Vogel sat there, watching this man who represented success and business wisdom far beyond Vogel's understanding. "What's it mean so far as Union Mill and Mining is concerned?" Vogel said finally.

"It means tightening our belts for a while," Sharon said. He leaned back and his sharp eyes fixed Vogel and held his gaze. "It means no new loans until I have a chance to analyze things and present them to the Board of Directors in San Francisco next month."

"That makes sense," Vogel said, "but I don't figure it ought to include me. I'm one of the Directors."

"Then be at the meeting in San Francisco next month and present your ideas there," Sharon said. He again returned to the paper work.

It was a dismissal and Vogel felt it. He flushed slightly. "I can't be at any meeting in San Francisco," he said. "I'll be logging full scale by then."

"I'm glad to hear that," Sharon said. "I don't want the Bank to be in any position to lose money by your failure to deliver on those timber contracts you hold. And there's another thing you might as well anticipate. I doubt we'll be able to pay you the agreed price, so you might as well start figuring where you can cut corners."

Matt Vogel always tried to hold his temper when he was around Sharon. He failed to do it now.

"You trying to squeeze me, Sharon?" he said softly.

"I'm trying to run a company," Sharon said without hesitation. "You're a part of that company, you participate in the profits, so you had better help us achieve those profits."

Matt Vogel licked his lips, for they were suddenly dry.

"Bill," he said, "I ain't got money enough to carry me through. I got a hundred men on the payroll. I been carrying them all winter so I'd have them ready when I needed them."

"I told you I thought that was a foolish idea when you suggested it," Sharon said.

Again Matt Vogel lost his temper. "I don't tell you how to run your bank," he said. "Don't tell me how to run the freighting and lumber business."

William Sharon looked up slowly. "All right, Matt," he said, "I won't tell you. But just remember that you're the one who came running to me, begging to be a part of this. I loaned you a half a million dollars of the Bank's money because I thought you knew what you were doing. If you didn't, don't come crying to me."

Matt Vogel stood up slowly. "I guess I know where I stand," he said.

"In the same shoes as the rest of us," Sharon said. "You said you could make money for the company and for yourself."

"I'll make it," Matt Vogel said.

"I sincerely hope you can, Matt," Sharon said.

This time the door was closed in his face and Matt knew it. To stand here or to press this discussion any further would only serve to make him appear in a weaker position than the one in which he now found himself. He turned abruptly without saying goodbye and left Sharon's office.

Sharon stared at the closed door. He had grown increasingly dissatisfied with Matt Vogel through the long winter. At times he caught himself wishing he had never met the man. But he did want desperately to control the lumber business and especially the freighting business.

He was going to do it, too, he knew, either with Matt Vogel or without him. At the moment he didn't much care which way it went. He had too many other things on his mind to worry about it.

* * *

Matt Vogel went directly to his own freight yard. He had been startled by Sharon's blunt refusal to lend him the money, but he wasn't frightened by it. Union Mill and Mining was much too powerful an organization to be stopped for very long by the failure of one mine. The entire thing was predicated on total control of the Comstock. They already had it, so far as the mills were concerned, and through the mills, they controlled most of the mines. Union Mill and Mining still had to have timber and transportation control to make the picture complete, and that's where Matt Vogel came in.

"There's just nobody else can handle it except me," Vogel said, and he startled himself by speaking aloud.

He hadn't gotten where he was by backing down from temporary setbacks—and that's what this was: temporary. Sharon, as Secretary-Treasurer of Union Mill and Mining, would go to that Directors meeting in San Francisco. He would tell them just how everything was and they would again give him a vote of confidence, just as they had always done before. Sharon knew the importance of Matt Vogel's freight wagons and his woods crew as well as Vogel knew that importance. Sharon would come back to Virginia City and everything would be exactly as it was before.

Vogel, at heart, was an optimist. Beyond that, he was a man of supreme self-confidence. He was actually whistling when he came up to his office at the freight yard. What, moments before, had seemed a stunning blow, was

172

now only one more manifestation of big business—the kind of big business Matt Vogel didn't pretend to understand. He had always been a one-man organization, running things his own way. He was continuing along these lines. Sharon complained now and then about the type of men Vogel was hiring; he complained about something he called "the Bank's image." Vogel hadn't really given it much thought. Produce, keep his end of the bargain, and everything else would be forgotten. He knew that was so.

The freight yard was a beehive of activity. The air was filled with the ringing sounds of sledge against anvil, the duller thud of sledge against cherry red iron, the hissing burn of a tong-held horseshoe plunged into a sawed-off barrel of water. There was a smell of neat's-foot oil coming from the harness shop. It mingled with the aroma of the grease buckets. Overall, was the ammonia smell of the horses and the mules, and now someone was moving harness, and collar bells were making a musical chime as the man walked along.

This was Matt Vogel's life, for every sound and every smell represented money, and eventually, when there was money enough, it would represent power such as few men knew. There was no end to the mines and no end to opportunity if a man would grab it. There would be some losers, but Matt Vogel had no intention of being one of them.

He found Bruce Cameron at the office, going over some payroll sheets with the paymaster. The thin labor recruiter looked up and grinned. "From the looks of the weather, maybe you'll start getting something for your money, Matt," Cameron said.

"About time," Vogel muttered. "Larson and Pete Wilson back yet?"

"About an hour ago," Cameron said.

"Why in hell ain't they here?" Matt demanded.

"Larson went over to the tool shed to check on some axes he bought," Cameron said.

173

"How about Wilson?"

"I don't keep track of Pete Wilson," Cameron said. "He's your boy."

Vogel allowed himself a chuckle. "He's quite a kid, all right," Matt said. "Reminds me of myself when I was his age."

He went outside, and as he walked through the wagon yard toward the corrals and barns he found himself thinking again of Pete Wilson. The boy had come a long way since Matt had first hired him last fall. He was developing an instinct for reporting exactly what Matt needed to know. Even bigger than that was the fantastic loyalty Pete gave to his boss. The lad took orders from no one except Vogel, and he never questioned those orders. Matt had the distinct feeling that if anyone was to say anything against him, Pete would use that gun he now always carried. It was a good feeling, having someone think that way about you. It was about like having a son of your own, Vogel thought. He was genuinely fond of the boy—even to the point where he sometimes worried about him getting too cocksure of himself.

He went on to the tool shed—a sizeable structure with neat racks for saws, axes, sledges, wedges, ropes, various sizes of block and tackle and a dozen other items. There were half a dozen pedal-operated grindstones here, and as many loggers were sharpening their axes. Neil Larson was personally supervising the activity, for during the winter Matt had made Larson head woods boss.

"You getting what you want, Larson?" Matt asked.

"The best money can buy, Matt," Larson said. "That's what I like about you."

"I told you from the first, this ain't no two-bit operation," Matt said.

"I'd hate to be paying for it," Larson said.

"You just get those trees cut and I'll worry about paying for it," Matt said.

174

He went out toward the corrals, and the momentary uneasiness that had been in him down at Sharon's office was
completely gone. Here, Matt Vogel's self-confidence was
full blown. He was the best teamster in the Comstock
and he knew it, and that was something for a man to be
proud of. To prove it to himself, he quite often took out a
sixteen-mule outfit on his own, and it was almost in-
variably on a job that someone had described as impossible. Once, on a bet, he hauled eighty-four thousand
pounds of ore a distance of eight miles, using twelve
horses and four wagons, hitched in tandem. He knew
the names of almost every animal he owned, and he
boasted that he could match vocabularies with any mule
skinner alive.

He found Pete Wilson squatted on the top rail of a corral fence, watching one of the teamsters train a pair of
young mules. Pete jumped down from the fence when he
saw Vogel coming.

"Figure on taking up mule training, Pete?" Vogel
said.

"I figure the more I can learn the more I'm worth to
you," Pete said, grinning.

Vogel chuckled. "Never quite satisfied, are you boy?"

"You told me once when a man gets satisfied he quits
going forward."

"That's pretty good advice, boy," Matt said. "You remember it." He looked off toward the man training the
mules. "Put a gee string on 'em and hitch 'em up to a
team," Vogel shouted. "They look to me like they got the
makings of leaders."

The man in the corral waved that he understood and
moved off with the two young animals. Pete looked at
Matt and shook his head.

"You can tell just by looking at them?" he said.

"Get so you can, pretty well," Vogel said. "I miss once
in a while, but not often."

"Hard to believe," Pete said.

19 "DAD BERN IT, Pa," Hoss Cartwright said, "I've been all the way from Lake's Crossing down to Carson City. I've talked to everybody who would listen to me. I hired exactly six hands, and I ain't sure they amount to much, either."

The Cartwrights and their foremen had just finished the noonday meal and were sitting around the dining room table while Hop Sing quietly removed the dishes. Ben looked around at the others—Joe, Jim Willy, José Bettencort.

"Afraid I didn't have much better luck," Little Joe said. "I even went up and talked to the Miners' Union. I figured with the Hale and Norcross closed down maybe there'd be some miners out of work."

"It was a good thought, anyway, Joseph," Ben said. He looked across the table. "Jim Willy?"

"I told my relatives if they didn't work I'd quit feeding them through the winter," Jim Willy said. "At that, I won't have as big a crew as I had last year."

"Any of them good at carpentry?" Ben asked.

Jim Willy shook his head. "I wouldn't trust them to work on the flume, Ben," he said.

"You don't have to worry about my crew, Señor Ben," José Bettencort said. "I gamble with them all winter. They owe me so much money they got to work."

Ben chuckled. "I won't inquire into your methods, José," Ben said. "Just so the cattle get moved."

"We got 'em moved, eh, Little Joe?" José said.

"Not we—you," Joe said. "I'm going to be riding guard, same as last fall."

"Wait a minute," José said, a note of protest in his voice. "You not gonna take four of my riders, are you?"

"Afraid I am, José," Joe said.

"Ay, Chihuahua!" José complained. "Why pick on me?"

"Because you're the only one with a full crew, José," Ben said quietly.

The foreman of the cattle operation shrugged his shoulders. "I can't win for losing," he said.

"Could we have some more coffee, Hop Sing?" Ben asked. He shuffled through a pile of papers in front of him and came up with the sheet he wanted. There was a scowl on his face as he looked over the figures on the page. He looked up then and spoke directly to Hoss. "Suppose we offered to top the wages Matt Vogel is paying?" he asked.

"Don't reckon it would do much good, Pa," Hoss said. "Matt's been feedin' that bunch all winter, charging it against their wages. Some of them will be working for Matt Vogel for the next three years."

Hop Sing came in with the coffeepot and poured for all of them. Ben took a sip of his coffee and said, "Well, boys, I guess we all know where we stand. It's just going to mean longer days for all of us."

"You can count on the woodcutting crew, Ben," Jim Willy said.

"I know I can, Jim Willy," Ben said.

They finished their coffee and all stood up. José Bettencort said, "Señor Ben, you care if I take Kirk with me on spring roundup?"

"Did he ask to go?" Ben said.

José Bettencort grinned. "That old coyote he don't have to ask to go. He punch cows so long he's two thirds *vaca* already. He see the green grass, he's got to get in a saddle."

179

"If you think he's up to it," Ben said.

Little Joe gave his high-pitched laugh. "Kirk?" Joe said. "I got a feeling he could whip Hoss if he made up his mind to it."

"I ain't gonna push him far enough to find out," Hoss said. "Come on, Little Brother. We got some horses to break."

Ben sat there for some time after they had all left. He wondered if they just didn't realize how tight things really were or if they were merely trying to keep everything light, just to ease his worry. He thought of the four of them and knew that the latter was the case.

Hop Sing said, "More coffee, Mister Cartlight?"

"What?" Ben said. "Oh . . . no thanks, Hop Sing."

Ben went back to his papers and Hop Sing stood there, watching him. Mister Cartlight had plenty of trouble, Hop Sing knew. Mister Cartlight needed people to work for him.

Hop Sing hadn't been to Virginia City for a long time. He would go soon, he decided. He wanted to go to the joss house and say prayers for his ancestors. After that he would talk with friends of his and ask their advice. He did not want to stand idly by while the Ponderosa was in trouble.

Hop Sing went back into the kitchen.

* * *

Hoss and Little Joe were saddled and ready to ride out to the breaking corrals when they first saw the surrey coming down the long lane toward the Ponderosa headquarters.

"Reckon we ought to stay around?" Hoss asked.

"Pa didn't mention anybody coming," Joe said.

"What's the matter?" old Kirk said drily. "Them buckin' horses get to looking big all of a sudden?"

"Maybe you'd like to go break 'em out," Joe said.

"You think I couldn't?"

180

Joe looked at the old man and didn't see the crippled body. He saw only the fierce eyes, the jutting jaw and the blocky chin. Joe grinned. "Nope, Kirk," he said. "I think you could."

"Joe!" Hoss said suddenly. He was peering off down the lane. "That's Jim Fair driving that surrey. I'd recognize those shoulders anyplace."

Joe turned to look. "Your eyes aren't that good," he said. "What you recognized was the team."

Kirk, too, was squinting off into the distance. "Got two people with him," he said.

"Did you spot that fly on the side of his nose, Kirk?" Hoss asked.

Kirk fixed Hoss with his steady gaze. "Yeah," he said. "Wonder how it got a broken leg?"

The old man turned and walked off before Hoss could answer, and Joe let loose with his distinctive cackle. "That ought to hold you, Big Brother," Joe said.

"Sure should," Hoss said, his face screwed up into a mass of wrinkles as he squinted into the distance. "I would of swore old Kirk couldn't see that broken leg."

Joe drove his fist into his brother's ribs. "I give up," he said. "You want to stick around?"

"Yeah," Hoss said. "The way things have been going, maybe we better."

They mounted and rode across to the house where they tied their horses and then went inside. Ben was working at his desk.

"Pa, you expecting Jim Fair?" Hoss asked.

"He said he'd be out one of these days when I talked to him about a month ago," Ben said.

"This must be 'one of these days' then," Joe said.

The three men went outside and now the surrey, coming at a pretty good clip, was close enough that there was no doubt about its occupants. Ben's face was a picture of puzzlement.

"I'm not surprised to see Mackay," Ben said. "They're

181

together most of the time. But what in the devil is Beth doing with them?"

"You want to be alone with her when you ask her?" Hoss suggested.

"Very funny," Ben said. He started walking out toward the approaching surrey.

"Don't break into a run, Pa," Little Joe called after him.

Ben stopped and turned around and he was the picture of the severe parent.

"Did it ever occur to you two little boys that your father can still wield a hairbrush just as efficiently as ever?" Ben said.

"You better quit pushin' it, Joe," Hoss said, loud enough for Ben to hear. "You know how he gets when he's been cooped up too long."

"That's mighty sound advice, young man," Ben said. The surrey was just pulling up before entering the yard.

"Jim and John! Beth!" Ben called out. "What a pleasant surprise!"

Fair was pulling in on the lines. He looked across at Joe and Hoss and scowled a hello to them. To Ben he said, "With a couple of big louts like them around it looks to me like you could get some of the chuck holes in your road fixed."

"That's my partner," John Mackay said. "Always looking for the chuck holes in the highway of life."

"Partner?" Ben said.

Hoss had moved up. "Ma'm," he said to Beth, "my Pa hain't had good fetchin' up. Iffen you'd allow me, Ma'm, I'd be delighted to help you down."

Joe, too, had moved in and he swept off his hat and made a deep bow. "We apologize for our father, lady," he said. "But if you . . ."

"Ignore these clowns," Ben said to Fair and Mackay. "They get this way every spring."

"I'd drown 'em," Fair said, and he could have meant it.

He looked at Hoss and Joe. "Any charge for taking care of the team?"

"Nominal, Mr. Fair," Joe said. "Nominal."

They waited until Ben had helped Beth down and the four had headed for the house. Joe stood there, holding the team, looking off after them. "Did you get the feeling we weren't invited?" he said.

"I told you not to push it too far," Hoss said. "Now we got to break them dad berned horses."

*　　*　　*

Hop Sing brought some small cookies and some coffee. The amenities were barely over when Fair said, "We're here to try to get some money, from you, Ben."

Ben glanced at Beth and started to grin. "I'll say one thing, for you, Jim," he said. "You come right to the point."

"Don't believe in beating around the bush," the burly Irishman said. "I leave that up to John here."

"This business about you two being partners . . ." Ben started.

"John, I think perhaps you ought to start from the beginning," Beth said to Mackay.

"In other words, you're telling me to shut up," Fair said.

"Jim, how does your wife put up with you?" Beth said.

There was a certain excitement in all three of them and Ben had sensed it the moment he saw them. He leaned back in the sofa and waited for Mackay to begin.

"Ben, do the names James C. Flood and William S. O'Brien mean anything to you?"

Ben searched his memory and found the names. "You don't mean the two who run the Auction Lunch on Washington Street in San Francisco, do you?"

"Why shouldn't he mean them?" Fair said.

"Because with the way things are, I'm not anxious to finance a saloon," Ben said.

"They don't need financing," Fair said. "They're doing fine."

"Jim, will you please let John get on with the story?" Beth said.

Fair grunted and dug his chin into his chest. "Don't see why you don't get to the point," he muttered.

"All right, I will," Mackay said. He paused, looked at Fair, then at Beth. "Ben," he said quietly, "Jim Fair is positive the Hale and Norcross shut down only a few hundred feet from bonanza."

Ben looked from one to the other. He could tell from their expressions that they expected him to leap for joy, but he couldn't quite see why he should. "That doesn't do us much good, does it?" he asked.

"It would if we owned Hale and Norcross," Beth said quickly.

"The Bank interests still own the controlling shares of the stock, don't they?" Ben asked.

"It's a drug on the market," Mackay said. "It's still being offered for forty-two dollars a share and not a taker in sight. Sharon's been selling off, confident he could buy it back at his own price if the mine started producing again."

"That's where Flood and O'Brien come in," Fair said.

Ben knew these two men well, and he knew that Fair's knowledge of mines probably surpassed that of anyone else on the Comstock. Fair had been Superintendent of the Hale and Norcross at one time and there was no reason to believe he didn't know what he was talking about.

"Go on," Ben said.

John Mackay leaned forward eagerly. "Ben, Flood and O'Brien's Auction Lunch is the most popular saloon and free lunch counter in the financial district. There isn't a broker in San Francisco who doesn't know them, and they count most of them as personal friends. They've been doing pretty good on tips they've been getting and they've

184

started dealing in stock on the San Francisco Mining Exchange floor."

"Mackay and I just got back from San Francisco," Fair said. "We explained to Flood and O'Brien what we'd found in the Hale and Norcross and offered them a chance to come in with us if they'd help us round up enough stock to give us controlling interest."

"How successful have they been?" Ben asked.

Fair and Mackay exchanged glances, then looked to Beth for the answer.

"We were waiting until we talked to you, Ben," Beth said.

Mackay said, "We told them to start buying as soon as we sent them a cipher message."

"What's your part in it, Beth?" Ben asked.

"I'm going in with them. As a partner," she said.

"You have that much faith in the mine?"

"I have that much faith in Jim Fair and John Mackay," she said.

"How much will it take?" Ben asked.

"I knew you'd see it, Ben," said the usually taciturn Mackay. "Believe me we can't miss! Fair will work as Superintendent . . ."

"Without salary," Fair said. "I'm willing to give promissory notes for my share. Mackay's got money and Flood and O'Brien are willing to borrow if need be."

"And you, Beth?" Ben asked.

"I'm putting in the stock I own and I've borrowed against the boarding house." There was a quick twinkle in her eyes. "Mr. Sharon seemed delighted to loan me the money."

For a long moment Ben looked at Beth then he threw back his head and burst into laughter. "Beth," he said, "if you're setting out to whip Sharon with his own money, I'll be darned if I want to miss going along!" He turned to the others. "Gentlemen, send that telegram," he said.

20 THERE WAS nothing subtle about the arrival of spring on the Ponderosa. At noon one day the sun was bright and warm with only a solitary, sullen, black cloud over the mountains, brooding that winter was gone. Then dying winter, in one last protest against a living world, launched a final assault, spitting snow and defying the earth to fight back. But the earth was tired of winter, and it refused to yield. The snow did not stay on the ground, and the next day it was spring.

The change of the season meant many things to many people. To some it was a time of planting; to others, the freeing of the passes over the high Sierra and the resumption of full-scale transportation from the freight yards of Placerville to the mines at Virginia City.

Beneath the earth, the miners knew no change of season, but above ground every activity was affected in one way or another.

José Bettencort and his crew were in the thick of it, branding and earmarking new calves, cutting out cattle to be sold for beef, sorting the herd that would be moved to the high country and the lush summer pastures.

Jim Willy and his crew were driving cord wood on the upper Carson, throwing cut wood into the river—now free of ice and swollen by spring freshets—goading it along with peavys and prods and breaking up jams until the precious firewood was finally backed up against the log booms at Dayton. There, men waded hip deep in the icy water, tossing out the wood to be piled in ricks and cords and tiers where it would be measured. And Matt Vogel's wagons, fresh down from Virginia City mines with loads of precious ore to be reduced at the Union Mill and Mining plants, stood empty and waiting to be loaded with the wood to be hauled back up to Virginia City.

Matt Vogel himself had not been seen in a week. He was personally supervising a mass movement of men and equipment into the forests around Lake Tahoe, and already the ring of axes and the rasp of saws was shattering the stillness of the high Sierra air.

The Texas man who called himself Stevens sat tilted back on the porch of a saloon in Dayton, his broad-brimmed hat shading his eyes. He felt the spring sun, and there was an itch in his high-heeled boots. He was not a logger and he was not a teamster. He was a man who had been raised with cows, and when spring was in the air he felt, like old Kirk, the need to be in a saddle. He had quit his job with Matt Vogel just three days previous.

He raised his hat slightly and saw the fourteen-mule jerkline outfit with the big wagon and the smaller back action wagon hitched behind. It went rumbling down the street, loaded with mine timbers, headed up Six Mile Canyon.

It's a hell of a country, the man called Stevens said. *It's a place where timber is God.*

Down on the lower reaches of Clear Creek, Hoss Cartwright thought the same. With an almost skeleton crew, he was pushing the final construction of the flume, fully realizing what a tremendous part it could play in the economics of the Ponderosa. It meant an over-all controlled cutting of timber, and therefore the preservation of the beauty of the land itself, and it meant a reduction in the price of lumber delivered to the mills in the Carson Valley.

Idealistic and sentimental as he was, there was a hard core of practicality in Hoss Cartwright, and he knew that

187

in the swift movement of things today and in the competition between men and the huge corporations that were growing all around him, the ability to deliver on time and deliver at a price would be the determining factor in many a contract. Personalities could endure just so long.

William Sharon had arrived at that conclusion, also. He had come back from that first Board of Directors meeting in San Francisco completely shaken. Always before, with his sincere and honest belief in the future of the Comstock Lode, he had been able to sway the Directors with his eloquence. This time they had stared at him, hard-eyed, and even William Ralston himself had shaken his head. The Bank was over-extended. It was involved in so many things that its collapse could well wreck the financial stability of both California and Nevada. The failure of the Hale and Norcross, not necessarily fatal in itself, had nevertheless happened at exactly the wrong time.

William Sharon left that meeting with a vote of confidence, but it was a mighty feeble vote. And now, within two days, he would be headed back over the Sierra by stagecoach to attend another special meeting of the Directors of the Union Mill and Mining Company. He hadn't seen Matt Vogel in several days now, and in spite of the fact that Matt Vogel was a Director and entitled to vote, William Sharon made no attempt to find him. Vogel, in a surge of confidence, had given Sharon his proxy.

Pete Wilson, too, had avoided Matt Vogel, for he needed time to think. He had been so confident—so sure of himself . . . But when he had struck his wife this morning and sent her reeling into the corner of the room, something inside Pete had momentarily snapped. The voice of Roy Coffee rang like a gong in his head, saying, go back before you've pushed it too far . . .

But he couldn't bring himself to apologize, because she had told him that if he stayed with the job she would leave him and he had told her to leave him and be damned. He had stalked from the house, the gun holster tied low on his thigh, the long, black, box-back coat that he now affected buttoned tightly across his chest.

He mounted and rode away from the little ranch that had started out to be as real as a dream. He loved Ellen, he knew that, and he hurt inside and in every muscle of his body. But there was something more to love than just talking about it, and it wasn't something for which you had to suffer. A man had to show his love. He had to show it with money and power and he had to be in a position to say yes to whatever request a woman might make of him. When these things were so, then a man could sit back and enjoy his love.

Something close to a sob caught in Pete Wilson's throat. Why couldn't he have been born a Cartwright? he wondered. Why couldn't he have had the material things of life? None of this would have happened then.

He rode steadily toward the high country, avoiding the roads, skirting the Ponderosa, keeping to himself like a skulking animal. In time, only the horse under him and the gun on his hip was reality.

The buds of the dogwood were bursting and straining and the leaves of the hazel nut were delicately green. Maidenhair fern peeked timidly around exposed roots in winter-eroded cut banks. A thousand birds vied with each other in heralding birth and life, and prickly tufts of yellow-green needles on the uttermost tip of each pine bough raised inquisitive beaks to sniff out the newness of the season.

Pete Wilson saw none of this. He rode on, a man completely alone—a man haunted by his loneliness.

* * *

In the alcove off the living room that served an as office, Ben Cartwright, coatless, vest open, ran his fingers

189

through his hair and stood up suddenly, tormented by a surge of impatience.

Here he was, on a day like this, stuck behind a desk, going over musty figures, muttering about the lack of income the ranch experienced every winter, worrying about the tremendous amounts he had spent on the Hale and Norcross manipulations, plus the fixed operating expenses of the ranch, plus the fantastic expenditures on the flume . . . he caught himself up short. It was his own brand of spring fever. He wanted to get out into the open as he had in the old days, fill his lungs with spring and feast his eyes with the vastness and feel things growing beneath his feet. He had to shake the staleness of winter and get into the vibrant aliveness of spring.

As with any other truant, he needed an excuse, and he told himself he had best go see how Hoss was progressing with the work on the flume. A few weeks ago Ben had taken a contract to supply twenty-eight tons of ice to John Mackay's Kentuck and several other Gold Hill mines. The essence of the contract was time, and so, together with a couple of engineer friends from Virginia City, he had set about devising a way to deliver that ice rapidly and cheaply. The answer was in the flume.

The clear ice came from a man-made pond near Spooner Summit. Tahoe itself, because of its great depth, never froze, but many of the smaller lakes did, and in winter and spring they yielded a bountiful harvest to cool the sweltering men in the scorched mines of the Comstock.

Although the flume was not completed, the terminus was near enough to a road for wagons to be moved to the flume without too much construction effort. Working with the engineers, Ben had devised a platform to slope down from the V of the flume itself, here at the lower end of the canyon. His theory was that ice in two hundred to two hundred and fifty pound cakes could be moved down the flume from the thick-walled storage sheds up near Tahoe. These cakes would slide out of the flume, onto the inclined platform, and from there would be loaded into sawdust-insulated wagons and hauled up to Virginia City.

He had gone over every minute detail with Hoss and had every confidence in his son, but he needed to get out of the house.

He went out to the barn and saddled Buck. Kirk was down in the Washoe meadows with José Bettencort.

* * *

Joe, too, had decided to ride by the terminus of the uncompleted flume. He sat his saddle, leaning forward, his hat pushed back, a grin on his face, as he watched his brother Hoss doing the work of two men. Three men were wrestling a gigantic timber into place—two on one end of it, Hoss, alone, on the other.

"That's one way to save on help, Hoss," Joe said. "Of course now if you were to handle it just by yourself . . ."

Hoss straightened up. There was perspiration running down his face. "If you'd work half as much as you talk, Little Brother," Hoss said, "we wouldn't be short handed."

Little Joe put up a hand of protest. "I'm working every minute," he said. He tapped a forefinger against his temple. "With this."

"Then you're doing lighter work than I thought," Hoss said. He turned to his crew. "Come on, boys," he said, "let's keep it moving. We're gonna start slidin' ice down that flume first thing tomorrow morning."

Joe turned in his saddle and further down the canyon he could see another crew working with scrapers and drags, hacking out a rough road that would allow the big wagons to come up here and turn at the loading platform. The wagons were owned by a small independent operator

191

with headquarters in Carson City, but he, too, was experiencing the critical help shortage. Hoss, himself, would have to drive one of the big jerkline outfits.

Joe was serious now as he said, "I took a swing by the pond. This weather keeps up you won't be cutting ice more than two or three more days. Starting to get water on top of it right now."

"Yeah, I know that, Joe," Hoss said. "I'm doing the best I can."

"Which is about four times better than anybody else could do," Joe said.

21 THERE WAS a great big happy streak down the back of the man called Stevens. It was springtime, he was out of a job, and there was no place he had to go. To add to his contentment, someplace down below him was the sound of cattle.

He had given this country a fair shake, he figured. He had taken a job, threatened a man with a rifle, gotten into a few fights and stayed out of a few and sized things up in general. Nobody here seemed to care much whether you were from the North or the South and he liked that because he was sick up to his ears with war. He reined up and leaned on his saddle horn and looked across the broad expanse of the Washoe Valley and the sound of the cattle was like music to his ears.

He was a man who figured you shouldn't work unless you were hungry, and he had had a big breakfast in Virginia City. He liked talking, though, and people who worked with cows were usually hospitable in their way, if you understood them, and it was possible a man could find out a thing or two worth knowing. Just what it was he wanted to find out, he didn't know. Stevens was an opportunist. He took things as they came. He put his pony into a jog and rode on toward the swelling sound of the herd.

There was another rider angling across toward the herd, a man on a black and white horse. Something stirred Stevens' memory and then he had it. Joe Cartwright. The first time he had met him he had held a rifle on him. The second time he had met him he had seen him beaten senseless in the Bucket of Blood Saloon in Virginia City. Stevens scratched his chin and wondered if there was a chance Joe Cartwright might dislike him. Frankly, Stevens didn't much care whether Joe Cartwright did or didn't. He put his horse into a canter; with the angle he was taking, he would arrive at the roundup camp before Joe. He glanced across then and saw that Joe had reined up and dismounted and was now hunkered down, talking to a couple of cow hands. So much the better, Stevens thought. When in doubt, get there first.

He had an uncanny ability for spotting people, and the first man he saw was a tall, rather elegant California vaquero, so sure of himself as to seem overbearing, but the immediate reaction of those he addressed assured Stevens that the man was sure of himself only because he knew what he was doing.

Riding alongside the vaquero with the tassle hat was a broken man who had ridden more broncs than anyone would want to count—a man who had met nature at its worst, a man who had been trampled in stampedes. Stevens looked at the man and felt an immediate oneness with him. There, he thought, is a man who has lived a life.

He reined his horse in and rode quietly to where the vaquero and the broken old man were holding in their horses. They gave him a glance and nothing more.

"My name's Stevens," he said.

The arrogant vaquero looked around and said, "First name or last?"

"Maybe both," Stevens said. "Stevens Stevens. I'm from Texas."

The vaquero squared his shoulders and said, "My grandfather fought for Texas."

"So'd mine," Stevens said laconically. "Your folks lost."

He saw the faintest hint of a controlled smile pinch the corner of the vaquero's mouth. "You looking for somebody?" the vaquero said.

"The boss," Stevens said.

"That would be me. My name is José Bettencort."

"I smelled your cows, José Bettencort," Stevens said. "I'm ridin' the grub line. I'm lookin' for a job."

"What do you do?" José asked.

"If I told you, you'd think I was lyin'," Stevens said. "If I show you, it'll prove I ain't. Ponderosa cows, ain't they?"

"They're branded," José said.

"There's talk in Virginia City you're short-handed," Stevens said.

"There's talk in Nevada I shouldn't hire the first man that comes along."

The crippled little old man shifted his weight slightly in the saddle. "He's all right, José," Kirk said.

"Just like that?" José said.

"Just like that," Kirk said.

"We're moving the herd up to the high country," José said. "You start out riding drag and you work your way up."

"That'll take a day," Stevens said.

"You want to know about wages?"

"Nope," Stevens said. "I know what I'm worth and I expect to get it."

194

"Go over to the remuda and draw yourself a string," José said.

Stevens touched the brim of his hat and rode off. Old Kirk looked after him, almost longingly, as if seeing something out of his past. He didn't look at José Bettencort. He said, "José, you just hired yourself a hand."

*   *   *

Joe Cartwright finished checking the cows and rode up to the roundup camp where Kirk and José Bettencort were having a cup of coffee while they checked out some tally sheets. Joe dismounted, acknowledged the greetings of the two men and moved across to the big coffee pot. He helped himself to a cup of the steaming, black brew.

"We got lucky, Little Joe," José said. "I just hired a new hand."

"Oh?" Joe said, blowing across his cup. "Where did you find him?"

"Just drifted by," José said. "Like in the old days. You know the boys used to work the Southern California cattle then they'd move up to Mono and across to Esmeralda and through here and up to Elko and clear to Montana . . ."

"He's that kind, Joe," old Kirk said. "The best kind there is. And some day they're all gonna be gone."

"If you say so, Kirk," Joe said. He took a deep drink of his coffee then froze as he slowly lowered the cup from his lips. He was staring over toward the rope corral that held the large horse cavvy. "The one in the blue shirt," he said. "Where'd he come from?"

José and Kirk turned and looked off and José said, "That's the one I'm talking about. That's him."

Joe Cartwright set his cup on the ground. He wasn't wearing a coat, and without thinking about it, he adjusted his gun belt. He took off his gloves and tucked

195

them in his back pocket and he walked slowly across toward the rope corral where Stevens was twirling a lariat, picking out an obnoxious looking grulla dun that was kicking at everything in sight.

Joe came to the rope barrier and stopped. He stood there with his feet apart and his hands down at his side. "Hello, Stevens," he said.

Stevens pulled in the rope and let it settle into the dust and then he coiled it neatly before turning around and Joe saw he had coiled it with his left hand and his right hand was ungloved and free. Stevens tossed the coiled rope over a post and he stood there facing Little Joe while the horses moved off to huddle in a group behind him.

"First time I seen you," Stevens said, "you told me your name was Joe Cartwright. Second time I seen you I heard a bartender mention it. Sort of stuck with me. I remember you plain now. Howdy, Joe Cartwright."

"What are you doing here?" Joe Cartwright said.

"Got me a job," Stevens said.

"I'm part owner of this ranch."

"Figgered as much."

"You think I'd hire a man who tried to kill me?"

Stevens kept his right hand at his side. He lifted his left and scratched his chin. "I don't reckon I tried to kill you," he said. "If I had of, you'd a been dead."

"You and your bunch tried to beat me to death," Joe said.

"That ain't so either," Stevens said. "I didn't figger it was any of my business to butt in, but you can't say I punched you."

"Get off the ranch," Joe said.

"Why? Ain't I doin' my work?"

"I don't like the man you're working for."

Stevens shrugged. "I reckon that's your taste, not mine. Down in Texas there was a time nobody liked any Mexicans. This one seemed all right to me."

Joe hadn't noticed José and Kirk moving up alongside

196

him. José said quietly, "He's a vaquero, Joe. We need him."

"He works for Matt Vogel," Joe said.

Again Stevens scratched his chin with his left hand. "There you go again, gettin' me all wrong," Stevens said. "I quit him two days ago. I don't like his trees or his wagons or his mules and it could be maybe I don't even like his ways, but that would be my business and not yours. I got lonesome for cows and I smelled these and I asked for a job. Your segundo here give me one. Your segundo hired me and I'll quit when the segundo fires me." He went over to the fence post and got his rope and started shaking out a loop.

Kirk moved up alongside Joe and watched the tall, lean man in the corral. "I've known you a long time, boy," Kirk said to Joe.

"That's true, Kirk," Joe said. "A long time."

"Take my advice for once," Kirk said. "You got a Ponderosa hand yonder. Keep him."

Kirk turned and went limping away. Joe glanced around and José was looking at him, a little worried, waiting for orders. Joe tugged his hat down over his eye and he spit at the ground. "You heard Kirk," he said to José. "You got yourself a hand there. Make sure he keeps busy."

He went back to his horse and mounted and rode out.

*   *   *

So far as newspaper work went, winter, summer, fall or spring made little difference except for the type of story. In the fall, if you ran out of something better to do, you could lie about the amount of wood being stored up against winter. The Indians were always good for a dozen tales about predicting the severity of the season ahead. If all else failed, one could pump up the power of the Washoe Zephyr until everyone believed there were donkeys and prospectors sailing through the air overhead, and one look at the tin roofs of the shanties below

197

D Street hurtling through the atmosphere made it seem almost true. Dan de Quille had little trouble filling his columns, regardless of the weather, for as accurate a reporter as he was, if filler copy didn't happen he had a way of making it happen.

It was two o'clock in the morning and his pen flew rapidly as he finished the yarn to explain why all the rivers of Nevada either pour their waters into lakes which have no outlets or just sink into the earth or dissipate in the evaporation that goes on in this region during the greater part of the year. Not one river gets out of the state or through any other river reaches the sea. Dan claimed he had found the answer.

It was a simple tale, once you looked into it. The Almighty, at the time he was creating and fashioning the earth, got along to this section late on a Saturday evening. He had finished all of the Great Lakes like Superior, Michigan, Huron, Erie and those, and He had made the Ohio and the Missouri and the Mississippi rivers. Now, as a sort of wind up, He was about to make a river that would be far ahead of anything He had yet done in that line. So He started in and traced out Humboldt River and Truckee River and Reese River and all the other rivers, and He was leading them along, calculating to bring them all together into one big boss river and then lead that off and let it empty into the Gulf of Mexico or the Gulf of California, as might be most convenient. But as he was bringing down and leading along the several branches—the Truckee, Humboldt, Carson, Walker and those, it came on dark and the next day was the Sabbath. So instead of trying to carry out the original plan, He just tucked the lower ends of the several streams into the ground where they have remained from that day to this.

Dan de Quille put the proper flourish to the end of his story and called it a day. He stretched then and yawned and decided to drop by the Bucket of Blood to see Don McBride for a minute, but before he could move from his chair, Scotty McCoy, proprietor of the Sweet Heather of Scotland, came bustling into the office. Almost automatically, Dan reached for a quarter, for Sweet Heather of Scotland had not proved worthy of its name.

Scotty McCoy held up his hand. "Danny boy," he said, "you've done me a lot of favors. This time I'll do one for you."

"Another mine, Scotty?" Dan said.

The little prospector shook his head. "You ken that the lad at the telegraph office is a nephew of mine?" he asked.

"Yeah, I knew that," Dan said.

"Then here's news for you," said Scotty, "and I'll cross my soul it's true. My nephew just got the telegram."

Dan leaned forward in his chair, sensing a story. "What kind of news, Scotty?" he asked quietly.

"The four Irishmen, Ben Cartwright and Beth Kelly have just taken over control of the Hale and Norcross mine," Scotty said. "Even Bill Sharon himself don't know it yet."

22 MATT VOGEL hadn't heard of the Hale and Norcross coup either, but even if he had, he likely would have paid little attention. Vogel was a man who gave full attention to the business at hand, and the business at hand was logging.

Three crews of forty men each were slashing their way through the sugar pine forests at the north end of Lake Tahoe. Five minutes never went by without the sound of a forest monarch crashing to the ground, and the ring of axes, the shouts of the teamsters, the rasp of the saws and the clang of the blacksmiths was everywhere. Matt worked as hard as any man on his crew.

This was like the old days when the giant nozzles were washing out the earth and making him money across the mountains. There was a savage brutality to logging that got into a man's blood. He yelled at the tallow boy to start greasing the skids, and he whipped up his tandem-hitched team of six mules.

There were four logs, butt to butt in the level log chute. Matt turned the team over to Neil Larson and watched the big woods boss face the large iron hook into the butt of the last log in the chute. The hook was secured by trace chains to the mules. Larson cracked the buckskin popper. The mules started out at a trot with the tallow boy running ahead of them, slopping brushfuls of animal fat onto the running surfaces of the log trough.

The team continued to the top of a steep bluff, where the hook was thrown and the logs plunged over the rim of the canyon wall and down another chute. Matt watched Neil Larson accomplish this without ever breaking the stride of his team. It wasn't always so. Only yesterday a "breaker," as the driver was called, failed to free his hook in time. The mules were dragged down in a writhing mass.

Matt Vogel shook his head. You expected to lose men and animals in this business, especially if you were in a hurry. And Matt was in a hurry. The first payment on that half million dollar note at the Bank was coming due soon. He had no intention of letting William Sharon get the upper hand on him.

Larson turned the team of mules over to one of the regular breakers and came across to join Matt. From down at the bottom of the canyon they heard the crackling, ear splitting report as a log hit the surface of the man-made pond on the Truckee. Larson grinned.

200

"Good sound, ain't it?" he said.

"The best," Vogel said. "How's the chute holding up?"

"I was just gonna look at it," Larson said.

They moved to the lip of the cliff where a team was pulling up, ready to dump its tow. The logs rolled free, hit the preconstructed baffles and fed themselves into the dry chute that dropped half a mile down to the river. They stood there, watching the tons of sugar pine logs move faster and faster, maybe sixty and then seventy miles an hour, leaving a rocket trail of sparks and clouds of smoke. A log broke free, made a gigantic leap into the air and started pinwheeling down the mountainside, tearing out young growth, smashing itself to splinters on the rocks.

Again there was that report, as if from a giant rifle, and an arching sheet of spray was driven into the air as the logs hit the water. Some logs shot off like projectiles, others smashed into each other, and one snapped end over end, leaping into the air, clearing the river entirely. It hit the opposite bank and buried half its twenty foot length a hundred and fifty feet up the mountainside.

"Seems to me we're losing quite a bit of timber," Matt said.

"You said you wanted it fast, didn't you?" Larson said.

"That's right," Matt said. "Fast."

Neil Larson looked off toward the grove where forty men were working at top speed. "Ain't nobody faster than me," Larson said. "When I was timber rustling I had to be fast." He shifted the cud of snuff he carried under his lower lip, gestured off in a general direction, down the slope. "I had only been loggin' four days there on the Ponderosa when old man Cartwright caught up with me, but even at that I done good."

"Trouble was, though, he caught up with you," Vogel said.

Larson looked him straight in the eye. "I couldn't stand

201

up to him because I was short-handed." He spit. "If I was in that timber down there I'd get twice as much out of this crew as I'm gettin' now."

He moved off and left Matt with his thoughts. Not all of them were pleasant. He was deeply in debt and the expenses were mounting by the minute.

He had made a poor contract, he realized now, and the difference between profit and loss was time and the distance he would have to haul those logs. When he had first gone into this thing he had been certain Ben Cartwright would agree to the logging of the Ponderosa, which would have meant, in most cases, hauling half the distance he was forced to haul now. The stubborn old fool, he thought to himself. He could not, for the life of him, fathom Ben's thinking.

He had never lost money on a deal in his life and he had no intention of losing on this one. He hated to leave, but he knew he had to talk to Sharon.

* * *

William Sharon had a bone tiredness in him that would not go away, and it had been with him ever since his recent trip to San Francisco. He didn't mind the boat trip down the river from Sacramento, but he hated with a passion the stage ride from Sacramento to Virginia City. Each way was nothing more to him than one hundred and sixty-two miles and eighteen hours of sheer, bone-jarring torture. To a man as fastidious as Sharon, it meant rumpled clothes, grime, dust, animal smells and mediocre food at the wayside stops. The majesty of the Sierra and the remarkable engineering feat of the road itself was completely lost on the foppish little banker.

This trip had been particularly trying because once more he had been on the defensive with a hostile Board of Directors. He had sensed a cooling in his relationship with William Ralston, and for the first time since the formation of Union Mill and Mining he had had to concede a number of points. He had to do something big and spectacular now, he knew, in order to restore his prestige. He thought he knew what that "something" would be, but it was such a bold, all-sweeping stroke that he had to have more time to think about it. William Sharon was considering building a railroad from Carson City to Virginia City, and later it would go up through Washoe and Steamboat Valleys and join with the Central Pacific, which was building over the Sierra and moving down the Truckee toward Lake's Crossing, which some were now calling Reno.

The thought was not new, for others had considered it before him, but in the whiplash mind of William Sharon what once had been only a possibility was fast approaching a reality of action.

He stood in front of his office now and heard the never-ending chime of team bells interspersing the thunder of his own stamp mills, and he saw the big outfit driven by Hoss Cartwright coming down the main street. Most drivers rode the off-wheeler, but big Hoss sat on the high seat, his feet braced, the jerk line gripped in his massive paw.

Sharon knew from the constant trickle of water that ran from the big wagon and its tandem back action that Hoss was hauling ice. He heard Hoss hoorawing his team, saw him toss a pebble at the off leader, and the mules looked as if they were executing a well practiced ballet as the first, second and third pointers went across the chain and the wagon started swinging around to go down the hill toward the ice house.

William Sharon expelled his breath and went into the office. There were two things he would have liked to have forgotten at the moment. The problems of transportation, and the Cartwrights and everything associated with them.

He had heard of the take-over of the Hale and Norcross immediately upon his return from San Francisco. He had trouble believing it, but a talk with Dan de Quille and a rapid check with his stockbroker convinced him that he was indeed on the verge of being voted off the Board.

There was nothing financially ruinous about the loss of control of the mine. Rather, it was an ego shattering humiliation. To be bested by a quartet of unknowns such as the four Irishmen—to be whipped by two ex-muckers and a couple of ex-bartenders turned stockbrokers was a little more than a man like William Sharon could tolerate. Added to that was the indignity of knowing that the soft-spoken and almost pitiful acting widow, Beth Kelly, had used the Bank's own money against him.

He thought of the Cartwrights then, and they had to share the animosity he felt toward the Irishmen. Sharon had hoped and fully expected that Ben Cartwright would leap at the chance of adding the Ponderosa to the gigantic complex of Union Mill and Mining. The fact that he hadn't and wanted to stand alone was understandable and even admirable to Sharon, but it did not lessen his desire to own the property, and he still dreamed of ways of getting Cartwright into the corporation. To William Sharon, business was business, first, last and always. He sat down at his desk and took a deep breath. He hoped sincerely that Matt Vogel would feel the same way, for he had some bad news for the big teamster.

*　　*　　*

It was approximately an hour before Matt Vogel arrived at the Bank office, and in this time William Sharon had had a chance to organize his thinking. He had gone back over every word of what had transpired at the Board of Director's meeting in San Francisco. He knew he could be calm, objective, even sympathetic. He stood up and offered his hand. "Good to see you, Matt," he said. "Sit down and make yourself comfortable."

Matt Vogel should have known then and there that he was through.

An hour later, William Sharon was still patient, still unruffled. His voice was quiet, and he was even solicitous. "I understand your position, Matt," he said, "but you also have to understand mine and the position of the corporation."

Matt Vogel was sweating profusely. "I'm gonna lose money even at the price that's on the contract now," he said. "I come here to ask you for a raise and you're telling me I got to cut the price on delivered lumber!"

"Matt, please be patient with me," Sharon said. "I'm not personally trying to tell you anything. I'm telling you what the Board of Directors have decided."

"You were voting my stock," Vogel said. "Did you vote along with them?"

"Matt, this is a democracy," Sharon said patiently. "There are eleven men on the Board of Directors. The majority voted that we have to institute certain economies . . ."

"I asked you how you voted," Vogel said flatly.

"With the majority," Sharon said.

"To protect your own neck," Vogel said bitterly.

"Not at all, Matt," Sharon said. "I'm Secretary and Treasurer of Union Mill and Mining. My job is to do what I feel is best for the corporation."

"You better think about the half a million dollars I owe the Bank," Vogel said. "If I try to deliver lumber from where I'm logging now at the price you're telling me you'll pay, the Bank won't even get the interest on that half a million dollars back."

"That would be most unfortunate, Matt," Sharon said. "There would be nothing left for us to do but foreclose on your transportation company. The Board discussed that possibility."

Matt Vogel stood up slowly. "That possibility be damned, Sharon," he said. "I ain't whipped yet. Not by a long shot. I'll deliver your lumber and I'll deliver it at your price. And I'll get rich doing it."

"I sincerely hope you do, Matt," William Sharon said. "I wouldn't want to see you get hurt."

"I won't," Vogel said. He turned and left the office.

Sharon looked after him, shaking his head. It was pitiful, in a way. Matt Vogel was in too deep to back out and Sharon doubted seriously that Matt had the ability to compete with the group of millionaires that made up the Board of Directors of Union Mill and Mining.

Sharon went back to his work and dismissed Vogel from his mind as completely as if the big teamster had never existed. There were a thousand other details to occupy his attention.

23 IT HAD STARTED out as a business meeting here in the living room of the Ponderosa, but now that it was winding up, there was almost a party attitude about the group that had executed the coup on the Hale and Norcross.

Beth Kelly was radiant, and Ben Cartwright had trouble keeping his eyes off her. John Mackay was as relaxed and contented as a tomcat in a milk house, and even James Fair had lost a great deal of his gruffness.

There was no complaint in Fair's voice when he said, "Now the work starts."

"With you as Superintendent, Jim, I won't lose any sleep over it," Ben said.

They had decided among themselves, with telegraphed agreement from Flood and O'Brien, that the first thing to do was to call a special meeting of the Board of Directors of Hale and Norcross. There was no doubt about their having enough votes to assume control. The next thing, then, was to strike into the bonanza that James Fair was so sure was there.

"We got to move fast," Fair said. "I got no more money to put into this. We'll have to have timber—lots of it—and we'll have to have it at a price."

"If the flume was completed I could deliver lumber to the mine at twenty-one dollars a thousand instead of the twenty nine dollars you're paying now," Ben said.

"What will it take to finish the flume?" John Mackay asked quietly.

"Forty men," Ben said.

"You'll have 'em there," Fair said. "The best timber men I've got in the mine. You'll have to pay 'em Union wages—four dollars a day."

"I'll pay it," Ben said.

Hop Sing padded in, bringing the iced champagne Ben had ordered earlier. Ben took it and popped the cork and filled the glasses himself. Beth raised hers to Ben and their eyes met and a message passed between them.

"Success, partner," she said softly.

"Success to you, Beth," he said.

*   *   *

Little Joe Cartwright welcomed the chance to make a trip to Virginia City, even on an errand as prosaic as executing some routine banking business for his father and picking up a buckboard load of groceries for Hop Sing.

The constant patrolling of the boundaries of the Ponderosa was a boring and endless task and at times, Joe thought, even a useless one. Up until now, at least, Matt Vogel and his crew had not shown the slightest indication that they planned to cross over onto Ponderosa territory. Joe had wondered to himself several times just what he would do if they did decide to make a mass invasion. He had talked to his father about it and Ben's answer, as usual, had been a logical one.

"It's the mere fact that they know we're watching them that keeps them from trying anything," Ben said.

Joe came in once a week to report to his father, and on this occasion, since Ben was going to be busy with Fair and Mackay and Beth Kelly, Joe had drawn the assignment of running the errand to town.

He had had a long visit with Roy Coffee, and had hoisted a few beers at Don McBride's Bucket of Blood, and now, as he drove back toward home, one foot cocked against the dashboard, his hat pushed back, he was humming a little tune and feeling at peace with the world.

When he came to the road that led off to Pete Wilson's place, he started to go on by, then suddenly pulled the team to a stop. He had thought of Pete constantly; he had worried about Ellen. And yet, he had avoided them both just as if he were guilty of some crime. The devil with it, he said to himself. If Pete isn't going to make the first move, I will. He turned the team down the lane and felt a further lifting of his spirits.

He realized now that Pete and Ellen had been even more on his mind this afternoon than was usual, and he knew it came from the fact that Sheriff Roy Coffee had been unable to tell him whether or not Pete was still working for Matt Vogel.

"He's got so many gun toughs on his payroll now," Roy Coffee had said, "maybe he figures he don't need an amateur like Pete."

He had been hoping that was exactly so, Joe realized, and now he intended to find out. The dog came out to greet him as he drove down the lane, and a flock of chickens went squawking out of his way.

He pulled up at the house and wrapped the lines around the brake and called out a "Hello!" There was no answer, and the place gave the appearance of being deserted.

"Pete? Ellen!" he called again. "It's Joe!"

He got down from the wagon and went across to the door and knocked. The sound of his knocking echoed back and forth, but there was no answer. They must have gone into town, he decided, and he was sorry he had missed them. Maybe he and Pete could have sat down and just had one beer together and in that simple gesture captured some of the old comradeship that had always been between them.

He turned to leave, but as he did he went by the window and a movement inside the house caught his attention. There was someone in there.

He stood there a moment, puzzled, then turned again to knock on the door. Still there was no answer, but this time he tried the door and the knob turned easily. He pushed the door open and went inside.

He saw her, then, lying on the couch in the corner, her face toward the wall. She was completely covered by a blanket, except for her blonde hair. Joe said, "Ellen?"

There was no answer and he went across and kneeled down beside her and he spoke her name again.

"I don't want to see anyone, Joe," she whispered. "Please try to understand."

"I can't understand, Ellen," he said. He reached out and put a hand on her shoulder.

Her voice trembled and she said, "Please, Joe, for God's sake, leave me alone."

"I can't, Ellen," he said. "Not if you're in trouble. I told you a long time ago if you ever needed help I'd be there."

"I don't need help," she said.

She was still lying with her face toward the wall.

"Look at me, Ellen," he said.

She did not move, so he reached out and he put his hand under her chin and he gently turned her face toward him. Her eyes were red from weeping and there were tear streaks on her cheeks, and as he stared at her in disbelief he saw the discoloration, the fist bruises, and the lips he had once kissed, now swollen beyond recognition. He said, "My God! Oh my God!"

She started to cry and she said, "Joe, I begged you to go away."

"That filthy bastard!" Joe said.

She said, "Joe, you don't understand."

"That's right," he said. "I don't understand and I don't want to."

"He needs me, Joe," she said. "He needs me."

"He needs a bullet between his eyes," Joe Cartwright said.

She said, "Don't talk that way, Joe."

"You get some things together," he said. "You're coming home with me."

"I couldn't do that."

"Get your things together," he said. "I'm not leaving you here. Come on, you're going home."

She got up slowly, moving as if she were a machine. Joe went outside and filled his lungs with spring air. He felt if he stayed in that room one more moment he would be sick to his stomach.

* * *

Ben Cartwright stood in the middle of the Ponderosa living room, both hands raised in that characteristic gesture he had. "All right, Joseph, all right!" he said. "I understand everything you say and I'm in full sympathy with your objective. I am merely saying that people think twice before they interfere between a man and his wife!"

"A man?" Joe said, his voice shaking. "Did you look at her face? Did you see what he's done to her?"

"Yes, Joseph," Ben said. "Of course I did."

"Then how can you stand there telling me that I'm interfering in a marital affair?"

"Because you are."

"Then just exactly what do you want me to do? Take her back there? Leave her in that house where she doesn't even have energy enough to build a fire to heat it? You want me to let her wait there, cowering in a corner until he comes back to pound her face into a pulp again?"

"Joseph, listen to me," Ben said. "I am merely telling you that you have to consider the consequences of what you are doing here."

"I'm considering the consequences," Joe said, getting control of his voice. "I told him I'd kill him if he ever hurt her and he's hurt her more than I ever expected."

Ben moved across and put his arm around his youngest son's shoulder. He held him close for a moment and said, "Did she say she would like to have you kill him, Joseph?"

Ben felt his son's shoulders sag under his embrace. Joe slid down into a chair. He stared into the deep embers of the fireplace and said, "Pa, this is what I don't understand. She says she still loves him." He looked up quickly, handsome, intense, those brown eyes burning and questing for an answer. He said, "Pa, what in hell is love all about anyway?"

His father sat down slowly. He folded his hands and looked into the fireplace. "How many times have I asked myself that question?" He looked up suddenly and there was his youngest, a grown man, asking for an answer to a question to which there was no answer. In that moment, perhaps, it ceased to be only father and son and became in addition two men who were friends. His rich baritone voice was quiet as he looked at his son and he said, "I don't know the answer, Joe." He stood up and went across to the table. "Do you want some coffee?"

Joe said, "Yeah, Pa. I'd like some."

They were sitting there, sipping their coffee, when Ellen came down the stairs. She had freshened up, and because Joe and Ben had talked it out this far, they were able to ignore the bruises on her cheeks and the dark violence where Pete's fist had closed her eye. They saw only the wealth of her golden hair, brushed back; they

211

saw only a girl they had known and loved for most of her life.

Ben said, "Coffee, Ellen? I think Hop Sing has some cake."

"I just wanted to say thank you, that's all," she said.

Ben said, "This has always been your home, you know that."

"Don't try to be kind to me, Uncle Ben," she said. "I made every mistake in the world, didn't I?"

Joe didn't look at her. He sat there, hurting inside. *You made every mistake?* he thought. *I'm the one who made the mistakes. Why didn't I ask you to marry me?*

"I'd like to sit in front of the fire a little while," she said. "I used to sit there when I was a little girl and I'd see pictures in the flames. Do you remember?"

"Yes, I remember," Ben said.

She came across and sat on the sofa and spread her hands to the flame. She didn't look at Joe and he didn't look at her, because they knew they didn't dare. Here, together, the memories were too close.

Hop Sing came in and said, "Someone to see you, Mr. Cartlight."

There was a puzzled frown on Ben's face as he stood up and saw Matt Vogel standing there in the doorway. There was a mixture of self-confidence and guarded reserve about the big teamster. It was the first time he had ever been in the Ponderosa ranch house. He looked from Ben to Joe and then let his gaze linger a long time on Ellen Wilson.

"Hello, Ellen," Vogel said. "I didn't expect to find you here. Pete said you were at home. I was going by there later to see if there was anything you needed."

"She's visiting with us for a little while," Ben said quietly. "Did you want to see me about something?"

"Yeah, I did," Matt Vogel said. He took off his hat and came into the room and Hop Sing closed the door behind him.

24 As she hurriedly excused herself and left the room to go back upstairs, Ellen hoped fervently that Matt Vogel had not noticed the bruises on her face. She felt sick, down to the pit of her stomach, as she thought of Vogel telling Pete she was here with the Cartwrights. She wanted to help Pete. She had told him so, over and over, but now, once more, it seemed, she had done exactly the wrong thing. She promised herself she would leave here first thing in the morning and go back home where she belonged.

Joe looked after her as she hurried up the stairs, then, making half-veiled excuses about a lame horse and things that should be checked in the blacksmith shop, he hurried out into the late afternoon.

Hop Sing went about his business, paying no apparent attention to Matt Vogel. He said nothing, and he heard everything.

Matt said, "Maybe you're surprised to see me here."

"Yes, I won't deny that," Ben said. "Won't you sit down?"

Ben went across and sat behind his desk and the teamster drew up a chair. Neither man had said so, but the attitude and position of both indicated they both knew this was not a social call.

"You got a nice place here," Vogel said.

"A tombstone to my accomplishments," Ben said. "Isn't that the way you put it?"

Vogel chuckled. "Just a way of putting things, that's all. Me, I never put much stock in land."

"Would you care for a drink?" Ben asked.

"Yeah, I would," Vogel said. "Providing you'll have one with me."

Ben lifted the brandy decanter that stood on the corner of his desk and held it up for Vogel to see. "This all right?"

"You ain't gonna find me too hard to get along with," Vogel said.

"That's fine," Ben said. He poured two glasses and set them out. There was a long silence during which Ben tasted his brandy and then put down the glass. "There's not much sense of you and me beating around the bush, is there, Vogel? What's on your mind?"

"Always did like the way you get right at things," Vogel said. "You and me always know where we stand."

"On opposite sides of the fence, generally, don't we?"

"Yeah, I suppose we do," Vogel said. "You suppose we have to?"

"I doubt either of us is going to change much."

"Maybe that ain't so," Vogel said. "I'm here to talk business, and like I said, I won't be hard to get along with."

Ben hesitated a long time, trying to think ahead of the man, failing. He said softly, "I've never been known to fail to listen to a business proposition."

Matt Vogel relaxed noticeably. He was a man of great self-confidence and the mere fact that Cartwright hadn't backed away from him gave him the feeling there was a good chance of getting someplace with the big rancher. He laced his fingers across his barrel chest and leaned back in his chair.

"I said once I figured the Ponderosa could be bought if somebody offered enough money," Matt said.

"You were wrong," Ben said.

"Yeah, I know that now," Matt said. "Like I told you,

I never held much to owning ground. I realize now you do."

Ben was more confused than ever. "I guess everyone goes his own way, Matt."

"Yeah," Matt said. "When I was leasing that timber land up at the north end of the lake I run into it over and over. Folks wanted their ground cleared off. I leased a hundred and sixty acres for two hundred and fifty dollars and maybe I could of got it for less. But I had to guarantee soon as I was through logging, I'd turn that ground back to the owners." He nodded his head. "Yeah, now maybe I see how it is with people like you."

"Do you, Matt?" Ben said.

"Yeah, I do," Matt said. "So I'm ready to make you the same sort of deal I made with those farmers up around the lake. I don't want the Ponderosa, Ben. All I want is the timber."

He accepted Ben's silence as interest and hurried on.

"You don't have to touch it. I got the crew, the teams and wagons to haul it out with—everything. You and your boys do the cruising and I'll accept your board foot count. If you want, I'll buy up what lumber contracts you got and take over your cord wood contracts too. Give me a month's credit and after that I'll pay cash for every stick I cut."

Ben had recovered his composure but the effrontery of the man still astounded him.

"I thought I made it clear the Ponderosa wasn't for sale," he said, "and I thought I heard you say you understood that."

Vogel was carried away with his own enthusiasm. "That's the point of it, don't you see?" he said. "You'll still have the land, if that's what you got to have."

"Stripped of every tree and every living green thing on it?"

Vogel looked at him intently. "Look, Cartwright," the big teamster said. "I'm offering you more than anybody

215

else ever offered you. I ain't trying to take the land away from you. When you die, it'll still be here, like that tombstone I was talking about, if that's what you want."

"I'm not interested, Vogel."

"You gonna just leave those trees standing there?"

"In many cases, yes."

Vogel expelled his breath. "That timber is a crop, just like hay's a crop. It's got to be cut and hauled to market before it amounts to anything to anybody."

"No," Ben said quietly.

Vogel sat there a long time, gathering his thoughts. He said, "Cartwright, I'm gonna put it to you another way. You remember when we all sat down up there in the Washoe Club and you had a chance to go in on the Union Mill and Mining Company?"

"That's right, I did," Ben said. "And you remember I didn't go along with it."

"I think you made a big mistake," Vogel said. "I did go along. I got every pound of freighting and every inch of lumber that goes into the corporation."

"Good for you, Vogel," Ben said. "It still doesn't have to concern me."

"That's where you're wrong, Cartwright," Vogel said. "It does have to concern you. I got my whole life—every penny I ever made and a lot more tied up in this. You got a lot of trees on your place. They could make you and me both rich. You gonna set there and tell me you ain't gonna take advantage of it?"

"Yes," Ben said.

"That ain't right, Cartwright," Vogel said. "That ain't right at all. I've signed my name on notes for a half a million dollars and I've signed contracts for the delivery of three million dollars more in lumber and you set there looking at me and say you just want to see those trees grow. That ain't right."

"I'm sorry, Matt," Ben said, "but that's the way it is."

Matt Vogel stood up slowly. "No, Cartwright," he said,

"that ain't the way it is at all. I'm not gonna let you stand in my way and I'm not gonna go broke."

Ben got to his feet and the two men faced each other across the desk. "Are you threatening me?" Ben asked.

"You take it any way you want," Vogel said.

He turned abruptly and started toward the door and as he did, Ellen Wilson came down the stairs. She stood there on the landing, trying to decide if she should go back. She realized it was too late.

Matt Vogel looked at her and said, "I'll tell your husband I saw you."

He went outside and Ben heard him wheel the buggy out of the yard.

*   *   *

Logs came down the skid road to the top of the precipice, into the chute to slide screaming and smoking and showering sparks in their plunge to the Truckee. Neil Larson was doing a good job. The vibrant sounds of the camp reached Matt Vogel's ears while he was still two miles away.

He didn't understand Ben Cartwright. He understood no man who refused to take a quick profit. He only understood his own desperation and his own determination to save his fortune and to multiply it until he was equal with Sharon and the other Directors.

He came up to the camp and he looked quickly over the operation. He thought of the expense of transporting the logs and the lumber across the miles down to Virginia City and he knew that was where he would sustain his loss. He thought of Pete Wilson, young, eager to please, ambitious and in love with a gun. He thought of the Virginia City "chiefs" who had loafed through the winter on his payroll . . .

He went over to Neil Larson then and he said, "How's it going?"

"We could do better," Larson said. "If the trees were
217

bigger and four times thicker and we were closer to the mill."

"All right," Vogel said. "Skim the cream off of it here and we'll move."

For a long time Larson looked at Vogel and the hint of a grin tilted the corner of his mouth. "On to the Ponderosa?"

"If that's where the trees are thicker."

"They are," Larson said. He looked at Vogel a long time. "Those Cartwrights carry guns," he said.

"So do some of my boys," Vogel said.

"Maybe my crew won't work so good with somebody shootin' at 'em," Larson said.

"Maybe nobody will be shooting at them," Vogel said. "Maybe I plan to keep the Cartwrights so busy someplace else you'll be through logging before they ever know you're down there."

Larson was looking off into the distance. "I been real anxious to get back on that Ponderosa," he said. "Real anxious."

He turned and walked off, a swaggering man who liked trouble. Matt felt a weakness in the pit of his stomach. He had committed himself now, he knew, and there wouldn't be any turning back.

He went to find Pete Wilson.

25 PETE WILSON had made up his mind to quit. He knew now that there was no way he could make Ellen understand his ambitions, nor could he make her realize that everything he did was being done for her.

218

Once they had shared dreams. Or had he only imagined that, too? Now there was no communication between them at all.

He would have to leave this part of the country, he knew that, but there were a thousand places a man could go. In another place he and Ellen . . . and there his thoughts bogged down. Would she go with him? He wanted her to, desperately, but when he thought of the violence of their last encounter he became actually sick to his stomach. There, for those few moments, he knew he had been completely insane, and he knew how it was that one person could kill another.

He would go to her, he decided, crawl on his hands and knees if need be. But she had to give a little, too. She had to forget that worthless piece of ground that had been given to her father as a gesture of charity by the all-powerful and benevolent Cartwrights.

Again Pete felt his anger rising against a fate that had allowed him to be born poor. Matt Vogel's voice said, "From your expression I'd say you've made up your mind to hate the world."

Pete turned swiftly, and he realized that this, too, had become a habit. Every sound, every voice made him jump. He rubbed the palms of his hands on the legs of his trousers and tried to manage a grin. "I guess my mind was off yonder someplace," he said.

Half a dozen crude buildings had been thrown up hastily in a logged-off clearing. The largest one served as a mess hall, and the others as harness and tool sheds, and one was a powder magazine, for Neil Larson did not believe in going around an obstacle if you could blow it out of the way. In most cases it meant pure and unnecessary destruction of young timber, but that was the least of Neil Larson's worries.

Vogel looked at Pete and said, "Come on over to the mess hall. I want to talk to you."

Now was the time to tell him he was quitting, Pete

knew, but he couldn't bring himself to it right at this moment. When Vogel turned and moved on toward the mess hall, Pete fell in beside him.

There was a gallon coffee pot on the stove and Vogel poured two cups, motioning for Pete to sit down. They were alone in the place. Vogel kicked out one of the long benches and sat across the table from Pete. "Anything new in town?" he asked.

There was nothing wrong in making his final report, Pete decided, although he did at times now feel exactly like what Ellen accused him of being—Matt Vogel's errand boy. "Lot of activity at Hale and Noreross," Pete said. "They're going to take it down another level."

Vogel brushed the information aside imperiously. "That ain't very important news," he said. "What are the Cartwrights up to?"

For a long moment Pete hesitated, then he pressed the fist of his left hand into the palm of his right and he cracked his knuckles. "Jim Fair sent forty timber men up to help them on that flume."

"Pete," Vogel said suddenly, "I'm going to start cutting on the Ponderosa. I already gave Larson orders to move camp."

Pete Wilson stared at his boss. He had thrown this at him so suddenly and Pete realized now that was the way Vogel always did. Catch you off guard and you would agree to do something before you even knew what it was you were going to do.

Pete said, "I've seen that tried before, Mr. Vogel, when I was working on the Ponderosa. Nobody's ever got away with it."

"Suppose the Cartwrights didn't even know about it until it was too late?" Vogel said. "Suppose they were busy every place else except around here?"

"I don't know if that's likely," Pete said.

Vogel chuckled. "You're a smart boy, Pete. That's why

I've brought you along the way I have. That's why one of these days you're going to wind up being a partner with me. The time will come."

"Mr. Vogel, there's something I wanted to talk to you about."

"What I like about you is, you give me ideas," Matt Vogel said. "That flume, now. That means a lot to old man Cartwright. He's got a lot of money tied up in that crazy trough. To me it don't amount to nothing."

"Mr. Vogel, I——"

"You know anything about powder, boy?"

Again Pete was caught flat-footed. "I worked in the mines for a while," he said. "I've blown up stumps on my wife's place."

"I want you to blow up that flume of Cartwright's," Matt Vogel said.

And there it was again—flat, head on, unexpected. Pete Wilson took a deep breath. "No," he said.

"Why?" Vogel said. "Because it's the Cartwrights?"

"If you want that for an excuse, it will do," Pete said.

Matt Vogel sat back and stared intently at the youth across the table from him. "Well I'll be damned," Matt Vogel said. "I had you wrong. Right from the first I had you wrong. I thought that wife of yours meant a whole lot to you."

Pete Wilson's head snapped up. "What do you mean by that?"

Vogel shook his head. "So I'm wrong again. I just figured you knew. Figured that's why you beat up on her."

"What am I supposed to know?"

"That she's moved in with Joe Cartwright."

Pete Wilson was on his feet with the swiftness of a cat. He reached across the table and gripped the front of Matt Vogel's shirt. "You're a liar," he said.

"Am I?" Matt Vogel said with exasperating calmness. "You weren't out of the house five minutes, I bet, before she went running over to the Ponderosa. She and your friend Little Joe looked right cozy last time I saw them."

Pete Wilson's grasp on Vogel's shirt relaxed. He sat down slowly. "I don't believe you," he said, and even while he said it he knew he did believe Vogel. So now Joe knew and all the Cartwrights knew. The surge of resentment that rose in him was terrifying and savage. Everything that had gone wrong was because of the Cartwrights, and now they were paying him the final indignity. They were prying into his innermost secrets. They knew he had beaten his wife.

Pete Wilson's voice was shaking when he said, "You tell me what you want me to do, Mr. Vogel."

* * *

The terminus of the flume was only a little more than a mile away from its ultimate goal—a huge pond at one of the largest sawmills in the Carson Valley. Here, rough cut timbers and even logs, flumed down from Ben Cartwright's mill at the upper end of the flume, could be converted into finished lumber or hauled on up to the Virginia City mines. Most of the big mines had lumber mills of their own and finished and fitted the heavier timbers right on the premises.

Hoss Cartwright wiped the perspiration from his forehead. "Jim Willy," he said, "how come I got to work down here in the lower end of this canyon where there's nothing but rocks and heat and you get to loaf around up there at the sawmill where it's nice and cool."

"For two reasons," Jim Willy said. "Because I'm handsome and intelligent."

"And dog goned modest, too," Hoss said.

"Not really," Jim Willy said. "Just terribly honest with myself."

Hoss shook his head. "I'm telling you, an awful lot of my little brother rubbed off on you while you were growing up," he said.

Jim Willy grinned as he looked across to where the crew Jim Fair had sent from the mine was working on the low trestling that would level the flume out for its final stage to the mill pond. He turned to Hoss and said, "You got some mighty good boys there, Hoss."

"Yeah, they really are," Hoss said. "Takes a certain knack to timber a mine, I reckon, and it seems to have something in common with building a flume."

"When you figure they'll finish up?" Jim Willy asked.

Hoss grinned. "What's the matter? Getting anxious to turn a head of water into this trough?"

"I sure am," Jim Willy said. "Your dad put a lot of thinking and a lot of work into this. It's just got to pay off for him."

Hoss's voice was soft. "You think a lot of Pa, don't you?"

"About as much as you do, Hoss," Jim Willy said. "You stop to think of it, he's the only Pa I ever had." He moved away from the unaccustomed sentiment quickly and gave Hoss a short jab in the ribs with his fist. "Maybe you can stand around here twiddling your thumbs," he said. "Me, I got work to do. I'm going back up to the sawmill."

"Don't back into one of those saws," Hoss said. "Those things cost a lot of money."

"I'll try to remember," Jim Willy said.

He went across and mounted his horse and started riding up the canyon, following the rough construction road that paralleled the flume for a great part of its distance.

Hoss looked after him with real affection. Jim Willy was one in a million.

*　　*　　*

Pete Wilson took his time about picking a place to set the explosive. He had started at the upper end of the flume, keeping out of sight of the crew of Indians who

223

were working at the sawmill near that location. From there, he had worked his way down the canyon.

There was one good spot where the flume clung to the face of a cliff, but it was difficult to climb up there and it would be dangerous getting down in time to avoid the rock slide the charge was bound to cause.

He went around this rocky gorge, up onto the crest of a hill, and from here he could look down and see the V of new lumber with the catwalk along one side, stretching away down the steep canyon.

He felt a resentment that someone like Adam Cartwright could sit down with pencil and paper and envision a thing like this and lay out plans that would bring it to reality. In that moment, the flume became almost a personal enemy.

Pete rode down the slope of the hill, and there, where the flume crossed a deep gorge, he found the spot he was seeking. He dismounted and took the bundle of blasting powder and the coil of fuse from his saddle bag and moved across into the towering trestle work and the shadow of the flume itself.

The timbering rose almost sixty feet at this spot, and the charge, properly placed, should break the back of the flume itself and bring tons of lumber crashing down. It would take weeks to repair it, and that, Pete knew, was Matt Vogel's object. The more Ponderosa people he could tie up here and elsewhere, the fewer he would have to deal with up on the shore of the Lake.

Pete led his horse some distance back and tied him behind a rock, then, moving carefully, he climbed to where he could see the construction road that passed directly under the flume at this point. There was no one in sight.

He took the blasting powder and the fuse and went back to the trestle and started laying the charge. He was a mile or more up-canyon from the construction camp at the terminus of the flume, he knew, so it wasn't likely he would be discovered. He worked rapidly, and in spite of the devastation he was about to cause, he excused himself with the certain knowledge that he was not harming anyone physically.

Again he was thinking of Ellen, and he remembered how he had told her over and over that he had no intention of killing anyone. He packed a gun and practiced with a gun so that people would respect him and not try to start anything with him. "I am not a killer," he told her, over and over. And now as he planted the blasting charge he heard her answer, ringing in his ears. "But you will be," she said. "You will be."

Pete Wilson made one final adjustment, then struck a match and put it to the fuse. The fuse sputtered, and the thin, tar-flavored smoke curled upward. Pete ran back to his vantage point where he had left his horse behind the rock. From here he could see the construction road and suddenly his heart started pounding and his voice stuck in his throat. Jim Willy was riding up the road, directly toward the flume and that charge of blasting powder.

Precious seconds ticked by as Pete tried to figure what to do. He had known Jim Willy most of his life—known him as well as he had known Little Joe. But unlike Little Joe, Jim Willy had come from a poor beginning—even poorer than Pete Wilson himself. If there was one person on earth toward whom Pete Wilson felt no animosity whatsoever, that person was Jim Willy, the Paiute.

Pete scrambled to his feet and started waving his arms and shouting. "Jim! Go back, Jim! Go back!"

He saw Jim Willy looking around, trying to find out where the voice was coming from, and he came riding on until now he was just ready to cross under the flume.

"Jim!" Pete yelled. "Please, Jim!"

His voice did not make a feeble dent in the sound of

the shattering blast that reverberated through the canyon. Timbers flew through the air like match sticks. The trough of the flume raised up, and then it broke apart. Pieces of it came crashing down. Pete Wilson pressed his face against the rock while timbers and splintered debris rattled down like buckshot on a tin roof. In time there was silence except for the rebounding echoes of the blast racketing down the rocky canyon to dissipate finally in the air of the flat plains below.

Pete ran stumbling down the slope. One look was enough to tell him the horse was dead. Jim Willy was a short distance away. He was on his knees, his hands clutching his stomach, and he looked up as Pete approached him.

Pete dropped down in front of him. "Jim, I didn't mean it," Pete said. His voice was almost a sob. "So help me God, I didn't mean it. All I wanted to do was blow up the flume."

There was blood at the corner of Jim Willy's mouth. He nodded his head that he understood.

Pete got to his feet suddenly. From down the canyon came the sound of shouts and the pound of horses' hooves. Pete looked around wildly. "Jim, you'll be all right," he said. "I got to get out of here." He went running up slope, stumbling, falling.

Jim Willy thought of Hoss and Joe and Ben. I'm letting them down, he thought. I promised I'd run that mill for them . . . the world was a black, spinning ball, and there was no conception of time and the feeling was leaving his arms. He closed his eyes tightly and when he opened them, the familiar face of Hoss was there, only inches away, and Jim Willy was stretched out on a blanket.

"Pete Wilson," Jim Willy said. "That crazy darned Pete Wilson. He was blowing up the flume. He didn't mean to hurt me, Hoss. He didn't mean it at all."

"You're gonna be fine, Jim," Hoss said. "You're gonna be just fine."

Jim Willy managed a grin. "White man speak with forked tongue," he said.

He died in Hoss Cartwright's arms.

26 STANDING THERE by the side of the grave, each one remembered Jim Willy in a different way as Ben Cartwright closed his Bible.

Ben thought of the winter of the great freeze and of the hovels near the south end of Pyramid Lake where he had gone to try to find someone who would claim the half-dead infant he carried in his arms. He remembered the hatred in the eyes of the Indians as they stared at him and refused to understand, and the howling wind plucked at the water of the inland sea and sucked it up from the surface to toss it into the air in demon shapes of spume and foam. A few years later, Ben Cartwright was one of the hundred and five volunteers who rode with Major Ormsby against Jim Willy's people. Seventy-six of his friends had died that day, and for a long time there were many who cursed the Cartwrights for harboring a savage. It had only strengthened Ben's love for the foundling who had become almost a son.

Hoss thought of the comradeship and of the way he had teased Jim Willy about being an Indian and of the way Jim Willy had always given better than he took. They understood each other so well that the apparent insults between them were actually their way of telling their mutual respect for each other. Jim Willy had adapted completely to a way of life totally different from the one into which he was born. He had never lost the dignity of his heritage.

Joe raised his eyes and looked across at Ellen and he felt an old pain. He remembered the time he was going to take Ellen to a very special dance. He was excited about it and he had talked about it constantly with Jim Willy and then in a burst of enthusiasm he had offered to get a date for Jim Willy and they would make it a foursome. He would never forget that patient smile as Jim Willy said, "I don't think so, Joe." Joe had completely forgotten that there were people who thought an Indian was different. He had completely forgotten that Jim Willy was an Indian.

José Bettencort had taught Jim Willy to ride. Old Kirk had told him of the shining mountains to the east where the beaver ran free and the smoke of a man's fire was blue against the gold of the turning aspen. He had told Jim Willy of the other Indians there and of an Indian girl old Kirk had loved.

Ben Cartwright finished his silent prayer. Jim Willy wouldn't want this prolonged. They turned then and walked off toward the house and they took with them the memory of a friend.

* * *

The boss of the crew who had been working on the flume was an honest and reasonable man. He stood there in the Ponderosa living room, facing Ben, Hoss and Little Joe. He said, "Mr. Cartwright, there ain't a thing in the world we got against you, but Mr. Fair told us we were coming up here to build a flume. He didn't say we were coming up here to get a charge of dynamite set off in our face. Mr. Cartwright, I got a wife and five kids and most of the rest of the boys are family people. We

228

ain't cowards. We just don't see that any part of this is our affair."

Ben Cartwright looked at the man and nodded his head. "I don't blame you," he said, "and I have no right to make any extra demands. Tell your crew they'll be paid for a full day today."

"Thank you, Mr. Cartwright," the man said. "It ain't that we're cowards, you know."

"No explanation necessary, sir," Ben Cartwright said.

The man turned and left the room and Ben, Joe and Hoss were alone.

"That about does it, don't it?" Hoss said.

"What about Jim Willy's crew at the mill?" Ben asked. "Can we depend on them at all?"

"I think so," Hoss said. "Some of them, anyway." He glanced at the clock on the wall. "Why don't we wait until Pio and Jack Catfish get here?"

Hop Sing came in and said, "You drink so much coffee you don't sleep."

"I don't think we're going to sleep much anyway," Ben said.

Hop Sing started to leave then stopped and said, "Hop Sing hear man say everybody quit work. How you fix flume you no have men to work?"

"That's a good question, Hop Sing," Ben said. "If you find the answer, let me know, will you?"

Hop Sing gave a grunt and went into the kitchen.

*　　*　　*

The fluming crew had long ago gone back to Virginia City. Hoss and Little Joe sat facing Jim Willy's cousin, who had been second in command at the sawmill, and a young vaquero named Pio Gomez, who was José Bettencort's right-hand man. Ben stood by the fireplace, one arm on the mantle.

"You mean you don't know what happened or when it happened?" Ben asked the young Indian.

229

"Big saw he no go no more," the Paiute said.

Ben looked at Hoss and Little Joe. "If it was just an ordinary mechanical failure, Jack Catfish here would have fixed it," Joe said.

Pio Gomez said, "You know me, Señor Cartwright. I have been with this cows too many years. They do not run for nothing. Somebody scared them."

"A deliberate stampede, huh, Pio?" Hoss asked.

"Si, Señor Hoss," Pio said. "If José had been there, he would tell you the same thing."

"So he's decided to hit from every side," Ben said quietly.

"You figure it's all Matt Vogel?" Hoss asked.

"He's the only one who could gain a direct advantage from all this," Ben said.

"How about Sharon?" Joe asked.

Ben shook his head. "No. Not by the furthest stretch of the imagination. William Sharon is one of the shrewdest and toughest business men I've ever known, but he doesn't hire gun crews and he doesn't wreck sawmills and he doesn't stampede cattle."

Pio Gomez shifted uneasily in his chair. "Señor," he said, "I think maybe I ought to go back down to the cow camp to make sure everything is all right."

"Of course, Pio," Ben said. "And thanks for coming by." He shook hands with the wiry little vaquero and Jim Willy's cousin stood up too.

"You need us, you say so," Jack Catfish said.

"You just try to get that sawmill working," Ben said.

The Indian drew himself erect. "I get sawmill working," he said, "but Jim Willy was my blood. If you do not want us to fight by your side, we will fight alone."

The Indian turned abruptly and stalked out of the room. Pio Gomez waited just one second. He shrugged his shoulders and said, "Jim Willy was my good amigo, too." He didn't have to say anything more.

The three Cartwrights watched him go, then moved across to the sofa in front of the fireplace. They sat there silently for a long time, staring into the embers, and then, without looking up, Hoss said, "Well, Pa, you might as well say it."

Ben said, "I just didn't want to involve everybody on the ranch."

"Matt Vogel's got a hundred men," Joe said. "The three of us can't face them alone."

"Especially not if they keep hitting us from a different angle every time," Hoss said.

"The cattle and the sawmill are a cover-up," Ben said. "The timber is the only thing that's important to him."

"What do you figure our best move is?" Joe asked.

"Hit him head on," Ben said.

They stopped talking suddenly as Ellen came down the staircase. She was wearing a robe and her hair was brushed back and most of the bruises were gone. She said, "I want to talk to you."

"Come over here and sit by us," Ben said softly.

Ellen said, "Hoss, you were there. I've waited for you to tell me and you haven't. I have to know."

Hoss said, "Ellen, why don't you just put all this trouble out of your mind?"

Joe stood up and the muscles were tight along his jaws. He said, "Tell her, Hoss."

"Yes, Hoss," Ellen said. "Tell me. Pete was there, wasn't he?"

Hoss had never felt so miserable in his life. He looked at his younger brother and he looked at his father and then he looked into the coals of the fire. He didn't want to do it, but he knew she had a right to hear the truth.

"Yes, Ellen," he said, nodding his head. "Pete was there. It was him who blew up the flume."

Joe heard her catch her breath and he almost felt the pain that stabbed through her. He wanted to go to her and put his arms around her and try to help her, but he knew he shouldn't.

Hop Sing came in and set a glass of hot milk on the coffee table. "You drink that, Miss Ellen," he said. He looked from one to the other, sensing the tension.

He went padding off to the kitchen. Some way he would help. He didn't know how it would be, but he would find a way.

*   *   *

The horses were saddled. There were rifles in the scabbards and the three Cartwrights wore holstered guns. Hop Sing came out packing a flour sack of provisions in either hand and he handed them to Joe who tied them behind his saddle.

The man who called himself Stevens leaned against the barn wall and scraped the backs of his fingernails with a knife blade. He had seen things like this shape up before. A member of the family had been killed. Someone would have to pay. He saw José Bettencort and old Kirk come walking out of the bunkhouse and they, too, wore guns. He saw them walk over to the Cartwrights and he knew Ben was telling them they did not have to go.

The man called Stevens snapped shut the knife. He adjusted his gun belt and sauntered across to join the others.

Joe looked at Stevens and said quietly, "You hired on for a cowhand's wages and you more than earn them. We don't expect more."

Stevens looked at Joe and said, "Where I come from, if you ride for a brand, you fight for it. I'll get my horse."

He moved off before anyone could answer.

It was six o'clock in the morning and the sun was hitting the highest peaks. Ben, Hoss and Little Joe swung

232

into their saddles and José, Kirk and Stevens rode up alongside them.

"We're supposed to swing by the mill," Kirk said. "Jack Catfish said him and four of his boys are going along."

"You know my cousin?" José said. "He's got five nephews. They gonna join up with us."

Kirk said, "We gonna set here all day?"

Ben Cartwright didn't try to answer. His voice would have sounded odd around the lump in his throat.

They rode, and when they stopped at the mill Sheriff Roy Coffee was there. Ben looked at the Sheriff and said, "Don't try to stop us, Roy. You got no authority here. It's not even your county."

"Well now, who was fixin' to stop you?" Sheriff Coffee said. He reached down and unpinned the badge from his shirt pocket. He tossed it in his hand, then reached back and dropped it into his saddle bag. "I'm way past due for a vacation," he said. "I figured I'd take it now. No fun spending it alone, so I guess I'll ride along with you."

27 PETE WILSON had to grip one hand with the other to keep from shaking. He had waited two days for Matt Vogel and now he saw Vogel standing there in front of him, and yet it was as if the man had never existed and he was standing in front of a stranger. "I blew it up," Pete said. "Just like I said I would. It was like it went into a thousand pieces. I don't know how they'll ever fix it. I don't think they ever will."

"That's good," Matt Vogel said. "We've laid up their sawmill and stampeded some of their cows." He was staring intently at Pete, almost as if trying to look a hole through him.

Pete Wilson started to break. "I killed Jim Willy," he said. "I didn't have nothing against him. How did I know he was going to ride up there?"

"What are you worrying about?" Vogel said quietly. "He was just an Injun."

"It wasn't my fault," Pete said. "I didn't have nothing against Jim Willy. He was the only one of that whole Cartwright outfit that was any good."

"You figure there was enough of a disturbance there to keep their mind off of what we're doing here?" he asked.

"I guess so," Pete said. "It will take a long time to fix that flume." He looked at Matt then and his voice sounded like the voice of a little boy. "They can't fix Jim Willy. He's dead."

Matt reached out and put a hand on Pete's shoulder. "I wouldn't worry about it, son," he said. "When you're in big business, there's some things can't be helped. You're gonna go a long ways with me, boy. Don't you forget that."

"I'm gonna quit," Pete said.

"What do you mean, quit?"

"Like I said. You've treated me good. I tried to do my job."

"You've done more than your job."

"Maybe I ought to quit."

"I've tried to be more than a boss to you," Matt said. "I've tried to be almost like a father."

"I appreciate that."

"If I didn't feel the way I do, I wouldn't even mention your wife. I figure that's your affair."

234

"I don't see where she's got anything to do with it."

"No, I don't suppose you do," Matt said. "But she does. She's got a lot to do with it." He looked off to where Neil Larson was giving orders to a bunch of teamsters who were moving their animals off down the slope. He didn't look at Pete as he said, "A man's married to a woman, loves her, promises her everything in the world, tries to do everything he can for her, then she runs off with another man."

Pete Wilson's teeth were clenched. "My wife didn't run off with anybody," he said.

Matt Vogel shrugged. "Don't guess it makes much difference one way or the other. If she run off with Cartwright or he run off with her." He clapped Pete on the shoulder. "Like I say, I'm awful fond of you, boy. I wouldn't hold you to nothing. You make up your own mind." He turned to face Neil Larson who had moved across to join them.

They were high on the shoulder of a hill and they could look down and see the blue wealth of Tahoe shimmering there below them. There was a promontory that extended out into the lake and the trees there grew taller and more majestic than anywhere else.

"I'd say that's the place to start," Matt Vogel said.

"Yeah," Neil Larson said. "Looks good to me."

Pete Wilson stood there, following their gaze, and he said, "That's where Joe's mother is buried."

Matt Vogel turned slowly. "Something wrong with that, boy?" he said.

Pete Wilson thought of Ellen and he thought of Joe and he thought of Ellen sitting in that big living room at the Ponderosa, telling of the way he had beaten her. He thought of her sitting there, liking it, knowing it was more than her own husband could ever give her, and he thought of the smugness of the faces of the Cartwrights.

"No, there's nothing wrong with that," he said.

*　　*　　*

235

Ben, Hoss and Little Joe rode side by side as they came across the shoulder of Mt. Rose and looked down through the trees to the whispering glimpse of Lake Tahoe. The wind was quiet up here, but it made itself felt, and they shrugged deeper into their coats.

Ben turned in his saddle and saw José Bettencort and the man called Stevens. Little Kirk was hunched down in his saddle, but he was there, and in his smallness he was somehow more powerful than the others. Behind Little Joe was Jim Willy's cousin and four of his relatives, stolid, expressionless, and for the first time since Ben had known them he thought of them as Indians— implacable and relentless. Ben glanced across at Roy Coffee, sitting there, squinting into the distance, and he saw Pio Gomez and his nephews. Seventeen men against a possible army. Ben didn't consider the odds.

"Pa," Joe said quietly.

Ben looked at his youngest son. He saw Joe looking off into the distance, and he knew without following Joe's gaze what Joe was seeing. They had been here together, many times.

"Yes?" Ben said.

Joe hadn't shifted his gaze. "There at the far end," he said. "Where the big grove starts."

"I see it," Hoss said.

"I promised your mother nobody would ever touch a tree there," Ben said softly. "Not one tree. It was her grove when she was alive. It's still her grove."

Ben Cartwright turned slowly in his saddle and looked at all the others. "I told you before, you can turn back any time you want."

He touched the flanks of the big buckskin and rode down the slope, his sons on either side of him. He didn't look around. He didn't need to. The others were right behind him.

Ben glanced across at Hoss and saw the set of the big man's jaws. It was not the mother of Hoss whose grave was being desecrated down there, but it made no difference. It was an indignity to the memory of someone all of them had loved.

The Cartwrights and their followers rode down on the newly established logging camp at the edge of the lake.

28 NEIL LARSON, the woods boss, worked with the destructive intensity of a man fired by revenge. He had never forgotten the beating Ben Cartwright had given him, and the fact that he had half killed Ben Cartwright's youngest son had not been satisfaction enough. Neil Larson prided himself on the fact that never in his life had he been whipped, and he did not consider himself whipped now.

He watched his crew slash into the giant sugar pine and ponderosa and every bite of the axe was as satisfying as if it had been biting into the flesh of Ben Cartwright.

He moved across to where Matt Vogel was standing with Pete Wilson. "Now this is what I call loggin'," Larson said.

The timber-rending crash of a falling pine was like a punctuation mark to his statement.

"How long will it take you to clear out this stand?" Vogel asked.

"You keep Cartwright and his crew off of my back for a week and there'll be nothing left here but stumps," Larson said.

There was a cracking and snapping of wood fibers, a

cracking and groaning as the life cords of a living tree were wrenched from the stump that had wedded itself to the earth. There was a sighing moan, as if from a wind of despair, and then a tearing of branches and a crescendo of sound ending in a broken, terminal shudder as a ton of lumber hit the unyielding earth.

"Dropping one every three minutes," Larson said proudly. "You done anything about getting a road across the Ponderosa?"

"I'll do it," Matt Vogel said.

"You'll never get a road across the Ponderosa without killing the Cartwrights themselves," Pete Wilson said.

"So?" Matt Vogel said.

He moved off, leaving Pete standing there.

*　　*　　*

Ben and the two boys rode side by side. The thundering crash of falling trees seemed everywhere, and the ringing bite of the axes chimed incessantly. The three men did not look at each other. They were not even aware of the small army at their back. At this particular moment, they knew no formal law. They knew only that the sanctity of their belief was being violated. They rode into a clearing and at a signal from Ben, they reined up.

"The land runs right out into the lake," Ben said. "If we move in on this end of it, they either have to come straight at us or back off into the water."

There was not one other word spoken. The men started separating, and they all started riding toward the now almost deafening sound of the logging operation.

Neil Larson was the first to realize that something might be wrong. Trees were falling, trimmers were slashing away at the branches, saws were starting to twang and teamsters were moving in to snake out the cut logs. All of his operation was right, but an old instinct—or perhaps an old habit from the days when he had been a gypo timber rustler—alerted his senses. He moved away from the major logging operation and climbed up on a stump. He saw only the movement of a horse, but that was enough.

Neil Larson was an opportunist. If you could do something on your own without calling for help, it could only be a feather in your cap. He went back to where he had left his mackinaw and he picked up a rifle that was there. It was not an unfamiliar weapon, for he did a lot of deer hunting, and this particular gun, cut down to carbine length in the Western style, was a special pride of his. He levered a shell into the chamber and moved back out into the choke of undergrowth.

He paused from time to time, and now there was no doubt about it. There were horsemen moving in through the trees, secure in the knowledge that the logging operation would cover any noise they might make. Neil Larson felt his heart beating against his rib cage. Deer hunting was one of his favorite pastimes. He had never before stalked a man.

He threw himself flat on the ground as he heard a horse approaching, and now, so intent was he on his quarry he could shut out the sound of saws and axes and falling trees and hear only the sounds he desired to hear. The horse went by, and Neil Larson came half erect. Crouching, he moved on through the underbrush.

He stopped suddenly, and there ahead of him was a buckskin horse and a big man whose white hair showed from under the sweeping brim of his hat. Neil Larson started to chuckle silently. He had never lost a fight in his life.

Slowly, he raised the rifle to his shoulder, and then gave way to one moment of conceit. He stepped out into the open and he said, "You should of tromped me when you had a chance, Cartwright." He squeezed the trigger and saw Ben Cartwright fall from the saddle.

He heard the explosion of his own rifle—or he thought that's what it was. It was a tearing, smashing thing that

239

slapped against his brain and pounded at him like a sledge hammer. The world was suddenly curtained by a mass of red blood, and then blackness.

Ben Cartwright picked himself up from the ground. The smoking six-shooter was still in his hand. He had thrown himself from the saddle, rolled and fired, all in one movement.

He looked down at the body of Neil Larson, and that was all the time he had, for the two shots, blending into one, had acted as a signal, and now guns were blazing on every side of him.

This was the way it must be in war, Ben Cartwright thought. There was nothing personal about anything. There were people shooting at you and you shot back. He saw a man he had never seen before in his life go spinning backwards, crashing into a tree and falling grotesquely on the ground, and Ben knew he had killed that man and he didn't even stop to reason why.

He heard someone scream, loud and wild, as a child might scream, and then someone else was shouting, "No, stop it! Don't! I don't have a gun! Stop it!"

The only point of realism was Matt Vogel's voice, high-pitched and near panic, shouting out, "Move in on 'em! What the hell you think I been paying you for?"

And again Ben heard that voice crying, "Stop it, stop it please! We don't have guns!" He saw thirty or forty men then, milling around crazily, like panicked cattle. They had their hands in the air and one man he saw was sobbing like a baby.

Ben called, "Hoss! Joe! Hold up!"

He found himself in the middle of a sudden dead silence.

There was a total lack of reality to the scene as Ben dismounted. Four men he had never known were dead on the ground, and now he never would know them. Another man he didn't know stood before him. He was shaking all over and his teeth were chattering.

"I'm just a logger, Mister," he said. "That's all I am. I work where my boss tells me to work. I don't ask for trouble and I don't want none. I don't know what this is all about, Mister, I just don't know what it's all about."

"All right," Ben Cartwright said.

Another man said, "That fellow over there on the ground. He had the bunk next to mine. He read books all the time. He never meant to hurt nobody. You couldn't even pick a fight with him. I tried it once and he just laughed at me and that's how we got to be friends. I don't see why he had to get killed."

Ben felt sick to his stomach. He, too, wondered why these men had needed to be killed, and immediately he was thinking of Matt Vogel. He said, "You men get your gear and move on back to where you were working last week. You're on private land here, and that's what this is all about."

"We didn't know it," somebody said. "We just didn't know it at all. We'll move back. We rightly will."

Ben turned, and as he did, a rifle cracked and a bullet buried itself in a tree trunk inches from his face. He threw himself to the ground and saw the loggers scatter and he put them out of his mind. There was an angry exchange of shots from someplace beyond his vision. And then there was quiet again, and across a small, logged off clearing, he saw Hoss and Joe and Roy Coffee, on foot now, herding six men in front of them. The six had their hands in the air, and now the rest of the Ponderosa crew was gathering. As the prisoners approached, Ben recognized every one of them as notorious gunfighters from Virginia City. Looking at them now, it was hard to understand how they ever earned their reputations as "chiefs."

Roy Coffee ordered them to halt about ten feet away from Ben. He searched them, quickly and professionally, and he threw away guns and knives; then while Hoss and Little Joe guarded them, Roy looked them over.

"I don't see a dog gone one of you here that I don't want for something or other," the Sheriff said, scratching his chin. He screwed up one eye. "Of course, you got me at a disadvantage," he said. "This county ain't really in my jurisdiction and I'm sort of on a vacation, as the feller says. But you were shooting at me, and that's a pretty serious crime." He stopped and seemed to puzzle about what he should do. "I could shoot you," he said, "and I could turn you loose, but that wouldn't be much of a favor, because if I was to ever see any of you in Virginia City again I'd jug you and make sure the Vigilantes knew where you was." He jerked a thumb across his shoulder. "I'm gonna give you a chance," he said. "California's that way. But I wouldn't stop there. I got friends there and I aim to send word ahead."

The disarmed men moved off silently.

"You're letting them go?" Joe asked, incredulous.

"Rather turn 'em loose my way than let a judge turn 'em loose his way," Roy said.

"Anybody see Vogel?" Ben asked.

"He lit out right after the shooting started," Hoss said. "Couple of Catfish's boys have got Pete cornered back there in the timber. If it's all right with you, I'd like to try to talk him out."

"Let me," Joe said.

Hoss shook his head. "No, Joe. And you know why."

"He's right, son," Ben said quietly. "Go ahead, Hoss."

Hoss moved off. He was out of sight, but they could hear his voice.

"Pete? Pete, it's me. Come on out. It's all over."

They heard Pete Wilson's voice.

"Where's Ellen?" Pete asked.

"At our house, Pete. You come on out and . . ."

The sentence was cut in two by a rifle shot. The men heard a thunder of hoofbeats and they all ran forward.

They found Hoss Cartwright lying there on the ground. There was a bullet hole in his chest.

29 BEN AND LITTLE JOE sat in a cheerless corridor of the Sisters of Mercy Hospital in Virginia City. They had done everything that could be done. They had staunched the flow of blood as best they could and they had brought Hoss here for the most expert help available. They had talked to the doctor—an old, old friend of the family—and they had received a noncommittal shrug.

"We're doing what we can," the doctor said.

"We got to do more," Ben said.

The doctor turned as a nun came down the corridor. He put a hand on Ben's shoulder. "That's being done too," he said.

"Hoss wanted to help Pete," Joe said, a note of desperation in his voice. "When he walked out there, when he wouldn't let me go, he was thinking he could help Pete. Hoss never had another thought in his mind."

"I know, son," Ben said. "I know."

"Don't tell me to hold back any more, Pa," Joe said. "Don't tell me, because I won't do it. He beat Ellen and he killed Jim Willy and now he's shot Hoss . . ."

"I blame myself, Joseph," Ben said, his voice barely audible. "Perhaps if I had gone another way. If I hadn't put so much stress on preserving the Ponderosa the way I, myself, believed it should be."

Joe looked at his father in amazement. "Do you think I ever thought of it that way? Do you think Hoss did?"

"Is the Ponderosa worth one drop of your brother's blood or of yours or of Jim Willy's?"

Joe forced his father to meet his gaze. "Do you really doubt it, Pa?" he asked.

One of the sisters came out of Hoss's room and Ben and Joe were immediately on their feet. The nun smiled and said, "I wish I had news for you. I don't. I love him too, you know."

"Thank you, Sister," Ben said.

She said, "I don't know what I would do if it was my son or my brother in there." She pursed her lips and gave it some thought, then nodding her head she said, "If I was a man, I'd probably go have a drink." She went on down the hall.

* * *

Matt Vogel's hands trembled as he read the copy of the *Territorial Enterprise*. He couldn't believe it, but there it was, under Dan de Quille's by-line. William Sharon and the Bank of California group were going to build a railroad from Carson City to Virginia City, and they were proposing a spur that would run up to the new station of Reno on the Central Pacific line. Later, they claimed, they would extend another spur south into the rich farm land around the town of Minden.

According to Sharon's statement, he had already hired the best surveyor on the Comstock—Superintendent James of the Sierra Nevada Company. In the short span of one month, during which time Vogel had been out of touch with Sharon, the Virginia Truckee Railroad had been laid out. Sharon had bought out previous grants; he had ordered rails from England and he had obtained a new charter from the Legislature.

The figures swam in front of Vogel's eyes. Legislative authority for the issuance of $500,000 in bonds by the counties of Storey and Ormsby had been secured by

244

Sharon as a free gift to the railroad. The mining companies, thinking of business rather than their personal feelings toward the Bank, had subscribed another $700,000. An original work crew of seven hundred and fifty men had already grown to one thousand two hundred, working out of thirty-eight camps between Carson and Virginia City.

Matt Vogel's eyes remained fixed on that last paragraph of Dan de Quille's:

As magnificent as this project is, one cannot help but feel a sadness as he realizes he will soon see the passing of the teams and the big freight outfits that have so long been a part of our lives. Team bells will give way to the clang of the locomotive bells; the picturesque speech of the teamsters will be drowned forever by the hiss of steam and the clatter of steel wheels against steel rails. A part of our past is being lost as Virginia City and the surrounding mines and mills rush on to an even more glorious future.

Matt Vogel let the paper fall from his fingers. He had gone to the office of the Bank at C and Taylor—the Bank of which he had, for a brief moment, it seemed now, been a part. William Sharon was not in, he was told curtly, and then and there he faced the realization that he had never been a part of this at all. The Bank was a separate, impersonal institution. It wasn't teams and wagons and a man's life and blood and sweat. It was like a kite, and William Sharon was one man clinging to a long, long string. It was a powerful kite that tugged and pulled, and behind William Sharon were other men, and finally, at the end of it all, was William Ralston, digging his heels in and holding them all. Matt Vogel had never even had the slightest grasp on that string, he realized now.

245

He hadn't had a drop to drink, but he was reeling when he left the Sazerac. He was broke, alone, and he had failed, and he had no idea in the world how he was going to face up to it. He thought of Ben Cartwright and a rage started growing in him, choking him with its intensity. He went lurching blindly down the street and Pete Wilson's voice said, "Matt?"

Matt Vogel stopped. It was the first time the kid had ever called him by his first name, but he had never heard such a welcome sound in his life. He put his arm around Pete's shoulder and held him close.

"Don't you worry, kid," Matt said. "We're gonna make it big, you and me. I promised it to you, didn't I?"

"Sure, Matt," Pete said. "I just don't know how to think . . . Maybe if Ellen and me went away."

"Yeah, I been thinking about that," Matt said. "The three of us. All this talk about the railroad. That's crazy. They'll never do it. It will break this country. But this ain't the only place in the world, boy," Matt said.

"I think maybe I'd like to strike out on my own," Pete said.

"That's what I was saying," Vogel said. "You and me. You want a drink?"

"Yeah," Pete Wilson said. "I guess I do."

They walked down the street then and they went into the Bucket of Blood Saloon. Don McBride looked up and saw them enter and he stopped in the midst of mopping the bar.

"Whiskey," Vogel said.

Don McBride's hand trembled slightly as he shoved out a bottle. People had started drifting out of the saloon. McBride moved away as Vogel poured for himself and Pete, and it wasn't until then that Vogel realized he and Pete were alone at the bar. He half turned and he saw Ben and Little Joe, sitting at a table near the window that looked out over the lower part of the town.

Matt Vogel sighed deeply. He didn't think the Cartwrights had even noticed him yet, but he figured he might as well get it over with. "Hello, Cartwright," he said.

Ben and Little Joe turned quickly, then slowly stood up.

Matt Vogel's lips didn't move as he said to Pete, "Stay with me, boy. We're gonna make it yet." His hand was completely steady now as he lifted his drink.

Pete tried to lift his glass, but he spilled the liquor. He looked at Joe and said, "It doesn't have to be this way."

Joe said, "You know better, Pete."

Matt Vogel had the shot glass half way to his lips. He reached out suddenly with his left hand, grabbed the bottle and sent it crashing through the window, inches from Ben's head. As Ben ducked, Vogel's right hand went into his coat pocket, and without ever revealing his gun he twisted his coat and fired through the fabric.

Ben had seen the move. He whipped his gun from its holster and fired twice and now Pete Wilson was crouched against the bar, his lips pulled back tight against his teeth, and he was firing and firing and firing until finally his gun was empty. He fell forward on his face, and Little Joe stood there looking down at him and there were tears running down Joe's cheeks.

Pete Wilson had fired six shots into a blank wall. He had fired them after he was dead.

Ben put an arm around Joe's shoulder. They sat down at a table, neither of them able to say a word. Don McBride brought a bottle and two glasses across to them. They were sitting there like that when Sheriff Roy Coffee and Dan de Quille came running in.

30 "Hoss looks good, Joe," Ellen Wilson said.

"The big moose," Joe said.

They had just come from Hoss's room and were standing in the corridor of the hospital. The nun who had been with them said, "He asked for a glass of buttermilk, a steak and a beer for breakfast."

"That's my brother," Joe said.

He and Ellen moved on down the hall and out onto a porch where they could look over the sprawling, teeming mass that was Virginia City. There was a hurt and a pain between them, and they both felt it, and finally Joe said, "Ellen, I don't even have a right to ask this, I guess, but I don't want you to hate me."

"I don't want to hate you," she said. "In time I won't. But I loved him, Joe. In spite of everything."

He took both her hands and turned her to where he could meet her eyes. "Don't think about it now," he said. "But when you get back to St. Louis and you're living with your aunt, if you ever want to write to anybody and say things that maybe you couldn't say to anyone else . . ."

"Thank you, Joe," she said. "I'll remember."

She moved off then, and he let her go, not even offering to walk with her to the stagecoach that would take her to Sacramento, the first leg of her journey to the East. He stood there on the porch and saw her come out of the hospital entrance and onto the street. He watched her walk up into the heart of town. Her figure became smaller and smaller, and he knew she was going out of his life.

Visiting hours were over, but he turned and went back into the room where his brother was stretched out on the bed. He sat down and managed a grin, and he said, "Hello, Big Ugly. How much longer you gonna loaf here?"

Hoss grinned back and said, "Don't push me, Little Brother, or I'll get out of here and whup you good."

*　　*　　*

It was a rare occasion when there were women in the Washoe Club, but this was a rare occasion. Mrs. James G. Fair and Beth Kelly were taking full advantage of their position.

Ben Cartwright was not self-conscious about it, but he was completely aware that he cut quite a figure in his ruffled-front shirt, the black string tie, and the well tailored box-back coat. He leaned across to Beth and said, "More champagne?"

When she looked at him there was a devilish twinkle in her eye and she said, "Can you tell me any reason why I shouldn't?"

Even the usually dour James Fair was in a good mood tonight. There was a current saying that Fair had a greater nose for ore than any two men on the Comstock. The rest of the saying was, if you don't believe it, just ask him. Fair baffled a belch against the back of his hand and said, "I told you there was still a bonanza in the Hale and Norcross, didn't I?"

"You told us," the mild mannered John Mackay said. "And I believed you even before you showed me."

"So did Flood and O'Brien," Fair said. "Why else you think they wanted to put up money? Because they know I got a nose for ore, that's why."

Ben Cartwright raised his glass. "To the four Silver Kings!" he said.

"Say, you know something?" James Fair said. "I kinda like the sound of that."

They drank, and then, as it had before this evening, the shadow of business—the one sour note—crept in to dampen the festivities. Beth, perhaps, felt it more keenly than the others, because she was sensitive to Ben's feelings, and she knew Ben's thoughts were never far from that shattered flume. Now that the bonanza was established, quick delivery of timbering was even more imperative.

Beth put a napkin to her lips and said, "The problem isn't going to go away, gentlemen. What are we going to do about it?"

Both Fair and Mackay tried to avoid meeting Ben's eyes. Fair said, "I loaned you forty men once, Cartwright. I'd do it again, but I got to have 'em myself."

"What help there was around is working on the railroad," Mackay said.

Ben Cartwright toyed with his champagne glass. "Gentlemen," he said, "I intend to fulfill my obligation. My sawmill is back in operation. I have enough cut logs to supply the timbers I promised."

"At the figure you quoted?" Fair asked. "Remember, it ain't just us now. We got stockholders. I'm Superintendent of that mine and I got obligations to run it. I can't figure on paying one price and then wind up paying another."

"I'm perfectly aware of that, Jim," Ben said quietly. "If I can't get help to complete the flume in time, I'll have to absorb the loss on the contract. It's as simple as that."

Everyone at the table was acutely uncomfortable. "I didn't want this to happen to you, Ben," John Mackay said.

Ben gave a soft little chuckle. "Frankly, John," he said, "I didn't want it to happen to me, either."

250

The meal came and they were jovial with each other, but none of them really felt it now. They were having their dessert when Dan de Quille came up the winding staircase. Joe Cartwright was following him.

Ben got to his feet immediately. "Is Hoss all right?" he asked.

Joe grinned at his father. "Getting better by the minute," he said.

John Mackay said, "You've got that peculiar look in your eye, Dan. Don't tell me Scotty Malloy has hit bonanza too."

"I doubt it," Dan grinned, "but I just invested another two bits in the Sweet Heather of Scotland, just in case."

"Fool and his money soon parted," Fair grumbled. "All right, newspaperman. You got something on your mind. What is it?"

"Exodus," said Dan de Quille.

The men looked at each other and Beth Kelly said, "Egypt again?"

"Virginia City," said Dan de Quille. "One hundred and fifty Chinese from lower town."

"Hop Sing's cousins," Joe Cartwright said. "With Hop Sing right at the head of 'em."

Ben looked at Joe and Joe gave one of his elegant shrugs.

"You don't suppose . . ." Ben started.

"It could be," Joe said. "You know Hop Sing."

"Will somebody start making sense?" James Fair said.

"When I can make sense of it myself," Ben said. "Beth —I've changed my mind. I'll have to get back to the ranch. May I take you home?"

* * *

He stood with her at the doorway and he kissed her on the cheek. "Thank you for a lovely evening," he said.

251

"Any time you need a dinner partner," she said.

He held her hands and looked deep into her eyes. "You're an independently wealthy woman now, Beth."

"Independent, at least," she said. "And so are you."

"What do you mean by that?"

"I mean we are still us, just as we've always been. If we ever need each other, we're here. But we're independent of each other, too." She smiled. "I'm making a rather bad mess of it, aren't I?"

"It depends, Beth," he said. "If you're giving me a definition of friendship, you're doing well."

There was a moment of wistfulness in her eyes, and then she looked up at him and said, "I wish it could be more, Ben."

"I do too," he said, "but is friendship so bad?"

"No, Ben," she said. "I think it's the greatest gift we could give each other."

He kissed her goodnight and then went directly to where Little Joe was waiting with their horses.

*   *   *

Ben and Joe sat their saddles and looked at the devastation Pete Wilson's bomb had wreaked on the flume. It was already starting to be rebuilt as over one hundred Chinese swarmed through the trestle work, nailing, pounding, sawing, hoisting beams and supports into place.

Ben looked down at the scowling Hop Sing and said, "Just where in the devil did you get this idea?"

"All lelatives," Hop Sing said. "All from See Yup Company," he said, naming the largest tong in Virginia City. "In China, all carpenter, you understand?"

"Yes, I understand," Ben said. "Or at least I think I do."

"All light," Hop Sing said. "You go way. I am straw boss here."

"Who's going to cook for us? Who's going to take care of the house?" Ben said.

"Number six cousin," Hop Sing said. "He be there to-day."

Ben looked at Joe. Joe raised his eyebrows and shrugged.

"Hop Sing," Ben said, "if we can help you . . ."

"Best help, you get out of way," Hop Sing said. He turned and padded off, screaming out a never-ending stream of Chinese. The men on the scaffolding seemed to know what he was talking about, and the tempo of their nailing and pounding and sawing increased.

Ben looked at his son and a big grin spread across his face. "Why fight it, son?" he said. "Let's go home."

They turned their horses and rode back through the living forests of the Ponderosa.

THE END

THEY'RE ALL HERE:

- **The Cartwrights**: Ben, the father, rancher, businessman—and dreamer. Hoss, dogged and devoted elder son. Little Joe, proud and tempestuous.
- **The explosive Nevada of the 1860's**: A battleground for determined men contesting for the buried treasure that was silver and for the timberlands that held the key to mining fortunes.
- **The dramatic excitement**: Ben and his sons come to grip with a ruthless grab for power which threatens their Ponderosa and their way of life.

All the elements that have made "Bonanza" the all-time TV favorite are here in "One Man with Courage" so you can savor fully all the drama and historical details of "Bonanza" days.

The imaginative skill and meticulous research of one of the most distinguished authors of historical fiction—Thomas Thompson—will transport you into "Bonanza" country. Twice winner of the Silver Spur Award and currently president of the Western Writers of America, Thomas Thompson was story editor of "Bonanza" at its inception and has written some of its finest episodes. In "One Man with Courage"—a story never before told—he brings you close-up to the people of "Bonanza," into the towns and forests and down into the mines of this pulsating time and place.

Read "One Man with Courage"—and you will be living in "Bonanza" country with the people who made "Bonanza" great.

FIRST IN THE NEW, ORIGINAL-STORY "BONANZA" SERIES